CAKE

A NOVEL

NICOLE BROOKS

Copyright © 2019 Nicole Brooks
First Erid Press Inc. Edition: June 2019
All Rights Reserved

Print book ISBN 978-1-7751554-3-0
eBook/.mobi ISBN 978-1-7751554-5-4
eBook/.epub ISBN 978-1-7751554-4-7

Print and eBook Cover Design by www.ebooklaunch.com
Book Design and Proofreading by www.ebooklaunch.com
Editing by www.naomiklewis.com

OTHER TITLES BY NICOLE BROOKS:

Just Because We Can (2018)

To the two most important women in my life—Julia and Erica. Their idealism inspires me.

"I come as one, but stand as ten thousand." — Maya Angelou

KEELY

1

I ran to escape the thoughts that plagued me. I just wanted to forget who I *was* and focus on who I was *going to be*. Looking back drained me of valuable energy and time, but once in a while memories tried catching up with me.

Short, short, long. Inhale, inhale, exhale.

I made the noise in and out through my mouth as my mind said the words. I concentrated on coordinating foot strikes with the beginning of every exhalation. Complete focus. My feet hit the pavement only as hard as necessary before springing me forward again. I didn't want to look like a galumphing elephant as I made my way around the park. Rhythmic breathing, correct form, and efficient movement led to the most effective workout.

Once I was in the zone, nothing else mattered. I was entirely focused on the flow of my breathing, on the rhythm of my heart. *The runner's high.* Of course, I also ran to keep my cardio health optimal. Lots of bodybuilders and fitness models focused only on their muscles, but I knew this was shortsighted.

I made my way around Queens Park three more times—my mind clear as a bell. I slowed as I reached the wooden bench that signalled the point when I started to walk one lap. A proper cooldown.

Man, it's hot! Hardly a breeze and only seven in the morning, I could tell it was going to be a blistering day. September in

Toronto was no stranger to heat waves, and the humidity off the lakes only added to the feeling of melting. Good thing I'd spend the rest of the day in the gym. Air conditioning was a godsend on days and weeks like this.

I stopped abruptly as a little boy raced across my path, following a little dog that had gotten away from him. "Excuse me!" I snapped.

"Oh! Sorry," a frazzled looking woman said as she too cut me off. I smiled stiffly at her as she streaked past.

After my cooldown lap, I came to rest at my favourite bench, where I did some stretching. My calves were particularly tight, and I leaned into a good, wide-leg lunge on each side, sighing at the feeling of my muscles relaxing into it. Endorphins now fully surging through my body, I embraced the feelings that they brought.

Accomplished. Strong. *Focused.*

Andrew could never understand why I did this kind of stuff to myself. Maybe that's where things started to fall apart. He was one of those naturally athletic guys who could pick up any sport he tried, but preferred to sit and watch TV and eat chips. *And not gain a single goddamn pound.* He could never understand why I set so many personal goals. He obviously didn't react—physically or chemically—the same way I did to conquering a target.

"Excuse me?" I heard a small female voice behind me say. I closed my eyes for a second, willing myself to not get angry with this person. I hated nothing more than being reefed out of my zone, and this was the second time in less than five minutes. Good thing for her I was almost done. I slowly turned around and saw a tiny, hunched-over old woman standing—well, curled over—behind me, leaning heavily on a cane. Her body was practically the shape of an upside-down question mark. *This is exactly why I take such good care of myself.*

"Yes?" I asked, trying to curb the impatience in my voice.

"Would you be a dear and help me fix my cane?" She nodded toward a little black piece of rubber that lay on the sidewalk about three feet behind her.

I took a deep breath and felt myself soften. I'd had a little old granny, not unlike this woman, whom I loved dearly. She died when I was only fifteen, and I would have given anything to see her again. I often wondered if things would have worked out better for me after high school if I'd had her to turn to after my parents decided I didn't exist anymore.

My throat clenched, surprising me. "Um, yeah. Of course." I took a couple of steps over, picked up the little boot, and brought it back. "Let's sit here and I'll see if I can get it back on." I automatically took her elbow and guided her toward the bench.

"Oh, you are just a dear!" she croaked.

You have no idea what you are talking about, lady.

I sat next to her and lifted the cane up, its black paint badly scratched. The little rubber boot had a crack in it, and obviously would not stay in place long. "You need a new cane. Or end cover, at least." I pushed it on as best I could.

"Oh, well, they are a bit expensive." She smiled at me, but I could see the "eleven" deepen between her sparse eyebrows.

"Well, they can't be more than fifty bucks or something?"

"I'm sure I can make this one work for a while longer. Don't they say duct tape fixes everything?" She looked up to me, her face heavily lined. Her hair was still pretty black. It was hard to say how old she was, but surely she had old age pension? RRSPs? Savings?

"Well, yes, you could tape it back on, but it would be pretty ugly."

"Oh, dear!" She touched my hand softly. "I long ago stopped caring for the looks of things. It's more about functionality. I wish I had learned that lesson sooner though. I should have taken better care of myself, like you obviously do."

3

I couldn't help but smile. Here I was, fifty years old, and could bench press circles around most women younger than me. I had created a plan, implemented it, and seen it through.

Had I been so focused, though, that I drove Andrew into the arms of another woman? And moreover, did I care? I was perfectly happy doing everything by myself.

"Dear?" The woman's voice brought me back.

I took a quick breath. "Yes. Sorry, I was lost in thought there." Actually, now I was irritated that my runner's high had been so quickly replaced by thoughts of my problems. I looked forward every day to the hour or two of inner silence that followed.

She reached over and patted my knee. "Don't waste too much time there."

"Where?"

"Lost in thought. Just do what makes you happy. It's a short life."

Her baby-pink blouse showed wear around the collar, and her brown slacks had a small stain on the right thigh. The sun suddenly popped out from behind the leaves of a nearby tree as a merciful breeze moved them. It was hot and bright, and I wished for sunglasses. I reached into my Nike runners pack, pulled out the two twenties I kept in there for emergencies, and pressed them into her small hand. "This should almost cover a new cane. It's probably not safe for you to not have a proper one, especially come winter."

"Oh, no. I can't take this." She started to push it back to me.

"Please. For my grandma." My voice hitched.

"Oh, sweetie. Thank you. This will buy the loveliest cane I've ever had."

I looked at her pale grey eyes for a long time, searching.

I sat in the Lexus for a long time thinking about the little old lady. "Could things have been different?" I asked myself. I had developed a strange habit of talking to myself since I had moved out of the big house and into my little two-bedroom rental two months ago.

"If I'd had my grandma to go to instead of losing everything I'd known, would things be different now?" *Of course they would, you idiot!* I scolded myself. But would things be *better* now? Certainly the kids wouldn't have been born because I would have never married Andrew. I guess I could have had different kids, but would I have accepted myself for who I truly was instead of living a cover-up life?

"Here's the conundrum. Is my life really a cover-up or is it the way it was all supposed to go?" I suddenly slammed both palms onto the steering wheel. "Who cares, anyway?" I screamed into the suddenly stifling air of the SUV, forcing every drop of air out of my lungs.

Why, at this point in my life, was I questioning everything? I had no option but to move forward. When Andrew told me, unapologetically, about his newfound love, I'd reacted with only a moment of rage before I realized he was giving me an easy out. Wasn't this what I wanted? To finally be left alone? My gym was doing really well—I wasn't the only person in Toronto obsessed with the way I looked—so I didn't even need financial support from Andrew. After only a day of deliberating, I released him to his new love and moved out of the big house in Rosedale. In some small way, I knew he deserved it. I hadn't been the easiest person to live with, and Andrew really was a great guy. A little needy? Sure. But he had a good heart.

And me? I wasn't sure my heart was so good after all, despite what cane granny thought.

I took a deep breath and started the car. I'd done what I did best. *Moved on.* Regret was useless, I reminded myself. I had made the choice to be here. I started every day purposefully.

With *intention*. And every day ended with the satisfaction of knowing I had accomplished what I set out to do.

Every day was mine to create. "Come on, Keely. Get it together," I told myself as I sat straighter and pulled away from the curb.

MICHELLE

2

I never allowed myself to think about the future. Why would I, with nothing to see except more of the same? Who would want to daydream about that?

I clicked the burner off and gently lifted each perfectly cooked, still intact over-easy egg onto two buttered pieces of white toast. I set the plate on the table next to the cutlery and a large glass of apple juice and walked toward the bathroom. As always, I said a little prayer, asking for today to be one of his good days.

"Ray?" I tapped lightly on the door. "Your breakfast is ready." I stepped back as the door opened. He looked at me for a second, no readable expression on his face, and then stepped past me.

Not great, but not terrible. I could live with that.

I sat down across from him with a cup of chamomile tea and waited. I was pretty good at the eggs now. It had been ten years, after all. But some days something didn't work out: the egg was off, or the heat was wrong, and they would be overcooked. Sometimes he let it slide, but more often than not, he exploded.

Today he silently scrolled through some newsfeed on his phone, making faces and grunting. He never actually complimented me on my cooking ability; the best he could manage was to say nothing. He shovelled the food into his mouth. I exhaled lightly and sat back, taking another sip of my tea.

He chugged the whole glass of juice in one, long gulp. When we first met, I found his love of apple juice cute and charming—almost childlike. And then I made the mistake of telling him that and sported a lovely black eye for a week after.

Women really do run into walls, it seemed.

And yet I stayed, even after that night in the kitchen as the glass cut into my back. Stupidly or ignorantly or lovingly, I found ways to see past his rage. I chose to remember the times he brought me fresh-clipped wild daisies or surprised me with a random but heartfelt "I love you, Shell."

I sighed again. The sunrise was particularly beautiful that morning. The orange glow it cast over the sixty-year-old kitchen was almost apocalyptic, and when I peeked outside, I saw the colours reflected back to me off several other houses' windows, amplifying the eeriness.

Now it had faded, and a hot fall day was upon Toronto. This was bound to piss Ray off. He worked for the city's parks department and hated the heat.

"Are you going to be able to stay inside today?" I asked quietly as I watched him over the rim of my old orange, chipped Home Depot mug.

He looked at me like I was the dumbest person on the planet. "Of course I am. It's supposed to be thirty-three today." He shook his head and went back to his phone.

Still okay. There had been much worse.

A memory from the day before flashed through my mind, and I couldn't stop the smile that slipped onto my face. I quickly forced the memory and the smile away before Ray could see it. If he saw any spark of life in me at all, he'd beat it out of me before I could say another word. I knew I'd been very stupid. Not only because of the consequences I would face if Ray found out, but because of what I had let myself feel.

I'd stepped onto a proverbial slippery slope by finally having sex with Andrew two months earlier. He had been so patient and kind—even telling his wife about us before we made love. He'd wanted to give her the power of deciding what happened to their marriage. He told me repeatedly that he wasn't a cheater and wouldn't act like one. What kind of man did that? None that I'd had the pleasure of knowing. It was practically knight-in-shining-armour gallant.

And I totally and completely fell for it.

I touched my temple where a couple of hairs had slipped out of the French braid. Andrew wouldn't come in tonight, which was probably for the best. Even though we always stayed at least a foot apart in public, it was a miracle that we hadn't been caught yet.

I still marvelled that Andrew had noticed me at all. It started one night when he came into the bar with his friends. A few nights later, he came back alone. That was six months ago, and he had been in three or four times a week since then. He said his wife didn't even wonder where he was.

The picture, or more a feeling, ripped through me from yesterday, refusing to be ignored. We'd only had one hour in the hotel room, all I could manage without attracting suspicion from Ray. But what an hour. Andrew had closed the door behind him and turned on me, his eagerness apparent. For a quick second, fear tore through me. I must have flinched, because Andrew smiled and put his hands on both sides of my face. Gentle yet tight enough to show me he wanted me more badly than I think I've ever been wanted.

Except, maybe, for Jonathan.

"What's the matter with you?" Ray barked suddenly.

"What?" *Shit! Had I said something?*

"You just made a noise." He frowned. "I thought you were choking or something."

My heart raced, trying to retrace what I may have done or said to give myself away. "Oh. No. Nothing."

Ray narrowed his eyes at me. "Where's your earring?" he finally said.

I automatically touched both of my earlobes, feeling the right one bare. *Oh no!* "I... I don't know. That's really weird."

"You've had the same earrings since I've known you and you lose one *now*? Only you could pull that off, Michelle." He pushed his chair back and got up.

I could almost feel Andrew biting my ear again, and I shivered. The earrings were only simple gold hoops, but the clasp was flimsy, and he must have opened it with his teeth as my head pressed hard into the pillows.

Ray grabbed his keys by the door. He called over his shoulder as he left the house. "Do *not* leave me shepherd's pie again for supper tonight. You've made it three times this month already. And I need some beer before you go to work." He turned and left, slamming the door behind him.

I slumped against the hard back of the chair, letting out the same huge breath I did every time Ray left the house.

Some days didn't go as smoothly as this one. What set him off never made sense to me. Just two weeks ago I had gone to work with a red mark on my face because apparently his egg was more "fried" than "over easy." I'd hoped that, in the dim light of the bar, the mark would not be noticeable. Like me.

I realized that some people went through their lives thinking they had choices. A nice idea, but for me—life just *happened*. No father, a mentally absent and emotionally abusive mother. From a very early age, I'd realized that bad things just happened to some people, and they had no control over them. I happened to be one of the lucky souls born into this kind of life. And then came the bad choices, which trapped me.

"Stop feeling sorry for yourself," I scolded myself as I cleaned up Ray's breakfast dishes. I had Cassie, and she was the one thing I had done completely right.

After Jonathan, I had tried to make it for several years on my own, but the debt and problems piled up. I met Ray when Cassie was eight, and he offered me a refuge. I knew he had a mean streak, but he had his good moments—in the beginning. And it wasn't like I had a hundred other men beating down my door. So I settled. Honestly, I did it so Cassie could have more, maybe even a chance at a post-secondary education. I essentially made a deal with the devil. But I would never, even on my deathbed, tell Cassie that. *I guess that's two secrets between us.* She still thought Jonathan had died in a car accident when she was two, that he had been a great guy.

I learned early on that it was just easier and hurt less to lie down and accept life. And thus the tone was set. So why, at the ripe old age of forty-six, had I allowed Andrew into the mix? I was scared and broken. Surely it was too late to be saved now? *No one actually starts living life this late in the game, do they?*

KEELY

3

My run-in with the cane lady a week earlier had really shaken me up. What if I ended up like her and needed someone to take care of me? Even as hard as I worked on my health, genetically it was a gamble. Or I could get injured in a horrific car accident. The two months since I'd left Andrew had been blissfully quiet. But last night, shuffling around my house, wandering from room to room, it was almost too much. I even texted Riley to see if she was coming over. At that point I would have taken her obnoxious Top Forty music blaring from her room over the silence that threatened to overwhelm me.

I sat crunching on my cucumber slices as I watched through the glass wall at all the people burning calories and exuding sweat in the fitness centre on Yonge Street I had built from the ground up eight years before. Suddenly, the thought of a delicious dark chocolate bar laden with coconut or tiny, ground up bits of espresso beans entered my mind. I could almost taste it while I imagined myself breaking the bar with a satisfying snap and popping it into my mouth. A side effect of the stress, I suppose. Being mad always left me unfocused and drifting when it came to diet. *Maybe on the weekend if you stick to it all week*, I bargained with myself.

My phone dinged a text. I had been beyond excited to get my hands on the Rose Gold iPhone 7. It was so *pretty*. I turned it so the light caught the colour just so. *I must get my next set of nails to match.* I was known around the gym for all of the different shades of pink I had used on my gel nail designs over the years. Right now, I was rocking "watermelon." I smiled, thinking of the time, a year ago, that I had been feeling crazy and showed up with "mint" nails. It was the trendy colour at the time, but I couldn't handle it and paid for another set only two days later.

Andrew: *We need to talk about the email you sent last night.*

I immediately responded: *I thought it was pretty clear.* What part of "I want to try again" didn't he understand? My stomach lurched as I wondered if I had done the right thing, rashly sending him a plea in a moment of weakness.

Well, yes. But you can't just come around saying you want to move back in and that you still love me after 2 years of ignoring me.

I sighed and waited to respond. I'd have to pull out all of my charms. I was pretty sure I had charms that worked on men once upon a time. But Andrew was tricky. He wanted more than a beautiful face to spend the rest of his life with. He wanted *a deeper connection* and *mutual interests.* I didn't leave him in search of greener pastures. Just quieter pastures with less annoyances and more time to think and focus. Andrew needed time to talk and bug me. How was I supposed to prepare for fitness competitions if all he did was whine that I didn't eat the special supper he made for us. Who had garlic bread *and* lasagna in the same meal anyway? I took a breath, trying to calm the thrashing emotions that danced inside me.

"Keely?" Amber appeared in the doorway, interrupting my inner fuming. "Marie, your ten o'clock, is here."

I transformed my face to customer mode in a breath and rose from my chair. As I passed the mirror on my wall, I stopped to make sure I had my business smile on correctly. *Engaging but not artificial.* Out in the reception area a plain-looking woman waited. "Of course! Marie, if you just want to wait for me in room two, I'll be right there." She nodded vigorously back at me, her limp bob, well, bobbing.

I quickly finished my text: *Just come by my place tonight ok, so we can talk? 6:30?*

He simply responded: *Fine.*

I unburdened myself of any thoughts around the tone of his response and entered the meeting room, closing the door to the metal on metal clank of weights coming down. I held out my hand and offered Marie my signature shake: firm grip, one strong pump, drop it. The working woman's handshake we learned at the entrepreneurial course I took years ago. Flimsy fingertip introductions were for McDonald's cashiers. You had one second to convince people you meant business. Immediately, she started gushing, "I'm so happy to be here! My friends were so jealous when I told them. You know, you are so well known in the industry and I just can't believe I got an appointment with you, Keely!" Her face grew pink, likely from the exertion of her breathless speech. A sign of her poor cardiovascular health and, more importantly, her potential. Marie stumbled, "Is that okay if I call you Keely? Or do you prefer Mrs. O'Connell?"

I stopped myself just in time from rolling my eyes. Anyone could get an appointment with me for a hundred and fifty bucks an hour. *Stay relatable.* "Keely is fine, Marie," I replied smoothly.

"Oh, great! I just have to say, your ads don't do you justice. There's no way you are fifty! I wouldn't put you a day past forty. Heck, I never even looked as good as you at eighteen!" Marie bubbled.

I smiled and tried to not look at the clock. *How long was this appointment for?* I sighed lightly. I'd seen this type of girl so many times. A little chubby, overenthusiastic. As if I was some rock star who could magically fix their weaknesses, restoring their lack of willpower. *And* get them competition ready in six weeks. Stupid buggers.

I crossed my arms on top of the table and leaned in slightly, making sure my pelvis tipped forward, achieving a good lumbar tilt. "I'll get straight to the point, Marie. There are no shortcuts." Her face fell a tiny bit. *I knew it!* "It takes months of hard work and dedication. No cheating on diet. No skipping workouts. Hard work! Willpower! *Desire.*" I tapped the brochure I had set in front of her that echoed what I had just said. A tiny, single rhinestone glinted from the end of my index fingernail, which I admired.

I really liked to see already-fit women I could take to the next level. Then I was more of a cheerleader than a drill sergeant. I despised nagging people.

Marie picked up the brochure and pretended to study it. She folded the corner of it over several times and asked, "So, say there's a birthday party. *My niece's birthday party.* Am I allowed to have piece of cake? You know, just for special occasions?" She looked up from the flyer hopefully.

My right foot started tapping beneath the table. I slowly, gravely, shook my head. "No cake. Especially if you're winding up for comp." Of course, there were cheat days in the program, but I wanted her to fully understand how hard this was going to be. If I told her now that, yes, she could have the cake, there would be no end to the "special occasions." Birthdays, holidays, Fridays, I-made-it-through-the-kids'-lame-Christmas-concert days.

Marie's shoulders slumped forward, which prompted me to add, "Plus, you have to do posture and presentation training." She jerked forward, straightening again, eyes alert.

As we ran through the rest of the formalities of the training and discussed cost, I could tell I was losing her. For the best. *No weak links.* I didn't have the most award-winning team in Toronto for no reason.

The appointment was supposed to last thirty minutes, ending with a tour of the facility. But I could tell after twenty that she had changed her mind. We shook hands as she left the room, promising to be in touch, but I knew I'd never hear from her again. So many people wanted the quick fix. The pills or the powders or the shakes that would make them magically thin. The only thing that worked in the long run was *a committed lifestyle.* I looked at the poster of myself on the wall, the result of my last ad campaign, that showed me in mock training, lifting weights and smiling beautifully for the camera. Tanned and styled to perfection. The photographer captured a fierce look in my clear green eyes. I smiled at how toned the (slight) airbrushing had made my abs. They were always my problem spot. *Having three kids takes its toll on a person, I tell you.*

I rushed home early from the gym to make dinner. Being strictly paleo, I had eaten flawlessly all day to prepare for the simple (aka white) carbs I would have to consume at supper for Andrew's benefit.

"You only get one body," I mumbled as I prepared his favourite meal, grilled steak and twice-baked potatoes. *And garlic bread.* Two servings of carbs in one meal. I made three kinds of vegetables so I could make my plate *look* full, but I would still suffer the consequences of this tomorrow. I was determined to keep my body as lean and mean as I could. I refused to be the seventy-year-old lady (sorry, cane granny) who couldn't walk up a flight of stairs without creaking and groaning and gasping. Or who couldn't pull off a killer pair of three-inch stilettos. I unconsciously twisted my ankle out and flexed my gastrocnemius and soleus muscles. The definition was on point.

At 6:40, the doorbell rang, and I pushed down my annoyance at his tardiness.

"Hello, Andrew." I smiled, opening the door fully to appear welcoming.

"I'm sorry, Keely. I had to run Riley to work," he puffed as he came in. I noticed he had grown a beard, which was surprisingly sexy with all its grey, even though it was a hipster trend.

When I had moved out in July, Riley decided to stay primarily with her father. I don't even know why I got a two-bedroom house, as she was hardly here. She had just graduated high school and was working for a year before deciding what to do with her life. That kid had never had any motivation. At least Emerson was in university, and Jacob was a hard-working, smart kid who jumped right into Andrew's company. Jacob would probably have to do some post-secondary training eventually, but if any of the kids could work their way up the ranks, he could.

Andrew looked around the clean and sparsely decorated house. I had lucked out and found a smaller place only a few blocks from the big house, a rare find in our upscale neighbourhood. "The kids said you hired Janae part-time to clean?"

I resisted the urge to defend myself. Andrew knew I detested cleaning, and we'd let the kids' nanny of sixteen years go when we separated. I thought it worked out well for both of us for me to hire her. Janae was older and had a hard time keeping full-time hours, and I was too busy with work and training to worry about dusty shelves and dirty floors. Janae and I were so used to working around each other, I barely noticed when she was around.

Andrew grinned while slipping off his runners. "Are you sure you don't want alimony to keep your life running smoothly?"

"No." I couldn't bite back my quick, hard response. I took a deep breath and continued, "The gym is doing very well, thank you. People will spend more than you can believe on their bodies."

"Oh, I can believe it. I footed the bill for years, remember?"

A scowl crossed my face before I could stop it. *I really need to work on my automatic responses.*

Andrew sighed and crossed his arms, stopping in the hallway. "Really, Keely. What do you want to talk about? Because you just gave me that look. Have you actually changed your mind?"

The scowl. In the last year of our relationship, I tried really hard to cut back on the scowl. It seemed anything he said annoyed me. Or irritated me. Or exasperated me. And it all came with the scowl. The frowning, eye-squinting, pursed-lips face that suggested he was a total idiot. I knew I did it, but I wasn't sure if it was just an automatic reaction or due to the fact that I no longer cared what he thought. I sighed and forced my shoulders down. They constantly crept up towards my ears, contributing to neck wrinkles and headaches.

"Sorry. It's just that I had a bad day." I actually opened up and told him about the fight I'd had with Emerson that afternoon. She insisted on becoming a nurse and was in her third year of university. I had tried to tell her it wasn't too late to switch streams. That some of the courses would probably transfer to a more useful degree. "What the hell could possibly be more useful than nursing?" she had yelled at me over the phone. I knew nursing was a noble occupation and someone needed to do it, but there was no space for personal growth there. No glass ceilings to shatter. Nowhere for a driven woman to go. Millions could not be made tending to broken and dying people. Not to mention that doctors and nurses were notoriously overworked and didn't have the time or energy to tend to the upkeep of their own bodies. Their eating habits were usually atrocious, based on those who came through the gym.

"But it's in her personality, Keely. She's always wanted to help people. She was meant to be a healer. You can't deny that." Andrew walked past me into the kitchen, suggesting he was giving me another chance to play nice.

I sighed again and thought of all the animals Emerson had begged to adopt. "No, I can't. But she could have so easily been a model." I could tell he was rolling his eyes, even though I couldn't see them, by the exasperated noise that escaped him.

"You can't put your unrealized dreams on her. It's not fair. She's never cared about her looks." As he turned back to look at me, the pinched look on his face revealed the unfinished part of that statement. *Unlike you.* He ran his hand over his head, an old habit from when he had beautiful, wavy brown hair. He said he didn't have time to waste on styling it now, hence the clipped look.

Strangely, I was overcome with affection for him. Sometimes it snuck up on me like that. He always saw things so clearly. So easily. He always valued people for who they were, not what they looked like, even though he himself was attractive. I knew sometimes my obsession with good looks was a curse. And maybe I wasn't beautiful in a traditional sense, but I was certainly handsome. *Striking* was what the scout said all those years ago. My parents didn't let me accept the modelling contract offered to me at fifteen, but insisted I stay on the farm and work for them. Along with my father's parents, they worked tirelessly at anything that brought in money. Some years it was the cattle that did well, other years the crops. They had a lot of land in rural Saskatchewan and kept their fingers in many pots to avoid a bad year when one avenue dried up. But I was not a farm girl at heart and had left after the blow-up with Mother. Although I did acknowledge the work ethic that being raised on a farm had instilled in me.

I forcibly let it go. "Let's eat. Everything's ready." I placed colourful melamine bowls full of roasted vegetables and medium-rare rib steak on the table first, followed slowly by the potatoes and bread. As he reached for the steak first, I countered my irritation by reminding myself I would have plenty of leftover veggies to eat.

We enjoyed a fairly civil meal aside from the fact that Andrew kept sneaking glances at my uneaten potato. I forced myself to shovel a couple of small bites into my mouth while suppressing a grimace. My hatred of the act overwhelmed my ability to enjoy how delicious they actually were. I had put everything Andrew loved in them: sharp cheddar cheese, bacon, chives, and sour cream. He was so obsessed with *enjoying* life to its fullest.

He leaned back in his chair and patted his stomach. I knew, as soon as he asked, that his next question was a test. "Hey." He feigned nonchalance. "Do you want to go out for ice cream after?" I tried to control the wince I felt internally.

"Sure," I said as convincingly as possible, lifting my shoulders in a high shrug. There went my hope of a chocolate bar on the weekend, and it was only Monday.

After, we walked home as the cooler September evening started to settle in, replacing the heat of the day. The colours that had begun to emerge on the trees were quite beautiful. I realized that I rarely stopped to appreciate these kinds of things anymore. I had loved "Indian Summers" when I was younger. On the farm, the sun setting across the vast prairie landscape had been stunning in the fall.

The single scoop of cookie dough ice cream didn't sit as heavily in my stomach as I'd feared. A calmness settled on me that had eluded me for months. Or years.

I was surprised when Andrew suddenly said, breaking my trance, "That was nice, Keely. Maybe we can do it again?" He turned to me, and I saw that his smile was hopeful. My brief feeling of triumph was quickly replaced by hostility. I wanted to ask, *What about her?* But I wasn't so sure I wanted to hear his answer.

For now, I would just pretend she didn't exist.

MICHELLE

4

I do exist. I do exist. I do exist.

I kept repeating the mantra long after Ray's screams had left the house, along with his body. He had lost his mind when I, carefully and passively, asked if I could go back to school. I made sure everything was to his liking and waited until he'd had his second cup of coffee. Mornings had about a five percent better chance than evenings to get something near nice from him, and when he'd rolled over in bed that morning and draped his arm sleepily over my waist, I thought this was a good sign.

I'd never allowed myself this kind of ambitious thinking in the past, which I knew had been fuelled by Andrew's belief that I could do something great with my life, given the chance. It had gone over very, very poorly.

Ray had looked at me, his blue eyes dancing at the prospect of having a good reason to put me down. He made a disgusted sound. "Do you really think that you would get accepted into a program? You're forty-six years old for God's sake and have no skill set!" He slammed his cup down on the old, stained coffee table and focused his attention back on the TV, his hand wandering absently down to scratch his crotch.

He was likely right, but unknown to my husband, people had come to me at the bar with their problems for years. They always told me how great a listener I was, that I always gave wise advice. Ironic, given my real life. Kenzie specifically told me recently that I would make a great counsellor, but I knew the training for that would be too costly. Plus, I would be early-fifties before I graduated. And I didn't even know how good a student I would make. My marks in high school had been low, and I'd barely graduated. It was hard to get top grades when I spent half of my life trying to avoid the person who was supposed to be taking care of me, and the other half trying to survive.

Taking a quick breath, I summoned the courage to quickly say, "I took an online quiz and it said I would be good at social work based on my interests." I didn't add that I scored quite high on youth worker. This intrigued me and had me thinking about how my life would have turned out if someone had stepped into my teenage years before it was too late. A thought started to form that I couldn't dispose of. *I can do that for someone else.*

Ray barked, "A social worker! Ha! Look at you. You are *unnoticeable.* A social worker is someone who can stand up and speak out. Barely anyone in this world knows you even *exist,*" he spat, indicating that this conversation was over. Forever. He reached over as if to stroke my cheek, but then grabbed it into a pinch with his whole hand. He squeezed until I cried out and then, satisfied, let go and patted it gently. It always seemed as if Ray was trying to control a temper tantrum. It wouldn't be the first time I wondered if he had some kind of undiagnosed mental illness. Like he would ever go to a doctor anyway. The only time he'd gone in ten years was when he fell off the back of a picker truck while pruning trees and broke his arm.

Inside my head I screamed, *Fuck you!* Cassie knew I existed. The girls at the bar knew I existed.

Andrew knew I existed.

I usually had several hours to myself between the time Ray left for work in the morning and when I had to be at the bar, depending on whether I worked the afternoon or evening shift. I had been there for eight years and the place before that thirteen. I'd fabricated a lie to get out of the last place, since Ray wouldn't let me quit for my own reasons. Ironic when I thought about how many times I'd told Cassie to stand up to men. When she was in grade one, a boy kissed her, and I gave her my full permission to punch him. She was worried about hurting him and getting into trouble. But when my old boss kissed me without my permission? I hadn't punched him or caused a scene. All because I didn't want to cause any problems or get *him* in trouble.

I only wanted to get out of there quietly.

Thankfully, I was starting work at three today. I preferred the late shift not because of the tips, but because it minimized my time with Ray at home. And then I also had more time during the day to make sure everything in the house was in order and to his specifications.

Being Wednesday, I pulled out the bathroom cleaning supplies and got to work. Our little house only had one bathroom, but Ray's cleaning schedule dictated that I clean it twice a week. Wednesdays and Saturdays. As I sprayed cleaner on the floor, I shook my head, wondering if he ever actually got any of his urine *in* the toilet. I sprayed and scrubbed and washed every inch of the small washroom, including the old, greying grout between the brown-and-yellow flowered tiles in the shower. By nature, Ray was a slob and probably couldn't care less how clean everything was. As with everything, it came down to control.

I heard my ancient, blue Motorola flip phone bing. I finished up as quickly as I could in the bathroom while still achieving the state of clean required of me.

I pulled off the gloves. The text was from Cassie: *Stopping by tonight.*

I quickly typed: *Great.* I kept my messages as short as possible because it took a long time on this phone. Each button was for three letters, and you had to push it until the letter you wanted showed up. I always marvelled at Cassie's newer phone, which made texting a breeze. I decided that should be my next request of Ray: a new cell phone. Maybe in a month or two when he had forgotten about this morning, I could take a chance.

On my way to work, I passed a yoga studio. Even though I saw it almost every day, I always slowed down a bit and watched the people inside. I felt like an outsider, looking into in a perfect snow globe of a world—mesmerized by this alternate life.

They flowed from one pose to the next, so strong and confident. I never tried to stop the thought from coming. *I would like to try this one day.* I just let it come in and wander around my mind. I knew sooner or later, reality would evict it. But it was still nice to dream.

I crossed the road with all of the other pedestrians and walked halfway up the block. Jim sat on the sidewalk, leaning against the brick wall of the dollar store, like always. I slowed down as I approached and dug into my purse, fishing out the change I had put there the night before. I crouched down and said good afternoon.

"I only managed one seventy-five today, my friend. It was slow last night." I dropped the seven quarters into his palm. I usually tried to give him three or four dollars, enough for at least one meal that day.

He smiled at me. "Oh, Michelle. That is more than you'll ever know. It'll get me a day-old hot dog and a drink from Hassam." He grinned, showing a severe lack of teeth in his mouth, and nodded towards the vendor down the street.

I smiled back at him. Hassam was a good guy, and as long as Jim gave him something, he fed him. And many other homeless people around here, I suspected. Hassam was a refugee, and worked day and night to provide for his family. I asked Jim the daily question. "You going to go see Bonnie today?" Bonnie ran the drop-in centre down the street and provided services to get people like Jim back on their feet.

Jim rubbed his dirty hands together and nodded, slowly and deeply, making the same reply he did every day. "Yeah, Michelle. I think today might be the day." He looked up at me with his clear grey eyes and for a second, like always, I believed him.

"That's great news. Today's a good day to start over." My reply was also the same every day, but what Jim didn't know was that deep down, I hoped and prayed for him that this truly *was* the day. Somehow I never lost faith in him. I never gave up on the idea that one day he may follow through.

The bar was pretty slow again, and during a lull, Kenzie leaned over the countertop, her long blonde hair falling forward. "So?" The expectancy in her eyes was sweet.

I so didn't want to let her down. I forced a smile and said, "He said he'd think about it." I hated lying to her, but I just couldn't burden her with the truth.

She clapped, buying my fib. "That's great, Michelle! Think of how awesome it would be for you to get out of here." She took my hands and looked at me. "You can do more. It can be better if you take the steps you need to."

Children are so idealistic.

Kenzie moved along the bar to serve a customer, but she continued to talk about how great this news was for a full hour after. I didn't know what hurt more, the fact that my lie had been so convincing, or that someone could have such high hopes for a life beyond repair.

Cassie showed up shortly after seven. She breathlessly sat down at the bar. "Sorry! I had a last-minute study date for psych." She smiled.

I leaned over and kissed the top of her head. "That's okay, sweetie, I wasn't that hungry yet." I undid my apron, put it on the bar, and sat next to her.

On days when Cassie came to visit, she tried to come at my break time so we could eat supper together. The menu at the bar was small, with pub food, but still good. The manager insisted it was better to make fewer things well than many things poorly.

"Do you feel like nachos? I have a hankering for jalapenos!" She laughed, which made me realize how much she looked like me. Except that she was way cuter and seemed truly happy.

"Yes, that's fine." I looked over at Kenzie. "Can you order us some nachos, please? Oh!" I dipped my head. Kenzie was in charge when Jacob or Dexter weren't there. "Is it okay if I take my break now?"

Kenzie made a noise. "You don't have to ask me, Michelle. You're a better judge of the timing around here than me. The usual?"

I nodded. Our order of nachos must have looked ridiculous. Half of it was basically just chips and cheese. That was my side. And the other half was loaded with everything: cheese, tomatoes, onions, peppers, ground beef *and* sour cream, salsa and guacamole on the side. That was Cassie's side. And every time, she tried to get me to try a bite of hers. She insisted that I would love it. I could never bring myself to try the jalapenos; my tolerance for spicy foods was zero. Once Cassie had picked the pepper off and tried to get me to try, but I could still see the little pale ring it had left in the cheese and even that freaked me out.

I looked at Cassie and smiled.

"What?" she asked, suddenly self-conscious.

"Nothing. I just… I guess I needed to see you today." Whenever I was having a poor-me day, I loved seeing her. It made me realize that I had done at least one thing *epically* right in my life. I snickered at my internal use of one of Cassie's favourite words.

Cassie reached over and moved my hair off my cheek, making me blanch. I'd worn my hair down to cover the pinch mark. "What happened?" she asked, her jaw muscles flexing.

I sighed and told her the whole story. Well, not the whole story. Even though we had promised to always be honest with each other, I always smoothed over or left out the parts that I thought would hurt Cassie the most. I relayed the story about three quarters truthfully.

But Cassie was excited enough that she didn't clue in on what I left out. "That's a big step, Mom! At least you're planting the idea of you doing something different in his head. *And in yours.*" She lifted an eyebrow.

"Yes, yes." I chuckled. "Look at me grow." In that moment, I wanted so badly to tell her about Andrew. She would lose her mind with delight. I actually opened my mouth but then closed it again, forcing the revelation back down.

The truth was that one day I wouldn't hear from Andrew, and that would be it. There was no possible way this would work out in the end. But for now, I was going to try my best and enjoy it. Bringing Cassie into my little web of deception would only endanger her, especially if Ray found out.

Kenzie purposely let me go at midnight, knowing I could still catch a bus. If I stayed until closing, I would have to walk home, as I wasn't allowed to spend my tips on a cab. It was a good half hour walk from the bar just off Yonge Street to the house on Grange Avenue. The Blue Night Service ran late and into the morning, but the drop-off closest to my house was still several blocks away. Some nights, Ray picked me up. I never told Kenzie that I preferred to take my chances on the street just to have another thirty minutes to myself. Actually, walking alone at night (even though I'd been mugged twice in the past ten years) didn't scare me as much as Ray's moods did, especially after he'd been drinking.

Naturally, my mind wandered to Andrew as I walked home down the sparsely populated streets.

"I never thought I needed a man to rescue me," I muttered to myself, which made me blend in as I walked past the shelter. I mean, I had never known my father, as he abandoned my mother shortly after my birth. About the only descriptor she gave my father was "chickenshit loser." She couldn't handle the rejection and slowly turned to alcohol. She may have been a good person before, but by my fifth birthday, she was a full-blown, non-functioning addict, and we were living on welfare. Looking back, it's a miracle I survived my childhood. In hindsight, my heart broke for that child. Now that I had raised a daughter myself, I fully understood what I had missed.

By my seventh birthday, I knew how to completely care for myself. I would steal change from my mom and buy the cheapest food I could find, often expired. Or the neighbour moms would sneak me bites to eat here and there. I cleaned my own clothes in the sink and put myself to bed each night. As I grew up, I spent an increasing amount of time trying to avoid my mom. Her drunken rages became unpredictable and terrifying. I knew the police would have been on our doorstep many times if similar things weren't going on at the neighbours' in the rundown Mimico apartment building we lived in.

All the time, grubby-looking characters came and went from the apartment. Once, when I was about ten, one of them came into my room. I awoke to him standing over me, with the sheet lifted. The slack look on his face and the lump in his pants terrified me. I had made friends with a couple of older girls in the neighbourhood, and when I told them, they advised me to barricade my door at night because next time he may do more than look. They knew because it had happened to them. After supper, I wouldn't drink any more so I wouldn't have to pee in the night, and I moved a small dresser behind my door after I closed it. I heard the door rattle a time or two after.

Honestly, a lot of the things I had been exposed to were beyond inappropriate for a child. As a young teenager, Mom asked me to "service" a dealer in lieu of payment. She said, "If you loved me you would." The terrible thing was that I actually contemplated it. I did love her and wanted to do it for her. I chickened out and locked myself in my room for almost two days, terrified what she would ask of me in the name of love the next time I came out.

I avoided men completely until I met Jonathan when I was twenty-four. Even now it was hard for me to think about the brief slice of life that had almost been wonderful. The first year with Jonathan had been great, but I got pregnant soon into the relationship. Cassie was born, and things quickly disintegrated between us. He distanced himself from me in the beginning, wanting nothing to do with the baby, and by the time Cassie turned one, he had completely checked out. We became invisible to him, and I wanted more. I waited almost for a year for him to come back around, but he never did. He came and went from the house at strange hours, barely seeing us. He never laid a hand on either of us, even after I had provoked him into fighting one night. Even a slap would have been better than nothing. He continued to care for us financially, but it was more like we were roommates. I wanted love. So I left. I would regret that decision for the rest of my life. My selfishness had gotten me here, and I deserved it for wanting *more* than a roof over my head and food in the fridge.

I managed for several years on my own after leaving Jonathan, but it was almost impossible to raise a child on a barmaid's income. Ray was the older brother of a girl I worked with at the bar. He picked Tina up from work the day I noticed him. He had a rough cowboy look to him and the attitude to match. I guess starvation and having your phone cut off were great motivators, and he won me over pathetically fast. He had a good job with the city and a small house he had inherited from his parents near Grange Park.

Right away I noticed his mood swings, but I forgot them when he did something nice for me. I did my best to make him happy, and he provided me and my daughter with the necessities of life. And he had no nefarious interest in Cassie. As a precaution, when I went to work, I taught her the dresser-behind-the-door trick. It broke my heart to pass that onto her.

My life became a balance between protecting Cassie and pacifying Ray. He became the pole around which I danced.

So, I never expected a man to do anything good for me. I didn't read fairy tales growing up. Instead I learned how to make scrambled eggs and hide bottles from my mother.

I was an unintelligent, unattractive, pathetic excuse of a human. I wasn't even sure I qualified as a woman. I had resigned myself to what I had been given. Who could have predicted that I would be swept off my feet by a knight in shining armour at this stage of my life?

Well, maybe Cassie would have predicted it.

Cassie. Looking back, I wasn't exactly sure how, but I pulled it off. I nurtured her the way I had desperately wanted to be nurtured. And by some grace of God, Ray stayed away from her. If he ever looked like he might let loose on her, I stepped in and took it.

I know she saw more than I would have liked. And when she was accepted into university for social work, I pushed her to move into residence. I didn't want to be alone with Ray, but if I could save her any more pain, I could endure it.

She begged me to leave him. But how? Where would I go? Anyway, he would search for me and drag me back. I would never be truly free. It's called your lot in life for a reason.

I took a deep breath and quietly unlocked the door to the house. Back into the life, or rather the bed, I had made for myself.

KEELY

5

"**G**ood morning, ladies!" I spoke loudly over the chattering women. On one side of me stood the gym's sport psychologist turned life-coach-slash-nutritionist. Two trainers on the other side.

The twenty women settled down and focused intently on me. I stood a little taller. My power posing in the mirror this morning had helped shake off the funk I woke up in. Nothing cured an ice-cream-induced self-hate hangover like putting on your best workout clothes and tightening every muscle in your body for two minutes. Hands on hips, legs spread. Taking up as much space as I could. "As you all are well aware, Nationals are coming up and today we start our eight-week training program. We've all been here before and know what is necessary to achieve top form." I nodded to one of the trainers, who handed out the daily schedule.

I passionately launched into my "choices" speech. Really, this epithet could be used in any number of life situations, you just had to interchange a few words. "Your life is defined by the choices you make," I started, feeling my power rise from within me. *Harness it!* I coached myself. "You can *choose* to thrive instead of survive. You can *choose* to focus on what you want instead of giving yourself away. You can *choose* to hit the gym instead of being a fat slob who watches TV for five hours a night. You can *choose* to eat a whole cucumber instead of a whole bag of cookies. You can *choose* to honour the temple that you are instead of letting yourself go." I paused for effect, eyeing each of the women individually. They nodded deeply as my gaze passed them over. I wound up for the grand finale, taking a deep breath and spreading my shoulders back. "Don't *ever* let anyone tell you that you don't have a choice. Every second of every day, you make choices. A string of bad choices can ruin your life. And a series of good choices." I smiled broadly, sweeping my hands across the huddle of women, noticing the definition in my forearms as my hands twisted, the brachioradialis muscle popping beautifully. "Gets you here." I pointed aggressively at the floor. "Exactly where you want to be."

On cue, everyone cheered and clapped and high-fived each other. I stepped back and let Devon talk. "Now that Keely has pumped you up, let's get down to business. We are going to head straight to the gym and get started. We don't want to waste all that energy!"

I hung back, wondering why my words felt hollow today. They echoed in my brain, bouncing around instead of sinking in. I felt like I convinced the other women but not myself. Seeing Andrew last night had softened something in me that had become so hard over the years, but I couldn't quite put my finger on it. I had reached out to him mostly because I knew letting another woman take him from me so easily was not my style, but maybe there was more? I thought back to the day eight months ago that I felt a discernible tipping of the scales.

"Why are there so many cups lying around?" Andrew had grumbled when he got home from work. "The kitchen looks like a bomb went off."

I sighed. I knew I should have cleaned up before he got home, but I just needed to sit for a few minutes. "Riley had some friends over before soccer and they made themselves a snack."

"She's seventeen years old for God's sake, can't she clean up after herself?"

"Yes, but they were being crazy and not listening. I didn't feel like fighting with her. I'll do it in a bit." I tried to go back to my book.

Andrew stood surveying the kitchen, obviously deciding whether this was worth the fight. Finally, he muttered, "I'm going to the garage."

And that was when I felt something crack. *Am I here by choice?* I thought. *Do I really need to put up with this?* Sure, it was nice having a man around, especially a good-looking, successful one, but if I was alone I could just leave the girls' mess until after supper when I got a second wind and felt like cleaning. Or leave it for Janae the next day. No big deal. I didn't really have to listen to this every day. I wasn't some abused, broken housewife with no way out. Was this really the life I chose?

The answer my heart gave me was a resounding *no*.

That was the beginning of the end. After that, all I could see were the things I hated about our relationship. The things I loved faded into the background. The kids were grown, and I was on a new path. The gym was doing better than I ever thought it would, giving me financial freedom. I felt as though a new life waited for me to grab ahold of it. A life where I only had to worry about myself.

"Keely, you coming?" Devon disrupted my daydream.

I blinked. "Huh? Um… I'm not actually feeling so great."

"You didn't eat the yolks this morning, did you?" he joked.

I scoffed. "Of course not. I had the usual. Four scrambled egg whites and two slices of Ezekiel bread."

Devon nodded in approval as he stepped back to assess me.

"I think I'll go for a walk," I said suddenly, feeling slightly claustrophobic.

"A walk." He raised an eyebrow. "That's pretty tame for you."

"I don't know, I just don't feel like myself today." Funnily, I had a small hope I would see cane granny again.

He smiled. "Okay. You go walk. We can make up for it this afternoon."

I frowned, grabbed my white S'well bottle off the front desk and headed out.

I made it three times briskly around the park before I found an unoccupied bench to sit on. For me, it wasn't much of a workout, but it was still better than nothing. Birds annoyingly, happily sang and tittered in the tree beside me. The noise distracted me from thinking. My phone pinged, and I quickly read the message: *Please type C to confirm your appt at The Brow Lab for Wed Sept 13.* I quickly typed *C*. Riley's grad was this weekend, and I needed to get my eyebrows microbladed before then.

I sat back and watched the people in the park. An older couple shuffled past, her arm hooked in his. I smiled. I had imagined Andrew and me like that one day. Back when we were young and newly in love. Before kids and life happened. No one told me how much you change in those years in between. How you could become such different people. Well maybe not Andrew. He was the same old guy, but I was pretty sure I had found him endearing and loving in the beginning. When exactly did he become annoying and intrusive? Maybe when I quit work to try and stay home with the kids? I was sure I lost a lot of patience over those years.

I had gone back to work drafting after Emerson turned six months old and Jacob was two. That was a lot to handle, but we found a good day home. And then Riley came along unexpectedly three years later. So I quit my job, which I was sure delighted Andrew, and tried my very best to be one of *those* moms. The kind who stayed home and doted on her children. Taking them to the zoo, using a cookie cutter to make hearts and dinosaurs of their sandwiches, volunteering with the school's reading program. That lasted about four years, until Riley was old enough to start preschool. I literally woke up one day and realized I hated it. My life was about the kids and Andrew, and I hated it. There was no room for me anymore. I had gained about twenty pounds and let my wardrobe get "mommy comfortable." I was pretty sure I couldn't turn anyone's head if I tried. I was never the "overly loving" type of mom anyway. I was more of a "they'll survive" kind of mom. That's how I was raised, and I turned out fine.

One day I simply announced to Andrew that I was hiring a nanny *and* a personal trainer. And that he should also be prepared for a hit to the credit card. A new wardrobe was in order as well as a full day at the spa. He reluctantly agreed. It wasn't like we didn't have the money. He liked the soft mommy type, but I figured if he truly loved me, he would only want me to be happy. And if this was what it took, so be it. I conceded a bit and agreed to only a part-time nanny at first, but my gym obsession grew quickly, and having to quit in the middle of a ten-rep set of leg lifts to drive the kids to swimming lessons was a total pain. They didn't really need me to watch them anyway. All of the other moms just sat chatting with each other or staring at their phones, basically absent.

A bird hopped onto the bench beside me, breaking my memory jog. I went to shoo it away before it pooped near me, when it looked at me. Its little head twitched slightly, but I felt like it was trying to see me. Just some common type of sparrow, brown tones muted and unremarkable. Except for the black stripe on its head. *Probably a female, they are always the drabber of the sexes.* It reminded me of all the birds Emerson used to bring home dead, after useless efforts to resuscitate the filthy little things, so that they could have a proper burial in our small garden.

I leaned toward it and said, "Caw!" impersonating a crow.

The bird flitted away, past a woman walking toward me. Actually, scurrying would be a better term for her. I hated women like this, who purposely tried to take up as little space as possible, giving our whole gender a bad rap. She was about my age, but had made no attempt to slow the process, her dull brown hair obviously greying. *Au natural* I guess you could call it. Lazy, actually. She reminded me of the sparrow, or a mouse, the way her head hung forward and her feet moved in short, quick steps. I wanted to scream at her, "Stand up straight! And get your filthy coat cleaned!" But instead I sighed my disapproval heavily.

That'll be the day I look and act like that. As though I didn't know who I was or where I was going.

MICHELLE

6

I was going to be late for work, so I decided to take a shortcut through the park. I tried to avoid going through the park midday. It was always full of people who had leisure time and could relax into enjoying the fresh air and sunshine or even had enough energy to get some exercise. And always the young lovers, lying on the grassy hills, enchanted with each other. It just made me so sad for everything I would never have.

So I kept my head down and walked. Quickly. I couldn't help but smile at the lovely sounds the birds made. They seemed so happy. As I passed a bench I heard a woman let out a strange bird noise and then a disapproving sigh. I knew what she thought of me. Less than nothing. I wished I had time to just sit there and watch others pass. Time to let my guard down. If I wasn't working, I was scrambling around the house, cooking and cleaning and completing any other tasks that if left undone, might set Ray off. I suddenly saw myself walking on a tightrope, thin as dental floss, over a life full of everything sharp and hard and painful.

I stole a look at the woman from whom the noise had come and saw everything I was not. Her long, sleek black hair cascaded over one shoulder, her facial structure defined, her skin smooth and tanned. Even though she had sunglasses on, I was sure her makeup was probably perfect too. She had on exercise gear and colourful running shoes that matched her bright pink nails. Even sitting, I could tell she was a confident person. I was sure she wasn't trying to be mean, but I could see the faintest curl of distaste at the corners of her lipsticked mouth as she looked at me. I was certain she didn't mean to make me feel smaller than I already did in our brief passing.

I wanted to vanish. To be unseen, once and for all. What was the point of life anyway if this was all it had to offer me?

Forcing back tears, I snapped my head back down and hurried a little faster to get away from her.

"So, any more progress with Ray on Operation Michelle?" asked Kenzie as she moved glasses from the dishwasher to the drawer. It was nice of her to give my little idea a code name. Now she was pushing for me to work on getting my own credit card and start building my credit in case an opportunity to escape presented itself. But I knew I could never really give her the answer she wanted, and her happily expectant look fell as I told her how it was an inconceivable idea in the first place.

"Michelle." She put her hand on my arm. "Don't you ever get to do what *you* want?" She searched my face. Kenzie lived in the land of hope and courage, where inspirational memes flew around social media freely. I envied her. Even working at the bar, she was slumming it. A way to piss off her highbrow parents. Trying to prove she could make it without their chequebook and credit cards. Actually, come to think of it, I even envied her rebelliousness. She didn't know how much of a luxury even that was. Determinedly going against what her parents thought best for her. All the while knowing, deep down, they would always catch her when she fell.

No one, ever in my life, had caught me when I fell. Though I had never gotten high enough to actually fall. Nothing lay lower than the dull, cold, grey concrete basement floor where my soul lived.

I put on a false brightness; no need to bring this lovely girl down with my tales of woe. "Well, you know. It's not that bad. I like working here, and I'm sure I wouldn't actually make that good of a counsellor anyways." *And I can live vicariously through Cassie's career.*

"Bullshit," Kenzie spat, surprising me. Her perfectly sculpted eyebrows furrowed deeply. "That isn't you talking. That's him. You've listened to his garbage for so long, you actually believe it, don't you?"

I smiled weakly at her. *So she is more than a young face.* But this was the life I let become my reality. I had no one to blame but myself. Every time a doctor or nurse had slipped me a domestic abuse pamphlet, I thought about running. Especially as Cassie got old enough to understand what was going on. But on the flipside, she actually tied me down to him even more. Where would I go? How would I support us? How would I pay for her college? I knew I should have left Ray a year into the relationship. "But you can never go back," I whispered more to myself.

"No, you can't. But you can go forward. Go, now. Today. I'll give you all the money I have. Leave before he comes in to *collect* you tonight." Kenzie eyed me, her body leaning toward me.

Every muscle in my body flinched forward. Just a hair. It knew the anger in that word she growled. The truth of it. *Collect.* My body acted on its own accord, trying to seize the chance it saw. And before I could think further, the invisible grip Ray held on me contracted. It squeezed until every muscle cried uncle and promised they wouldn't try that again. "I can't." I sank back.

Kenzie sighed deeply and looked directly into my eyes, not backing down. "I saw that. Just so you know, I saw you take that offer and run. Even if you only moved a millimetre."

Unfortunately, I saw it too.

Andrew entered the bar later that night, making my breath catch in my throat. Although I had never gone to church, I crossed myself, just in case I was going to hell. It still shocked me that I actually did something like this. *Cheated.* Maybe there was still a flicker of life left in me. Had I truly been a lost cause, I wouldn't have even noticed his attraction in the first place. *Maybe I'm not as resigned to my life as I try and convince myself.* Quickly, my excitement at seeing him turned to fear. *Always with the fear.* I rushed up to him. "You can't be here tonight," I whispered.

"I suppose Ray is coming?" His tone surprised me, cutting hard through the din of talking and clinking and music.

"Well, yes. He should be here in half an hour." I looked at my watch quickly. It was payday. The one night that would guarantee a personal pick up from Ray.

Andrew squared up his shoulders and said, "What if I stay tonight?"

"You can't. Please, Andrew." I could feel a sweat break out along my hairline. He had no idea.

He relaxed a bit. "I just really wanted to see you tonight." He reached out to touch my hair. "The other day…"

A cheer broke out over at the dartboard, where a group of men stood. I smiled. "I know. I would love to see you too, but it can't be tonight."

He took a deep breath and blurted out, "Look, I want to be honest with you. I saw Keely last night."

He'd promised when it became apparent we would not be parting ways any time soon that he would be honest with me. He'd said he would do everything in his power to not hide anything from me or hurt me. That he wanted someone who would talk to him and share her life with him. I began to feel like a real partner in a relationship even though we had only been "courting" at that point. A partner who had the same amount of control as the other. It felt euphoric and terrifying. I didn't know how to be that person. He had promised he would help me learn.

"I hope everything is okay?" I finally said.

He rubbed the back of his neck. "You're concerned about her?"

"Well… I just don't want to see her suffer. I mean, she's a person too."

Andrew grabbed me and hugged me tight to his chest. "You're something else, you know that?" His voice cracked.

I relaxed into him for a split second before gently pushing him away. "Andrew."

He regained his composure. "I know. No public displays of affection." He paused and looked around before continuing. "She wants to get back together with me." His face swivelled back to me.

I wasn't surprised to hear this, but it still quickened my pulse. Of course she would want him back. Who wouldn't? She was crazy to push him away in the first place, and I'd always kept this possibility in the back of my mind. *Prepare for the worst and hope for the best.* But who was I kidding? Even hope was a luxury I couldn't afford.

He plowed forward through a speech I couldn't help but feel he had prepared in his head. "But don't worry, okay? I'm not getting back together with her. You can't have your cake and eat it too." His voice fell unconvincingly.

No, you can't. I caught a glint in Kenzie's eye as she pretended to focus on entering an order into the computer. She knew what was going on with Andrew and me, but we had an unspoken agreement not to talk about it. Same as Cass, it was safer for her to stay detached from this situation. Plus, an old-fashioned part of me was superstitious and was worried speaking about it would break the spell.

But it seemed Andrew's ex had broken the spell herself.

I lay in bed that night thinking how nice it would have been to run away with Andrew. I decided I should just be grateful for the small glimpse of happiness I'd had.

What did I ever do to deserve this? Maybe I was a horrible person in another life and this was my punishment? I tried to keep my breathing normal and light as the tears overtook me. Ray hated it when I cried, and he had already berated me outside the bar tonight for wearing a skirt that was too short. Apparently, anything above the knee was attire meant for sluts only. As soon as we got home, he demanded I take it off. After I handed it to him, he jammed it into the garbage can, staining it with coffee grounds, never to be worn again by anyone.

I cried as silently as possible as I tried to forget the dream life I'd thought I had a chance at.

KEELY

7

Be nice, I repeatedly told myself as Riley and I waited for Andrew to arrive. I could never understand fall graduations. I had been long gone by the time September rolled around and didn't give going back to attend a second thought.

I fussed over Riley's grad dress, which was almost *too* skater. Black and plain and ill-fitting. It was not her plump figure that bothered me. People could still be beautiful if they dressed to their body type. This was where Riley failed, though. Because she simply didn't care. At least she had let me flatiron her sleek brown hair into loose waves. Alarmingly, I felt a twinge of jealousy. What would that feel like, really not to give a shit about what was on the outside?

I pulled myself back together. *Neglectful.* That was what it would feel like.

Andrew pulled up, and Riley left the house ahead of me. She could be gorgeous. Riley was the female version of Andrew. As he opened the door of the Escalade for her and then for me, he frowned. *Keep it to yourself,* I internally instructed him.

"I know, aren't they ridiculous?" Riley openly laughed from beside me in the back seat. *Damn her!*

"Well… I wasn't going to say anything." Andrew reddened. "But what exactly happened to your eyebrows, Keely?"

I sighed deeply and closed my eyes for a split second. I was still mad at the microblading technician, but really, I shouldn't have had them done so close to a big event. "The girl microblading them was an inexperienced idiot." I crossed my arms over my chest and then immediately undid them. I didn't need more wrinkles in my décolletage. That habit was almost as bad as sleeping on your side. Nothing showed a woman's age more than the condition of the delicate skin between her neck, boobs, and shoulders.

"What the heck is microblading?" Andrew asked, his own eyebrows lifting.

"Something you should only have done if you are under twenty-five years old." Riley clamped her hand over her mouth in an actual attempt to stifle her comment. She shrugged her shoulders and looked to me, her own lovely eyebrows naturally full. "Sorry, Mom, but I couldn't help it."

I scowled at her. Jacob turned from the front seat and smirked that crooked grin that indicated he was holding back. Everything about his appearance screamed "milkman's kid" with his reddish blonde hair and clear blue eyes. Some long-lost recessive genes had kicked in when he was conceived. "Riley, leave Mom alone. She looks lovely with two black caterpillars on her forehead."

Andrew slid into the driver's seat. "Okay, you two, leave your mom alone." He turned backward and smiled at me. "But just for the record, I thought you had nice eyebrows before. Especially the tiny bald spot you rub when you're stressed."

"That was the worst part!" I said. "I hate that spot, and this has always worked before and you didn't notice. It's just this time it's a bit too heavy."

"And too perfect," added Jacob. "I don't understand it myself. It doesn't look real."

"Mom hasn't looked real for years," Riley said.

Wow, she was on a roll tonight. "Is this pick-on-Mom time?" I finally exploded.

"No, Keely. Everyone zip it." Andrew started the engine.

The car ride to the auditorium was mostly quiet. It seemed there was nothing to talk about unless I was the object of everyone's harassment. Finally, I said, "So, Riley, is Jayden meeting us there?"

Riley's exasperated look indicated I had missed something. "We're not talking about Jayden, remember Keely?" Andrew said, trying to save her from having to explain.

"Right," I said, but I couldn't help myself. I turned to her. "Why?"

Riley's face started to crumple, and I was immediately sorry I asked.

Andrew glanced sideways at me from the front seat, a look of exasperation on his face. He finally said quietly, "Last week. You know? Jayden decided at the last minute he was taking Olivia to grad instead?"

Shit. Why didn't I know this? She must have been at Andrew's when it happened. "I'm so sorry, honey," I said to Riley, gingerly patting her knee.

Riley levelled a glare at me. "Just for once, could my life be more important than your own?"

I bit back a defense. I knew, deep down, that there may be a shred of truth in her question. But they didn't remember how much I gave to them when they were little. So much that I almost lost myself. But of course they would forget that. They only remembered all the ways I had wronged them. I crossed my arms again, not caring about wrinkles, and remained silent, before I said anything more to make this whole thing worse. This was why I just wanted to keep to myself. I always seemed to say something stupid to my family. Some days I thought the only people who got me were my clients. *Other people like me.*

At the reception after the actual graduation ceremony, Emerson met up with us. She couldn't exchange her shift at the bookstore and had to miss the first part. "I'm so sorry, Riley," she breathed as she sat down next to her sister, squeezing her shoulder. Riley shot me a look that said, *That's how you do a real apology.*

As we listened to the boring speeches, I pushed my meal around on my plate. Now that I was in training, I was only allowed to eat good fats combined with lean protein. At least I could eat the chicken breast. I had done my best to scrape off the teriyaki sauce, but I left a couple of bites behind in lieu of the glaze I couldn't remove.

I watched intently as Emerson inhaled the pesto linguine with gusto. "What about your stomach, Em?"

Emerson laughed at me, wiping her lips with a red napkin. "Really, Mom. I'm not gluten intolerant."

"But you always had those stomachaches when you were younger. And you know…" I didn't actually want to say the word *diarrhea,* but if they pushed me, I would have to.

"Everything in moderation, Mother. Including moderation." Em rolled her eyes.

"I agree!" inserted Andrew, fork pushed into the air.

I looked at him. "But you remember how sick she was after eating too much bread."

"Maybe it was something else." He shrugged.

"Maybe you just convinced me that I was gluten intolerant as a way to control what I ate?" Emerson eyed me.

I felt the heat creep up my face. I looked at her, and something in her eyes suggested that she wasn't joking.

"But bread is so *bad* for you," I started emphatically.

"For your ass or your stomach?" she countered, tipping her head.

Both. I pursed my lips but didn't reply. I knew I was stuck. I was surprised to feel my throat tighten. The harassment of the evening was finally getting to me.

"Mom. It's okay. I was just bugging you," Emerson said quickly.

"It's fine," I whispered as I discreetly patted my eyes and focused back on the presentations. Had I really been that terrible of a mother? *But I was just being me.* I wouldn't have been doing my job if I let the kids stuff everything they saw into their faces. Someone had to try to make them appreciate being healthy.

"Here." Andrew slid a glass of wine over to me.

"Thanks." I smiled. Tonight, I deserved a caloric concession. Didn't I?

"I think maybe you should stop now," Andrew said, four glasses later, as the last speaker left the stage.

I looked at him, but past. My eyes not quite able to focus. I had miraculously survived the worst part, and I noticed a DJ setting up. I suddenly perked up. "When does the dancing start?"

"Mom!" Riley said. "Keep it down, okay?" She looked around nervously to see if anyone had heard me.

"Like I'm the only drunk parent here. This is insufferable!" I laughed too loud, attracting unwanted attention. Several people at the table next to us stared and then leaned in to whisper to each other. I stood up suddenly.

"Where are you going?" Riley asked, looking panicked.

"To pee. Is that allowed?" I wobbled a tiny bit before forcing my legs to contract and appear more solid.

"Of course, Keely," Andrew said, starting to stand.

"I can go myself. Jeez!" I said, a little too loud again. I walked away, concentrating every bit of energy I could into walking straight.

I was almost to the back of the auditorium when I saw her standing at the bar. Her eyes swept the room and stopped on me, an automatic smile coming to her lips. *Cadence.*

I was hoping to avoid her tonight. This was the last thing I needed. She waved, but I quickly looked past, pretending I didn't see her.

I hurried into the washroom and peed. I crossed my fingers, literally, that she wouldn't be standing outside the door as I left. To my relief, she wasn't, and I hurried back to our table, only allowing myself to briefly look toward the bar. Cadence was still in line for a drink, but looking around the room. Internally, I congratulated myself for escaping. As she turned back to the bartender, I noticed how much longer her naturally blonde hair was than the last time I saw her. Normally, Cadence wore a pixie-type cut, the kind of look only truly beautiful and confident women could pull off. Like Pink. But tonight her hair fell in soft curls past her shoulders. It was downright sexy.

I shook my head and turned back to Riley. "Can we go yet?"

Her right eye twitched. *She must get that from me.* "I thought you'd never ask."

I quickly grabbed my purse and started walking to the main door. The faster I could get out of there the better.

Feeling mushy from the wine, I leaned into Andrew's ear as he dropped Riley and me at home. "Maybe you should come in." I wobbled on my strappy black Manolo Blahnik stilettos as Riley disappeared into the house. They had been the perfect understated choice to go with my new white Michael Kors leather and lace dress. White always looked so good on me because of my black hair and tanned skin. And sleeveless. My arms were my best feature and I showed them off as much as possible. But Riley had freaked when she saw me, swearing she could see my panties through it. I laughed wickedly at her assumption. But after seeing her genuine distress, I finally caved and told her it had a nude liner so she would calm down.

Andrew bent over and said, "Here, take these off before you kill yourself." He stood up with the shoes in his hand. It felt better on the cool, flat, *unmoving* earth.

He sighed. "Why would I come in, Keely?"

I shrugged my shoulders in an exaggerated motion. "Maybe we could kiss," I slurred.

He burst out laughing and put his hands on his hips. "See, this is the Keely I miss."

"What's wrong with the current Keely?" I asked, instantly a little more sober.

He put his hand on my arm. "Nothing. You are an amazing, driven, successful woman, and I'm very proud of you." He looked up toward the rental house. It was painted a crisp white and had black shutters and shingles. *Clean lines*. Like me. "But you were different before the kids were born. We had fun together. Do you remember?"

I sniffed. "Yes. But life is serious business, Andrew. How am I supposed to become the amazing person I was meant to be if I just wander around looking for fun?"

He sighed deeply, shoving one hand in his jacket pocket. He looked absolutely smoking hot. "I don't know. But there has to be some kind of balance, don't you think?" Finally he added quietly, "All I ever wanted was to take care of you. You know it's what I feel I was meant to do."

I bristled. "I don't need anyone to take care of me." I tried to put my shoulders back.

He looked at me sadly. "I know. You've made that very clear."

I blurted out, my filter melted away by the wine, "Is that why you went to her? Is she some kind of damsel in distress? You knew I wasn't like that when we got married."

It took him a long time to answer. "I guess I'm just the kind of person who's happier if I'm taking care of someone. It's not a macho thing. I don't think." He frowned. "I feel like it just gives me a purpose. To help someone." I knew how Andrew had watched his mom die a slow death of breast cancer, and how his own dad had become her caretaker. Robert had even quit his job for his wife so he could be by her side twenty-four seven. Andrew had been twenty-six when she died, right before we met, and he'd told me with tears in his eyes of the true, unwavering love of his parents. He'd seen firsthand what it meant to love someone with your whole soul, and that was all he wanted in our relationship. I felt a wave of guilt wash over me. I couldn't give him what he needed. My emotional barometer was broken. That, or I was a man at heart. Even right before our wedding, I got cold feet and tried to cancel it, but Andrew begged me to stay. Sometimes, I really wondered what he saw in me. I told myself it was at least better to have a husband who cared so much than one who didn't care at all. I forced myself to try to change. To be what Andrew wanted, needed, and deserved. To be what I thought a good person looked like. But I failed.

I softened. "You're a good guy, Andrew. I've never doubted that. I just… I don't know if it's the way I have always been or if I changed with old age. People are allowed to change, aren't they?"

"Yes, of course."

"My parents were detached. Always focused on working. And maybe that's how I came to define success? All they ever said was that no one ever helped them, so they had to do it themselves." They had wanted children who were *tough* and *motivated* and *self-reliant.* They wanted children other people would look up to and respect. And I turned out to be the opposite. A wolf in sheep's clothing. A blasphemy.

"So they were a generation ahead of the self-help trend?" He smiled.

I suddenly felt deflated. And tired. The sag in my body must have been obvious. "Okay, enough chatting, let's get you inside." He put his arm around me and steered me up the sidewalk.

I let him help me into the house and onto the couch. He pulled a blanket up over me. As he turned to leave, I mumbled, "I never meant to let it go this far."

He looked back, frowning, and then shrugged, probably thinking I was completely incoherent. He leaned over and kissed my cheek. "I know. Everyone does the best they can with what they have. Remember that, Keely." His eyes flashed in the lamplight.

It bubbled at my lips—the thing I never told him. But even in my state, I couldn't bring myself to speak the deep, dark truth I hid. I wanted to tell him I couldn't silence the nasty voice that liked to remind me my *true* nature was never quite good enough.

MICHELLE

8

R ay was on a double shift with the city, cleaning up one of the parks for a big music festival, so I decided to leave for work early and stop by a bookstore on my way. The past few months, I would have used this chance to sneak in a visit with Andrew, but for some strange reason I wanted to do something just for myself. He had texted the other day telling me how great Riley's graduation had been, but I realized it was another chance for him and Keely to be together. Maybe I knew I should start letting him go. Release him *and* the dream. That way, when he inevitably initiated it, the pain would be less.

I didn't need to be more broken. That had been the one saving grace of not realizing, all of these years with Ray, what *could* be. I had purposely forgotten the brief respite with Jonathan. And now I knew the trouble I'd caused myself, falling for Andrew. All the old feelings came back, reminding me they were real. I would probably have been better off not getting a taste of it at all.

As I stood in line for a coffee, I noticed the other women waiting. Some had small children, some were alone, probably on a similar "me break" while the kids were at school. Or they were not mothers. I felt a pang of regret at dragging Cassie into this mess, but I tried to push it away. I wondered for a moment what kind of lives these women had. Were they at all like me? They didn't look it. They looked bright and happy. Not dull and sad. But, then again, maybe they hid something darker and truer.

Did they ever regret their choices?

As I sipped the ridiculously overpriced but delicious latte, I wandered around the store. I was not sure what brought me here, as I had little time to read. The last proper book I'd finished was *Charlotte's Web*, when I was still reading to Cassie before bed. A woman about my age stood looking at books in the self-help section, so I wandered over. I passed over books with titles like *Awakening to Your Life's Purpose* and *How to Start Living Your Perfect, Awesome, Sparkly Life* and *Create the Life Others Would be Jealous of.* I sighed. Did people really have the luxury of reading these things? Where was the section of books relating to me? *How you Became Such a Loser in the First Place* or *Punishment the Second Time Around For All of the Terrible Things You Probably Did in Your Previous Life* or simply *Escape: A One-Way Ticket Out of the Hell That is Your Life.*

The woman next to me turned and smiled, her teeth lined with braces. *I thought they were only for gangly teenagers?* It didn't fit with the rest of her polished appearance. "I could hang out here all day, couldn't you?"

"Um… yeah. Me too," I said, not wanting to scare her by blurting out the truth. Which lately seemed a little closer to the surface than ever. Old age must do that to a person.

She frowned, taking me in. Probably thinking, *What is a timid, beat-down little thing like you doing here, in the land of women who are awesome and slaying their lives? Women who are rising to the top echelons of society, previously places only men could occupy?* Even I was surprised at this sudden, internal snarkiness. I saw her look at my fingers, which were wrapped around the coffee cup, and I knew she was probably disgusted by how short the nails had been chewed down. I put the coffee down on the nearest shelf and pulled my hands into the sleeves of my coat. But she put her hand on my arm and said softly, "It's okay." Her soft smile revealed tiny wrinkles around her mouth.

Tears rushed up. Was it the way she looked at me, with pure pity? Or was it her genuine tenderness and concern too much for me to take? I made to leave, and she said, "Don't go. I'm sorry, I shouldn't have said that." She looked over my shoulder to another woman approaching. "Please forgive me, but I can see my old self in you. Beat down." I instinctively looked down. She reached over and grabbed a book off the shelf. "Can I please buy this for you?"

I was shocked and couldn't respond. Instead, more tears came forward. I had thought myself so weak my whole life, and the tears betrayed that this was in fact true. I couldn't even control them in front of a stranger. I looked down at the book she had pressed into my hands. *The Gifts of Imperfection.* I panicked. What would I do with it anyway? And if Ray ever found it, I'd get the mocking of my life. I shoved the book back at her and ran from the store. A full block away, I remembered my coffee on the bookshelf. I didn't have the courage to go back and get it, though I desperately wanted to.

I couldn't risk the look on that woman's face again, seeing me for what I really was.

Weak.

Back at work the next day, Kenzie asked, "Why the heck are you wearing a long-sleeved shirt, Michelle? It's scorching out today!" Her eyes grew large, and she clamped her mouth into a tight line.

I just shrugged my shoulders and said, "I had a chill this morning." I was boiling to death as it was unseasonably warm for September, but I couldn't even roll the sleeves up past my forearms. The thought of yesterday came crashing back into my head.

"Did you really think I wouldn't notice that you were sneaking money off your tips? Do I seriously have to come collect you EVERY SINGLE FUCKING NIGHT to make sure you're not screwing me over?" Ray grabbed me by both of my arms, just above the elbows. I could instantly feel the bruises he would leave with his fingertips. The explosion had caught me off guard because he had been in such a good mood when he got home from work. He'd actually hugged me.

"I wasn't taking extra," I sobbed.

"Then how do you explain the twenty I found in the bottom of your purse?" His face came close to mine. I could smell the tobacco on his breath that always disgusted me.

"I don't know. It must have fallen out of my wallet."

"Money doesn't fall out of a wallet, you stupid bitch." He shoved me against the wall.

I closed my eyes and waited for it. But he actually hesitated. Finally he spat, "You know, it gets really old dealing with you. Especially now that I've footed the bill for your dumb daughter to go to college. You'll be paying interest on that one for the rest of your life." He pointed to the bedroom. "Get undressed."

The usual disgust at myself for letting him treat me this way started to flood my system. But I soon found myself unable to move. *What is wrong with me?* This was going to make him even madder, and it would hurt more. The pain of him driving himself into me increased with his level of rage. As if he needed to hurt me more to relieve his own anger. "Why aren't you going?" he hissed, his face reddening.

And for the first time in a long time, I looked up and directly into his eyes. I knew I'd pay for it, but at the moment I didn't care. A conflict had been rising inside of me since I met Andrew, and the ordeal in the bookstore the previous day had seemed to turn up the heat. This new brave feeling and my old feelings of weakness were doing battle inside of me. Finally, my trusted old voice of reason piped up. *You'll never make it on your own.* I dropped my eyes. Again.

He snorted. "Yeah, that's right. Now get going."

I obeyed, forcing my body to move, but this time I actually started to think about why.

"Michelle?" Kenzie's voice brought me back to the present.

I blinked. "Oh. Hey. It's nothing."

Kenzie gave me a questioning look. "Michelle. I could help you. My parents, they have money. I'm sure if I told them, we could get you a small place…" Her high blonde ponytail swung as she talked fervently.

I smiled at her. "Kenzie, that's so nice of you, but I'm okay. Really, I am."

"You're not, though. I just want to help you." Her eyes grew shiny.

Why did I bring my stupid problems in here with me today? Now I had her all worried for no reason. And I couldn't tell her the real reason I couldn't leave. All the money in the world wouldn't stop Ray from finding me again. Money may buy a temporary escape, but it doesn't provide protection from the inevitable.

"Please, sweetie." I took her hand. "Don't worry about me. I made my bed." *My mantra.* I smiled and tried changing the subject. "What I would like to know is when are you going to get out of here and do something great? You're better than this place."

The look she gave me hurt more than I expected. "So are you."

I knew she couldn't let go, so I told her what she so desperately wanted to hear. "One day. One day I'll figure something out, okay? But it's not for you to worry about. Let's get this place organized before the after-work crowd arrives." I busied myself getting the bar organized.

I didn't turn back to see her reaction. I finally relaxed once I sensed that she had moved away.

I winced as a group of girls came in around eight. *Bridal showers.* Groups of drunk women, hell-bent on making the night memorable for the bride-to-be, were insufferable at best. All but the most desperate men even avoided them for fear of becoming a target of one of their "funny" tests and pranks.

I took a deep breath and approached the babbling table. "Hello, ladies." I put on my working smile. "What can I get for you?"

"A round of boilermakers!" the leader shrieked, her impressive cleavage on full display. I forced myself to not look down at my own droopy breasts. "And sex on the beach for this bitch!" She pointed to the girl decked out in white lingerie and a tiara. *Oh God, they are on a tear.* "You betcha." I turned back to the bar.

"Are they going to be a problem?" Kurt asked as I returned to the bar and told him their order.

"Possibly. Hopefully they're doing a pub crawl and will move on quickly."

He eyed the table as he prepared the drinks. One of the girls blew him a kiss. "Hopefully," he said sourly, while smirking and winking back at her.

But they didn't leave. Their demands for drinks grew louder and more obnoxious. "Another reason not to drink," I muttered to myself as I brought them another round. Being surrounded, at work and at home, by drunks was a surefire way to induce sobriety in a person.

As I approached the table near midnight, the bride was in tears. I wasn't surprised. Usually at least one of them was crying by the end of the night. Heaving and sobbing, she exclaimed, "It's not even a whole carat!" She held out her hand to show off her apparently tiny ring with the biggest rock I'd ever seen. It glinted and sparkled even in the dim light of the bar. "But it's a good quality stone, I can tell." One of her friends smiled, trying to cheer her up.

"But Mandy got a two carat, princess cut solitaire. It's gorgeous!" the bride wailed. Her friends tried to console her. "I thought he loved me," she continued. "Now I'll be the laughing stock of the group!" The princess bride dramatically flagged me down. "Bring me another shot!"

Sometimes I hated my job. I took a deep breath and said, "I don't think that's a good idea."

The bride turned her rage at her unloving husband-to-be onto me. "I said, bring me a shot. This is my stagette, and you'll do what I tell you to."

"We have a policy here…" I started, my stomach clenching.

"I don't fucking care about your *policies!*" she shrieked. "When I want a drink, you bring me a drink! Got it?"

Thankfully, Kurt was suddenly at my side. "As Michelle said, we have a policy here. You ladies have reached your limit. And if you keep talking to my waitress like that, I will not hesitate to have you removed." He crossed his arms and leaned on his left leg.

The bride's face softened into the cunning female look. I was always shocked how easily people could change to get what they wanted. "Oh, hotness!" She flipped her hand toward him. "I was just joking. We were just trying to have a bit of fun. A round of beers, then?" she fawned.

"One round. Then that's it. And no more shots." He turned and walked away, and as I followed him, I heard the bride hiss loudly. "If I ever become that lame, please shoot me!"

I tried to suppress the flinch as their shrieks of laughter erupted behind me.

When I arrived home after two, Ray was snoring on the couch. Kurt had insisted I stay until closing so he could give me a ride home, as it appeared that my husband had already forgotten his threat about picking me up every night. It was a Saturday and a full moon. "Not a good night for you to walk home alone, Michelle," Kurt insisted.

I crept into the bedroom and changed into pajamas. For some reason, I felt like pulling out the memory box of Cassie's things I kept in the closet. I gingerly picked up Ray's dirty underwear from the floor and dropped them in the laundry basket, then sat on the floor. I wiped the dust off the top of the box. Just a plain, brown cardboard file box, but it contained everything bright and happy and colourful. This box reminded me how much I was loved by at least one person in this world.

On the top of the pile was a macaroni Mother's Day card Cassie made at five years old. The dried pasta was arranged in a haphazard flower shape and then messily painted. Cassie's artistic skills had much improved over her lifetime. Inside the card, in blue wax crayon, it read *I Love You, Mom.* I sorted through many more such ritualized cards and drawings, sent home at the appropriate holidays. Even if Cassie made them in school though, somehow all of the Father's Day cards went mysteriously missing by the time she got home. I knew they were likely torn and muddied, lying in the gutter somewhere along her path. Like it mattered anyway. Ray never said a word about not receiving anything.

Near the bottom of the pile, I pulled out the note she had written me right before she moved out for college. I had not been able to read this without crying. Ever. Not because of what she said in it, but due to the realization that I may have saved Cassie from Ray's abuse, but I hadn't succeeded in saving her from the emotional pain. The short note had one simple line: *I will get you out.*

I felt like the worst mother in the world for having put such an enormous burden on my child. No kid should have to feel like it's their life mission to rescue a parent. They should be able to leave home and start their own life. For the millionth time I wished I had chosen more carefully. Surely there had been better options to secure Cassie's future? I had panicked and been rash. Desperation does that to a person.

There was only one way to ensure that Cassie wouldn't have to rescue me, but I was too chicken to follow through with such a plan.

I put the box away and climbed into bed, forcing myself to remember the night that should have sent me running.

The whole facade of my first year with Ray came crashing down one night after he'd been out drinking with friends. He wasn't wasted, but drunk enough. He showed up at my little apartment looking for love, and when I turned him down for sex, he flew into a rage.

He hurled a beer bottle at the fridge. "You're mine, and I'll fuck you when I want!" he hissed at me, his face contorted and ugly. "Especially if you expect me to support you *and* your child."

I'd seen enough drunken eruptions to know I was in trouble. But I couldn't force myself to move. Cassie was asleep in my bedroom, and I didn't want him to wake her. I tried to calm him down and told him I would do it, just to shut him up.

On the floor, in front of the stove, I let him have me. I told myself it would only be five minutes of my life. I told myself it was for the greater good. I told myself I was being dramatic and there was no rape in a relationship.

I quietly endured it as my back was cut in several places from the glass that had showered the kitchen.

After, he told me that's the way it was in relationships. When the man wanted sex, he got it. Whether the woman wanted it or not. He said that was how it had been since the beginning of time, and it was never going to change, regardless of how many rights those stupid feminist cunts pushed for. He married me and told me to get used to it.

I took his word as the ugly truth society hid. How was I really to know any better? I told myself Jonathan had been a once-in-a-lifetime chance. It would never come around again because I had been stupid enough to want more. I knew my mother had given it up for years for alcohol and drugs.

I guess Cassie was my addiction. And I was okay with it.

KEELY

9

I sat with the accountant as we went over the quarterly financials for the gym. I knew the recession may have had an effect on my business, but I thought since we had gotten through the worst of it, we were in the clear. I was wrong.

Matt said, "It's not the end of the world. In eight years you have done amazing. One bad quarter is okay. But I would advise you to maybe cut back on unnecessary purchases for the gym." He chewed on the eraser of his pencil and then picked up a stack of receipts. "And I'm not sure things like this can be written off. You spent... what did I calculate? Three thousand two hundred and sixty dollars in April for skincare?"

"Ugh! I was copying Kim Kardashian. She has amazing skin, and everything I purchased was a part of her daily routine." I could almost hear my mother sigh in disgust. She probably would have tried to tell me that a concoction of clay from the dugout mixed with cow piss was just as good, and free.

He flicked through the receipts and pulled one out. "Guerlain Orchid Longevity Concentrate for five hundred and ten dollars US? That could buy a family of four groceries for a month!" And then he pulled out another one. "Four hundred and ten dollars at the ICK Laser Clinic?"

I dug my fingernails into my palm. I hated justifying my purchases to *anyone*. Plus, the whole regime had worked beautifully. Between the Kardashian-approved products and having all of my sunspots lasered off my face, I swore I looked five or six years younger. I was surprised I hadn't received more compliments on my skin.

I snapped, "I have created the means for myself to live better than that. I don't pay you to question my purchases, just to hide them for tax reasons."

Matt breathed hard out of his nose. "Just maybe try and cut back on the frivolous expenses, okay?"

Frivolous expenses? I had none. Tanning was a must. Waxing was a must. Botox was a must. Competition fees and clothes (with coordinating high heels) were a must. Root touch-ups were a must. The best, cleanest, organic foods were a must. And, of course, the skincare products. Well, maybe the Lexus wasn't a must, but what was I supposed to drive, a *Ford*? Maybe Riley would skip college. That would help.

"You never did settle on alimony with Andrew, did you?" Matt raised his eyebrows.

"I don't need his help." I laced my fingers on the desktop and glowered at him.

"You may change your tune if things continue like this. I told you last time, once you sign that away you can never get it back. Better safe than sorry. And you could lose your condo."

The condo! "Crap." I rubbed my forehead, trying furiously to flatten the ever-creeping wrinkles. "I forgot about that."

"I know he was giving you that, but the maintenance fees are approximately twelve hundred a month."

Buying the condo in Saint Lucia was my wildest dream come true. Andrew had surprised me for my fortieth birthday. He wouldn't tell me where we were going, just that I shouldn't worry, Janae had the kids and we were going on a surprise holiday. As we flew into the island, I was delighted. We had been there a few times before and had fallen in love with it. When he blindfolded me and walked me into the four-bedroom, exquisitely decorated tropical paradise overlooking the ocean, I almost couldn't contain my excitement. And when he said, "Happy birthday, babe," I turned to him, disbelieving. "Yup, it's all yours." He grinned. *I used to love that grin.* That look he gave me when he'd hit the nail on the head for me.

The condo was the only thing I wanted in our initial separation agreement. He gave it to me willingly. I think it was a symbol of how hard he tried to make me happy. And failed.

"You might want to think about renting it out here and there, just to cover the monthly costs. Because I know you wouldn't sell it unless you were destitute." Matt grinned.

"Uh, no! I would move there before I had to sell, and I'm not renting *my house* out. I don't want other people occupying *my* space, looking at *my* things, sleeping in *my* bed."

"Okay, Gollum." Matt smirked. "But when you get over the shock of my suggestion, think about it."

"And I pay you to treat me like this?" I swung my head back and forth, breathing in.

"Yes, you do!" He collected his papers and stood up. "If it makes you feel better, you're not the only one. I've had to help close down three businesses this month already."

"No, that doesn't make me feel better. I don't care what other businesses are doing. I care about my business." I stood up as well. "Unless one of them is a gym. Then tell me who they are so I can steal their clients." I laughed.

I sat for a long time in my office thinking about what Matt said. Of course I *could* rent the condo, but that was a last-ditch option. "Maybe this is a sign that I need Andrew more than I thought," I muttered out loud, drumming my nails a little too hard on the desk. I caught myself and lightened up. The last thing I needed was to chip my new set of gels.

Even I wasn't too far gone to see that this was a very selfish reason to want to stay married. But seriously, I knew tons of women who stayed married for financial reasons or worse. Especially while the kids were still at home. It was the only way unskilled stay-at-home moms could make it. But I refused to be *stuck*. Living in a life I had no way out of because of money. That was why lots of moms started up with those pyramid schemes. They wanted some kind of financial freedom. Honestly, the workplace was not friendly to mothers. In Canada we got a whole year maternity leave, but they got nothing in most of the US, unless you counted twelve weeks unpaid leave. Who wanted to hire someone who left every couple of years? And had to call in sick all the time. And couldn't work overtime or weekends because the kids had soccer. Best to go at it on your own terms. No one ever got far sitting and waiting around for someone to take care of them, or worse, save them. I refused to let life just *happen* to me.

Matt's news really sucked. Sure, I could probably go back to drafting, but it would be hard work to get back up to speed. And the money wasn't great. And I'd have to find a new firm since I always worked at Andrew's. I could survive, but there would be a lot less designer shoes purchased.

"Maybe I should find a rich boyfriend," I muttered, twisting on my office chair, flexing my core as tightly as I could on each swivel. *Now this is multitasking.* But that would be too much work. *Just go back to Andrew,* the voice inside my head said. I did miss the big house. My rental house's facade may have been new, but the inside was a little more shabby than chic.

Emerson. She would know what to do. Even though she chose a path I didn't really approve of, she was always the most levelheaded child. I texted to see if she wanted to come for supper tonight. She responded *Yes* instantly.

I couldn't believe I was going to my twenty-one-year-old daughter for life advice.

Even though she spent most of her time at Andrew's, Riley's washroom was disgusting, and she wouldn't let Janae in to clean it, so before Emerson came over, I quickly went into my en suite washroom and took all the Post-it notes off the mirror. Em would just roll her eyes and make fun of me. *You're amazing* and *Don't ever doubt your ability to kick ass* and *Act as if you already have what you want* and *You are the creator of your life* were added to the pile with dozens of others proclamations.

I'd just finished tidying when the doorbell rang.

"Come in!" I yelled.

"Hi, Mom!" I heard from the living room as the door clicked. I heard a second, louder slam. *That's what you get with a rental, doors that don't fit properly into their frames.*

"Are you hungry? Dinner's almost done." I walked out of my bedroom. Emerson threw her sweater on the black leather couch and said, "Yes."

"It'll be about five minutes. Will you survive that long?" Emerson had been hangry half of her childhood. I figured she had gotten it from Andrew, because I could never understand the rage she would fly into at five if she wasn't fed properly. Some days when I was home, I wouldn't even talk to her until she'd been fed a burger or some other substantial meal.

"Yes, Mom." Em rolled her eyes.

"Anything new?" I pulled open the fridge and took out the strawberry spinach salad. "Hot, young men still beating down your door?" I didn't really know what my obsession was with the kids' dating lives. It was as if I wanted them to all be with a good catch. Which was strange, considering that I was now single on purpose.

"No, Mom." More eyerolls.

Does it ever stop? I wondered. I don't know what prompted me to ask next, "Any girlfriends?"

She stopped moving and raised her eyebrows. "What?"

I asked, "It's the modern era, isn't it? This kind of thing is allowed now, no?"

"Well, yes, it is. But it was just a random question coming from you. Usually everything you say and do is." She raised her fingers to do air quotes. "With purpose."

I made a dismissive noise. "Like you would be *that* anyway." I couldn't bring myself to say the word gay. "You could have any guy you wanted."

Emerson opened her mouth and promptly closed it. I waited. *There's no way.* That would just be fate playing a cruel joke on me.

"I'm focused on my studies," she finally said.

I nodded. "Right. Dating just gets in the way of life plans sometimes. Come sit then." I put the salad in front of her and went to the oven to remove the crustless quiche Lorraine. I always tried to make guests come to me for dinner—then I didn't have to navigate gluten-filled restaurant menus or try to pretend to love whatever nutritionless casserole someone made.

"How *is* school going?" I asked, once seated. I was trying to eat my dinner as slowly as possible, pushing and rearranging it around the plate.

Emerson brightened. "Great. But I'm glad next year will be my last. I want to get out there and start working. Actually helping people. Did I tell you I've decided to intern at a hospice next year?"

"Why would you want to surround yourself with the sick and the dying, Em?" I said before I could stop myself. "I mean," I stammered, "wouldn't you rather work in emerg or something? At least then you would be helping people live. More. Longer." I gave up trying to save myself from looking callous.

Emerson banged her hand down on the table, making me, and the cutlery, jump. "Life isn't always about what we *want* mom. Someone has to do what needs to be done. Like police officers and sanitation workers and waitresses. If there weren't all these people running the world behind the scenes, people like you wouldn't be able to make your glorious presence in the world known to everyone who has eyes to see it." She wobbled her head slightly as she spoke, mocking me. I held back from pointing out that the gesture made her look like some black woman from the projects.

My eyes widened. So she *did* have a spark after all. "Well, yes, I *know* that, Em. You don't have to take it out on me." I paused, noticing a change in her presence. Something I couldn't put my finger on. *Was she sitting straighter? Lost a couple of pounds?*

"Where has all of this come from? You seem... different." I frowned. She was a mini-me physically, although I always thought more beautiful. She had a softness that contrasted with my edges.

She held my gaze and asked, "Have you ever seen true suffering in your life, Mom?"

I put down my fork and looked directly at her. "Well, yes, of course I have! I had to milk cows in the dead of winter. Nothing freezes your hands quicker than getting them wet at minus thirty. And I had to take care of my annoying little brother since I was probably eight years old. He was too much of a bother for my mom, and she thought I had nothing better to do than babysit. I never had time to hang out with all the other kids at the arcade in town because if I wasn't watching him, there was some other kind of work to be done at home." I was scared the real truth would float up, but I kept unloading. "And then in college, I got myself into a tricky situation once. Too much booze and bad taste in men almost got me raped. Scared the crap out of me. And when you were born, I was fully dilated by the time I got to the hospital, and they wouldn't give me an epidural. I had to do the whole thing *naturally.*" The look on Emerson's face, disgust mixed with shame and possibly pity, finally made me stop. "What?"

"Oh, and let me guess. You had to fly coach to your condo once and it was horrendous. You've never suffered a day in your life what some people suffer in the blink of an eye." She sneered and muttered, "*Almost* raped. How *tragic*."

I didn't like how she was drawing out her words in an effort to belittle me. "Really, Em. Suffering is relative, isn't it?"

"No, it's not. Do you know I volunteered at a woman's shelter last year?"

Shit. Another thing about the kids I should have probably known. "No," I finally mumbled, taking a big gulp of wine.

"Well, I did. And I can tell you, from firsthand experience, that you don't know what suffering is." She pushed her chair back suddenly and jumped up.

"Where are you going? You're not done eating yet!"

"I've lost my appetite." She walked out of the kitchen. "I have to go."

"But I wanted to talk to you about your father," I added desperately. "I don't know if I've made the right decision. About leaving him, I mean."

She turned back to face me and asked levelly, "Do you *really* love him?"

"Yes," I answered immediately, hoping to sound convincing.

"Then do what's best for *him,*" she growled and left.

After cleaning up, I went out on the front porch to sit on the swing. The sun was almost down, and children were returning home from biking with their friends. I looked at my watch and wondered why they were out so late on a school night. Optimal rest was necessary to reach peak performance during the day.

"Speaking of bad parenting," I said to myself. "How the hell did I raise such a bunch of disrespectful brats?" In the past couple of weeks, Jacob was the only one who hadn't mouthed me off at me. Except for the caterpillar-eyebrow comment, but compared to the other two's attitudes, it seemed like a minor transgression.

Internally, I launched into a good old-fashioned back-in-my-day rant. I would never, ever have dared talk to my parents that way, or even to my grandma, who had a soft spot for me. If I had, I would have been on woodchopping duty for a year. But, something inside me argued, look where respecting them got me. Nowhere. I hadn't talked to my parents in over thirty years.

Just the way it was with every generation—the old ones thought the new ones were in for a world of hurt because of their sucky attitudes and disrespect towards their elders. But a small part of me had to admit where they all got their piss-and-vinegar attitudes from. I caught myself rolling my eyes and actually laughed.

What I really needed to work on was myself and a proper financial plan. The kids were adults now and could look after themselves. I thought about what Matt said and decided it was best to take at least some of his advice. Best case, he was wrong and then I would have extra money set aside. I didn't really want to think about the worst-case scenario. The recession had impacted the country, and especially Alberta, hard. People had less disposable income, and luxury items were the first to go. Not that I thought exercising was a luxury item, but to many people it was.

I sighed, realizing the matching workout clothes and shoes would have to be pared down a bit. I was going to have to settle on getting *two* seasons out of everything I purchased for the next while. And I would have to stretch the food budget a bit. No more boutique food shops for me—*Walmart, here I come!* I cringed. But even if I could save four or five hundred bucks a month, it should be enough.

I got up and went back inside to pour myself another glass of wine. I downed half the glass and refilled before returning outside. "Everything's better with wine," I whispered over the rim, inhaling deeply. I cringed at the memory of the last time I had said that, over a family dinner about six months earlier.

Emerson was enraged. "Think about what you're saying!" she yelled. "You're telling us, your children, that's it's okay to use alcohol to temporarily rid yourself of your stress and pain?" Of course, my gut reaction was to say *yes*. I mean, so many women I knew did the same thing. And hundreds of memes confirmed it.

Em had pushed up from the table and said, "Okay. That's great. I'm just going to get on with my miserable life and turn to booze when it gets unbearable. That sounds like the best life plan I've heard in years. Thanks for the wisdom, Mom!" I looked to Andrew in shock, but he just shrugged and went back to his supper.

I sat back heavily on the swing. Whatever. Even I could allow myself one vice. It's not like I was a bloody raging alcoholic. Emerson's moods lately suggested she was the one who really needed a drink.

Between her and Riley, I was almost done with my daughter's attitudes. Maybe I should try and work on a relationship with Jacob more, I thought. He was always the easiest kid to get along with. Maybe I was never meant to have a good relationship with another female. "Karma, I suppose?" I muttered to myself, pushing against the deck to move the swing slightly and then letting myself glide forward.

EMERSON

10

I stood in line at Subway deciding if I should have an entire footlong Melt. I was starving. I had barely gotten to the quiche before I stormed out of the house.

I stepped to the front of the line and automatically stated my regular order. "Footlong Melt on white." *Take that, Mother.* As I moved down the line, the man behind the counter asked, "Toppings?"

"Mustard," I said.

"No veggies?" He tipped his head.

"No thanks." I grinned to myself. Mother always thought she was being so sneaky putting the salad out first at dinner. *And right in front of me.* As if she hoped I would fill up on it first. "How can a person possibly fill up on vegetables?" I muttered to myself.

The guy behind the counter gave me a funny look and I realized I had said that out loud. I leaned over, grabbed an iced tea from the fridge, and paid.

A table by the window was free, and I sat down. Before I unwrapped my sandwich, I pulled out my phone and opened up Instagram, trying not to think about *another* failed attempt to talk to my mom like a normal person.

I knew what she thought. She thought I was young and idealistic. That one day real life would come around and slap me upside the head. And then I'd suddenly awake to what the world was *really* about. Money, looks, power, control. All the things she held dear. "*Me, me, me. I, I, I.* That's what makes the world go around now," I mumbled to myself as I unwrapped my sub and took a huge bite. Just to be a pain in the ass, I took the most ridiculous selfie I could, mouth wide open and the sub taking up most of the frame. I quickly posted it to Insta with the caption *eats carbs* hoping it would show up in my mom's feed—the black sheep among the other clean eating freaks she probably followed. I swore everything on her account was body obsessive.

Nursing school had been a real eye-opener for me. I hadn't realized the full extent of my protected little upper-class upbringing. In the hospitals and clinics, I finally got a taste of real life, and a lot of it wasn't pretty. I switched over to Facebook and started reading an article that Janine had shared about the disappearance of the middle class. I wondered where the fine point existed that determined what side of the curve a person would fall on. Race, gender, socioeconomic status, sexual orientation. The things a person was given. Sure, you could work hard and find yourself on the upswing of the curve, but what if you had everything stacked against you from the beginning? And on top of it all, the people who'd risen to the top of the pecking order had essentially learned how to cut themselves off from discomfort and suffering by micromanaging their lives. *Sounds like someone I know.* But the only thing this did was disconnect them from the reality of the world around them. People like my mom didn't even see people like the ones I saw at the women's shelter.

I realized I was being overly hard on my mom, that so many people were like this now. It was the great problem of our time. I knew deep down she wasn't a bad person. But this positive, affirmation-filled life left them unable to *experience* what life brought them by avoiding anything that was less than they *intended.*

I took another bite and tapped my finger on the screen of my phone, making the article disappear. "Dammit," I whispered as I had to go through the process of finding it again. Eventually I found the part that had induced the tapping. "But what if the ones who sank to the bottom of life didn't have the tools, not even one measly flathead screwdriver, to start digging themselves out of the life they were trapped in? And not only do these people have no tools, what if they thought they simply deserved *nothing*?" It made me think of people like my mom, who actually, truly believed they deserved everything this big and beautiful and sparkly life had to offer them. As if the universe *existed* to prostrate itself at their feet, begging to be used, ruthlessly and excessively, for their own personal gain. What, exactly, in a person's biological makeup determined these kinds of qualities?

Jeez, I was starting to sound like Cassie. I smiled at the thought of her as I nibbled around the sub's crust. I understood why Cassie felt the way she did. Her mother really had nothing. Cassie herself was lucky to have escaped without physical scars. But she carried her emotional ones silently. Lying in the dark, where Cassie could fully open up, she had told me so many times that one day she would have the resources to save her mother. "As soon as I'm done school and working," she always said, nodding deeply at the soundness of her plan. I knew it was the driving force in her life. And so many times, I had been on the verge of telling her how unhealthy that probably was. I thought of my own relationship with my mom and bit my tongue.

I turned my phone off and watched a group of teenagers storm the Subway. *Was I ever that loud?* They yelled and jostled with each other for the front of the line. Last year Cass had insisted I join her at the women's shelter where she volunteered. Honestly, I didn't want to go at first. Even though I was in nursing, I was scared I would see something that would truly break me. But for her, I went; that's how attracted I was. You do weird things when you're in love.

Although Mom asking if I was dating a girl had shocked me, I figured she was just trying every angle since I hadn't brought a guy home for almost three years. I could literally hear my mother groan at this revelation. The arguments would start with a discussion about nature versus nurture. Traditional versus trendy. Whatever. Adults always overthought these things. I never actually made a conscious decision to become a lesbian. It was simply presented to me. And maybe from a lack of any better choice. I smiled to myself, thinking of how I almost spilled the beans back at the house to Mom. The shock value alone was almost worth it. But this thing Cass and I had was no flash in the pan. I had to protect it.

As if trying to instill heterosexuality in me, my mom always told me the story of how she was immediately, physically attracted to my dad. Without even talking to him. I had never experienced that. Sure, I had a few boyfriends over the years. Sex was okay. And then the relationships ended. I met Cassie a year and a half ago, in my second year of university, when I was twenty, and we were immediately inseparable. The way only a deep female relationship could be.

And who was to say only men and women could hook up? That was the only approved option they had in the old days. The days when their brains were still wired for procreation. And their behaviours dictated by the mob. But a lot had changed in a short amount of time. People were no longer baboons on the verge of extinction. The planet had way too many humans anyway. The more childless couples, the better.

I took the last bite of my sub, stuffed to the gills, and crumpled the wrapper up, throwing it in the garbage on my way out. Driving home, the memory of how we'd met came to me. Actually, I thought about that day all the time. I was sure a stranger would think I was a lunatic because of the smile it brought to my face. Cass had saved me from one particularly annoying boy in a philosophy class. She and I clicked, and soon we were seeing each other every day, meeting for lunches and then after school and then on the weekends. I had realized one day how I felt as I watched Cassie talk about one of her other classes. She was taking social work and was more passionate about it than my mom was about posing onstage in tiny, rhinestone-studded bikinis and high heels.

How many times had I watched Cass doodle on the edges of her notebooks? I noticed one item among the hearts and stars that seemed out of place: tornadoes. I started to suspect that her life had not been as easy as mine.

One particularly beautiful spring day, we were studying outside beneath a large poplar tree when she started talking about her practicum with social services. She became so excited—her face all lit up—and I blurted out, "You're adorable."

She smiled warmly at me and continued talking, but a whisper entered my mind then. It said, *I love you.* The whisper didn't escape my mouth then, but it hung on the end of my tongue for months after that.

And then, miraculously, she said it out loud first.

I breathed for the first time in what seemed like months.

CASSIE

11

I walked to the front door, and Wilma followed me. I was shaken up by what Blair had just told me. *Gang rape. Forcible confinement. Isolation.* No number of terrible stories from these women would soften the next one's blow.

"Are you going to be okay, Cassie?" Wilma asked as I put my hand on the doorknob. I paused and breathed through my nose. *Hadn't I seen it all?* It would appear not. I couldn't understand why it had to be this way. "Why can't people just be kind to each other?" I whispered toward the door, not turning around. "Maybe kind is asking too much, but even decent would be enough, don't you think?"

"Yes. I would love decent," Wilma said, touching my shoulder. I turned around to see Wilma looking at me, her lips pressed together. How long did she say she'd been doing this? Forty years?

"No, it doesn't get easier," she said suddenly.

I wanted to ask how she knew what I was thinking but understood it must be what everyone wanted to know.

"Next week still? Tuesday?" she asked.

"Yes. Just after one," I said.

"Okay. You go home and get some sleep, love."

I nodded and left, walking down the block to the bus stop. I had been lucky enough that Mom and Ray helped me go to college. A car had been entirely out of the question.

It was a warm night, and I was grateful for the fresh air after being at the women's shelter all afternoon. A car drove past, slowing down so the male driver could get a good look at me. I flipped him the bird and saw a snarl cross his face as he sped away.

That would have made Em so mad. And she would have launched into a speech about single women out in the city alone, how I shouldn't antagonize "them." Honestly, it was nice the way she worried about me.

I wasn't stupid. I knew I had anger issues. And I knew exactly where they came from. My mom had tried to protect me the best she could from the turbulent life of my childhood. But coming out of it completely unscathed was not in the grand plan. I knew she did it to secure us financially, but shacking up with Ray was the worst mistake of her life. Eight years I'd had to live with him. And watch the way he treated her. He never physically abused me, but mentally, well, that was a different story. If he could pick me apart somehow, he did it. With glee. I swore sometimes that Ray was actually a psychopath. Or at least had some kind of mental issues.

When Em had given me a key to her place a few weeks earlier, I realized I was happier than I'd ever been. And not the twitterpated kind of happy, but the kind of happy that comes from finally feeling safe and content after many unstable years. I had known by about sixteen that I had no interest in men. I always attributed it to Ray. Or more specifically, hating Ray. If men were like that, I wanted nothing to do with them.

But now, I just thought I was meant to be with women. Maybe I should thank him, I thought, for helping me figure it out sooner rather than later.

"Fuck that," I muttered as I stopped at the bus shelter where another girl waited. That would be the day I ever thanked him for anything. Honestly, these had been the best years of my life. I was out of the house, I hadn't seen him in

over two years, and I was doing something I loved. If only I could get my mom out. I had written her a note when I left. I told her how much I loved her and hated seeing her treated that way. I specifically didn't say *let yourself be treated that way* because I didn't want to add to her feelings of self-hate. She had that in spades. I promised her, even if it was the last thing I did, that I would save her. Somehow, I would find the money to get us a place and get her out of there. I knew he would come looking for her, so I promised to be very sneaky about it. By then, I would be a social worker and would be able to work the system. And lastly, I told her I knew how much she had suffered for me. How she had put herself between him and me. And that I saw it in his eyes when he'd been drinking that he wanted to do something to me. And she took it. Once I actually antagonized him into hitting me, just so I could go to the cops and file a report. After that she never, ever left us alone. I saw her do that for me.

But I never sent that letter. It still lay beneath my mattress, where I pulled it out every night and read it. Instead, I wrote a short one to actually give to her: *I will get you out.* I knew the price she had paid, in advance, for me to get here. And I knew she didn't want to be repaid.

That is true love, right there. I felt a twinge of guilt in my chest, knowing Em didn't have that kind of relationship with her mother. Even with all that my mom and I had suffered together, what we had was unbreakable. My mother had never had that with her own mom, either. My heart broke for all the motherless daughters in the world. I knew it was good that Em had her dad, and that he had filled what could have been a huge void. But I could never tell her that it wasn't quite the same as having a mother, another female you were connected to more deeply than could even be expressed, who loved you fully and unconditionally.

I was capable of taking drastic measures to save my mom. I wasn't scared of him.

MICHELLE

12

M y phone buzzed. I had to open it up to read the whole thing: *Is Ray at work today?*

I responded to Cassie: *Yes, why?*

Can I stop by the house at 1? I want to take you somewhere. I can drop you at work by 3.

I hesitated before I texted back. What was she up to? Finally I typed: *Sure.*

Great, I'll see you then.

I had mostly avoided Andrew for a couple of weeks while the bruises on my arms healed. Either they must have been pretty deep, or my body had given up trying to fix me. I didn't blame it.

It hadn't been that hard to put him off, which saddened me, but I had felt a disconnect from him recently. Without him actually spilling everything, I understood where he was coming from. Even though he was unfaithful to Keely, he hadn't left, she had. So if she was offering a do-over, shouldn't he grab it? I was probably just a rebound anyway. Andrew had told me enough about his wife, how successful and beautiful she was, for me to understand that she was the kind of wife a guy like Andrew deserved. Even if I did get out of my marriage, what could I bring to the table that would make his life better? I couldn't think of a single thing.

I smiled sadly into my tea. *At least I had a couple months of happiness*. But now, would the feeling growing inside of me go away with him? I hoped so. I couldn't live the rest of my life with Ray if it stayed, I knew that for certain. Something whispered a truth to me. I didn't actually need Ray anymore, and Cassie didn't need me. As soon as Cass graduated, my debt to Ray would be paid.

I quickly finished putting the laundry away and pulled a meal out of the freezer, placing it in the oven for when Ray got home. All he had to do was turn the stove on for half an hour and a piping hot, homemade lasagna would be ready for him. A wave of sympathy for Ray washed over me, as it did once in a while. I'd caught a glimpse of the good person that lies at the core of every human. About a year ago, he actually told me he loved me. I hadn't heard that from him for probably five years. And the silly thing was, I felt that he meant it. The pained look on his face when I looked up from my dusting showed that it took a great effort for him to say it. I wondered how many times in his childhood he'd heard those words. Before Jonathan came along, I could count on one hand how many times I'd heard them. I told Cass I loved her every day. No child should grow up questioning their value in the world. Look where it got me.

Ray grew up in a violent home. His father took his anger out on all of them, no one was spared, not even Ray's little sister. She ran away from the family when she was fourteen and they never saw her again. At least I stopped the cycle for Cassie. Ray, for the most part, restrained himself from doing something terrible to her. His eyes only glazed over at the sight of her when he drank, which wasn't nearly as often as it could be. She went from his invisible stepdaughter to a female he could do terrible things to. On those nights, I instructed Cassie to do what I had been told so many years ago. Go to your room and push a dresser behind the door. I didn't sleep a wink on those nights. It was the best I could do for her, yet it still seemed to me a pathetic effort.

The doorbell rang at exactly one. I opened it and grabbed her into a hug. "Hi, sweetie," I whispered into her hair, noticing that she smelled of cinnamon.

"Hi, Mom." She squeezed me back.

I released her and asked, "Where are we going?"

Her smile played out mischievously in her eyes. "It's a surprise. Grab your stuff."

I laughed. "Okay, bossy pants!" As we got into a car, I said, "What's this?" I had assumed we were taking the bus.

"Oh! My friend let me borrow it." Cass blushed.

I closed the door and turned to her. "Tell me everything new about you."

"Here, this is for you." She handed me a plastic container with a cinnamon bun in it.

"This looks delicious!" I dipped my finger in the cream cheese icing abundantly covering the top of the still-warm treat.

"My friend made them," she said, and her head dropped a fraction.

I assumed *a friend* was code for something more, but I decided not to pester her. Cass always told me what she needed to say when she was ready, so there was no point pushing her. I took a bite and closed my eyes. "So good. Please thank your friend for me. Go on then. Tell me what's new."

I listened happily as she spilled everything else going on in her world. It almost drove me crazy trying to keep my questions to myself, especially when she mentioned the friend again. Cass pulled expertly onto Dundas in the little blue two-door car. "When did you learn to drive a stick?" I asked as she shifted. Even I had no idea how—I barely knew how to drive an automatic as I've never actually owned a car and didn't have a driver's license. Strangely, Ray had insisted on teaching Cassie how to drive and took her for her test when she was sixteen. He said a person was useless without a license and wheels, looking at me sideways.

Cass didn't answer, so I inserted, "The friend, right?" I reached over and touched a string of beads that swung from the rearview mirror.

"Mala beads," Cass said.

"Yes. They remind me of the yoga studio I walk past on my way to work."

"Yah. I've been a couple of times."

"Do you like it?"

"I do, actually. I didn't think I was going to at first. I just assumed it was a trendy thing for rich people. But it really is great. Very calming."

I knew Cass had a temper, so this news was good. "Maybe one day you can come with me," she added casually.

"Maybe…" I looked out the car window and saw homeless people milling on the corner as we crossed Shelbourne. I assumed Frank was among them. I wouldn't get to see him today since I wasn't walking to work. Suddenly, I laughed. "What the heck would I wear?" I mentally ran through my wardrobe and saw nothing that would make me blend in at a yoga studio.

"Oh, Mom. People don't care what you wear there. Sure, there are tons of Lulu moms, but really, shorts and T-shirts are as good as anything."

"One day," I whispered more to myself than her.

Twenty minutes later, we pulled up to a nondescript house in a residential area. I was still licking my fingers when Cass came around and opened the door for me. We walked up to the front door with its peeling white paint showing a light olive green beneath it and pressed the intercom.

"Hello?" a woman's voice asked.

"Hi, it's Cassie. I have my mom with me."

"Oh great! Come in ladies," the woman's voice said.

"What is this place?" I asked, quickly looking up and down the street.

Cassie turned to me. "Just trust me, please?" she begged.

I sighed, suddenly knowing what she was up to. I said quietly, "He'll still find me, you know."

"No, he won't. This place is super secure. He'd have to look pretty hard, and honestly, I don't think he'll bother."

My face fell, and she rushed, "I don't mean you're not worth looking for. I just mean I think he's too lazy to try that hard."

"I don't know about that. Good slaves are hard to come by." I forced a smirk for her sake.

The door opened after a series of locks were released from behind it. A woman about my age stood back as we entered. Once she had us inside and locked up again, she hugged Cassie. I could tell they had a warm connection, and it made me happy. I had always felt bad that Cassie had no other family members to connect with growing up. I had no family to speak of—my mom died when I was twenty, and Ray rarely spoke to his relatives. Cassie had no spoiling grandmas, no loving aunts, no good times with the cousins.

The woman turned to me and hugged me as well, freezing me. "Michelle. Welcome, I've heard so much about you." She stepped back and smiled warmly at me, her long grey hair twisted back into a bun. I noticed that she had a slight accent. *British maybe?*

"Um… that's great," I stumbled, casting Cassie a long look.

"It's okay. Cassie didn't speak of me because we try to keep this place pretty obscure. On the down-low." She laughed, throwing her head back at her own humour. She looked at me again seriously and said, "I'm Wilma." She touched my arm. "Let's go meet some of the other ladies, shall we?" She walked off down the corridor.

I tried to shoot Cassie another look, but she just winked at me and turned to follow Wilma down the hall.

In the living room, sitting together on a faded and worn burgundy couch, one woman was painting another's fingernails. They looked up when they heard us approach and both smiled.

"Blair, Mary, this is Cassie's mother, Michelle." Wilma sat on another couch opposite them and patted the seat beside her for me.

The younger of the two women jumped up and grabbed my hand. "I'm Blair," she said, shaking it excitedly, and pointed to the other one. "And this is Mary."

I was surprised at how vibrant Blair was. She didn't look and act abused, and she couldn't have been more than twenty-five. *Imagine if I had gotten help at that age.* Could I have turned my life around? Not met Jonathan and not married Ray? But then Cassie wouldn't have been born, and I realized I wouldn't change the way it went. It felt strange to realize that now. That given the chance, I would suffer it all over again.

As I sat next to Wilma, Mary spoke, barely lifting her head. Her voice was soft, almost inaudible. "So you have an abusive husband too?"

My mouth dropped open. Cassie quickly said, "I'm sorry, Mom. But please trust me, this is a safe place."

If any other person had tried this, I would have been angry, but I knew her heart was in the right place. "Is there any way…" I trailed off.

"He won't find out," Wilma offered. "Please don't worry about that. Only a handful of people know who I am or what I do. I actually have a couple of different identities to keep people guessing." She smiled widely, revealing a silver cap on one of her back teeth.

There was a strange feeling in the house. A kind of calm I wasn't sure I had ever felt before. Slowly my shoulders relaxed as Wilma launched into the details about the house.

"Before I start, I must insist you keep all of this a secret, Michelle. Telling even one person about us risks the very lives of the women that depend on us." Her eyes became solemn.

I knew, more than anyone, the importance of being able to keep a secret. I nodded deeply, and she continued. "Right now, we only have Blair and Mary, but we have room for up to four women." Cassie looked at me pointedly. Wilma continued, "You are allowed to stay here as long as you need. We provide food, clothing, and shelter, free of charge. We have the resources to help you with career retraining and starting on the path to your own financial security and personal safety."

Wilma went on, but my mind drifted on the word safety. Had I ever felt *safe* in my entire life? I couldn't think of a single time. Memories ran through my mind as I scrambled to find at least one instance that provided safety. I saw myself at six, cutting my hand with a paring knife while making supper, crying because no one was there to help wrap the wound up and clean up the mess. And then at eleven, turning a knife over in my hands, thinking of ending it all because I was being bullied at school so bad for my appearance, which screamed *I'm neglected.* I was still scared of the dark, as no one ever comforted me through childhood nights. I must have felt somewhat safe with Jonathan, and then Ray for the first while, until that night he turned on me forever and showed his real self. How many times had I been harassed and catcalled and pinched at work? I knew I felt safe with Andrew, but that didn't count because it wasn't a part of my real life. I shook my head and tried focusing back on what Wilma was saying.

"Why don't one of you tell Michelle your story?" Wilma said to Blair and Mary.

Mary dropped her head, and I could tell she had been beaten down for possibly more years than I had. Talking obviously wasn't so easy for her either. But Blair piped up, "I'll talk."

Wilma smiled fondly at her. "Go ahead then."

"I actually had a pretty good life. Pretty and blonde, living in the suburbs. In grade ten, I picked the wrong guy to date. The exact opposite of what my mom wanted, right?" She smiled broadly, showing her two lower front teeth were missing. I was surprised I hadn't noticed that earlier.

"Oh this?" she asked, pointing to the space where the teeth used to be. "A side effect of choosing said wrong boyfriend. Anyway. I knew he was part of a gang. But I was totally naive and what I didn't know was that initiation of a new girlfriend of a gang member involved sex. With several of them. In the same night." Tears came to her eyes as she looked out the window. "I should have gone to the hospital after that. It took a month to fully heal." She took a rattling breath and continued. "After that, I was nothing. To them or to myself. I was *so* easily broken. I thought I was weak and must have deserved it. Everything good I had thought about myself before that night evaporated. I started using drugs. Had sex with whoever came to me, whether they asked nicely or not. I became a pawn and a possession. I lost everything. My poor parents," she sobbed as Mary put her arm around her. "To have given me everything, and I threw it away to show them they weren't the boss of me. But guess what? I wasn't even the boss of me. *Patrick* was." She said his name with an acidic tinge.

"How did you get here, then?" I asked.

She laughed. "I woke up one morning and walked out of the house with nothing but the clothes on my back. I was ready to give up. I was headed to a bridge I knew was high enough to ensure my death. But Wilma has spies." She smiled at her. "They brought me here. That was six months ago."

"Did he ever come looking for you?" I asked.

She flicked her hand. "I don't actually know. Maybe briefly. But I'm sure another young, dumb girl quickly replaced me. I'm sure after a week Patrick had moved on." She pulled up the sleeve of her blue plaid shirt, revealing a scabbed-over tattoo. "I'm in the process of getting my brand removed." She grunted. "Like cattle, we were marked. Once this is gone and Wilma finalizes my move, I'll be ready to start again."

"Move?"

"I'm going to Calgary. I don't think I'll ever feel safe in Toronto. I'm going to school for medical administration, and I'm going to start over again. Once I'm there, I think I'll contact my parents, just to let them know I'm still alive." The smile that spread across her face almost convinced me that I could start over too.

We chatted for another fifteen minutes, and then Cassie showed me around the house. As we passed an empty bedroom, she paused. I looked in and saw a single mattress on the floor with simple white bedding on it and a small three-drawer dresser in the corner. Finally, she said, "This one is empty, you know."

"Okay," I said. My hands started shaking as I realized what she was suggesting. "Cassie, I can't," I finally sputtered.

She turned to me and grabbed me by the shoulders. I tried to withhold my automatic flinch at being grabbed that way. Her eyes were wild with hope and fear, reminding me of the look on Kenzie's face the other night. "Why not? Just walk away. Right now."

"But..." My eyes searched the sparse bedroom.

"But what? Do you have anything you *have* to go back for?"

I mentally scanned the house. Some simple clothes, cheap jewelry. Nothing I couldn't live without. I had no heirlooms, nothing of sentimental value. Except... "Your baby stuff. I kept some of my favourite clothes and some things from school. Pictures and love notes you wrote me. Ray almost threw it all out a couple of years ago when he found it. He was searching for evidence of my lying about something ridiculous. I begged him to let me keep it. He finally conceded. I need that. It's the only happy memories I have."

"I'll go back and get it," Cassie said quickly. She looked at her watch. "It's only two thirty. He doesn't get home until five, right?"

"Yes, but Cass." My eyes grew wide. "You're not doing that. It's too dangerous. Sometimes he comes home early."

"I'll take Wilma. She can keep a lookout. It'll only take me five minutes. Less. Please, Mom!" She begged, pulling on my arms like a child.

The forty-six years of anguish that had been rising in me the past few months finally crashed through the surface. I started crying uncontrollably. *Could I do it?* Maybe I could. All I needed was one moment of steadfastness and then it would be done. A fresh start was within my grasp. I felt it move the air just around my fingers in a gentle eddy. I held the feeling for what seemed like eternity. And then the thought of Ray pounding into the bar tonight, demanding to know why I hadn't come home came crashing into my mind. What was the first thing he would do? *Go to Cassie.*

I took the deepest breath of my life and whispered, "I can't." I pulled back from her.

Cassie started crying too. "No, Mom. Please," she pleaded. The look on her face killed me.

But I couldn't tell her why. She had already carried too much for me. I couldn't tell her that Ray would come straight to her, knowing she had something to do with my disappearance. I knew he had seen the glint of defiance in her eyes as she dared to oppose him once, shortly before she had moved out, after he demanded that she bring him his smokes. I saw him take in the calculated look on her face, because he hissed to me later that night, "I know you wouldn't be so stupid as to put your own daughter in a dangerous situation, should you ever decide to do something dumb." I knew exactly what he meant, and he saw it, satisfied I was still under his control. To seal the idea, he pushed my head down roughly to service him. The memory almost made me gag now.

And once I was "retrained and rehabilitated," where would I go? Calgary? I couldn't leave Cassie, although I was sure she would come with me, but that wasn't fair to her and the life she had planned for herself. I couldn't let her world revolve around me.

I stopped the feeling-sorry-for-myself tears that ran down my cheeks, and I pushed my shoulders back. "No. Take me to work, Cassie." I walked out of the house without saying goodbye to anyone.

The drive was the most agonizing twenty minutes of my life. I could feel her anger filling up the car as easily as my silence could fill up a room. Again, I considered telling her about Andrew. And maybe even the truth about Jonathan, her father. I was pretty sure the news about my boyfriend would give her some relief or sense of hope. But who was I kidding? Andrew might as well be out of the picture now. Which was again probably for the best, given my track record with nice-at-first men.

Cassie wouldn't look at me as I got out of the car. I glanced back through the window as I gently closed the door and saw her looking rigidly ahead, her eyes dry. I prayed that she would forgive me.

EMERSON

13

Oh, she's mad. I couldn't help smiling as I watched Cassie march around the apartment, clenching and unclenching her fists, grumbling to herself. She went down the hallway, turned at the bedroom door, back past the washroom, through the kitchen, and around the living room. My apartment was small, so the entire circuit only took about twenty-three seconds given her deliberate pace.

She had told me her plan to ambush her mother. I tried to tell her it wasn't a good idea. That you can't force people to do things they're not ready for. That everyone has to arrive on their own at the place they want to be. But I could see my philosophizing had only made her angrier, so I dropped it. I knew she felt she had to at least try. Maybe after this she could finally be at peace with the way things were.

"But I was so close!" Cass finally cried. "I had her! I could see it in her eyes." She stopped in front of me. "She wanted to say yes. But she couldn't. Because of *me*," she growled.

"What do you mean?" I asked, moving a hair off her face.

"She still thinks she has to protect me." Anger flared in her eyes again, making the gold flecks shine. "But I'm not a little girl anymore. I can take care of myself. Why can't she see that?" She began on her path again.

I honestly didn't have an answer for her. I had never known that kind of mother. Even though my mom thought I didn't remember the few years she stayed home doing all the proper good-mommy things, I did. And I knew she didn't love it. She didn't feel it in her heart like Cassie's mom obviously did. A twinge of jealousy rose up in me.

"You should be happy you have a mom who cares about you so much," I snapped at her back. Immediately, I felt my face grow warm. "I'm sorry, Cass. I didn't mean that. I know you desperately want her to get out. I do too." She turned to come back to me and I wrapped my arms around her tiny frame, feeling her rigid body soften.

I wondered if Cassie's mom hugged her like this. Like she meant it. *Wouldn't that be nice.* I tried desperately to sift through my memories, looking for anything that remotely resembled what I was feeling now. I could see many moments of my dad hugging me, gently making me disappear into his frame, not an easy task since I had inherited my mother's *solid* build. Even a few instances of me embracing my siblings flashed past. But not a single one of my mother. I didn't even know when she last touched me. I couldn't remember even the slightest brush of the arm or shoulder. I sighed and tried to let it go. *It is what it is.* Wasn't that my advice for Cass?

A siren sounded outside. You'd think after all these years living in this city I wouldn't notice ambulances anymore, but I do. *Maybe it's the nurse in me.*

Cassie pulled away from me and looked up into my eyes. "Have I ever told you how happy you make me?" Some of her rage had dissipated.

I pretended to concentrate, tipping my head for effect. "Hmm…" I finally said after thinking hard. "Not since this morning, I think."

"Well, you do." She pulled away from me more. "More than I think you will ever know." She patted my butt and walked into the kitchen. "Could you imagine the kind of love that would take? For a mother to stay trapped in her suffering for the freedom of her child?" she asked sadly as she opened the pantry.

"No. No, I can't." I suddenly thought back to the day I realized my mother cared more about herself than her children. That must have been when the hugging had stopped, if it had ever even existed at all.

Mom had been furious that I hadn't told her about my flute duet at the grade eight band concert that evening. I couldn't figure out if she was just embarrassed that she had found out from Brooklyn's mother or if she actually cared about my "big moment." Truthfully, I wasn't sure I wanted her there, scrutinizing me beneath the glare of the unflattering overhead lights. And I didn't want to let Brooklyn down and mess it up. I tried apologizing and asked Mom, slightly hopeful, if she was coming. She made the most exasperated sigh she could manage and stated that had I given her more notice, she could have cancelled her training session, but now it was impossible because she couldn't get a refund for last minute cancellations. Her hundred-buck workout was more important than my feelings.

Like a stubborn child, I pressed on, saying that one more training session couldn't possibly make a difference.

Her face had darkened, and I'd never forget what she said next. "It's always about you kids, isn't it? What about me? Do you know how hard I've worked to get this far? I could tweak a pose tonight that will make or break my mark in figure this weekend. I simply can't change my plans." She crossed her arms over her chest and her voice grew detached. "You should have told me in advance if you wanted me there. Anyways, do you think I really want to listen to a bunch of kids with squeaking instruments and no rhythm stumble through a performance? Listening to you practice that thing at home is torture enough, thank you."

With that, I had burst into tears. I couldn't help it. She sneered and said that she didn't want to see me cry, telling me to go upstairs and not come down until I could control myself. As I ran up the stairs, I had heard her call after me that I was not going to get very far in life if I couldn't learn how to suck it up.

And I hadn't gone very far in the direction she meant. *Nursing.* Mom said the word with obvious distaste when I had told her my decision in grade twelve. She tried to push me to drop out numerous times up until this past year and catch a modelling career by the tail. *Before it was too late.*

"Well, I'm not going to stop trying to get her out of there," Cassie said, interrupting my thoughts. "It's only one setback."

"That's my girl." I smiled at her.

If Cassie could keep pushing forward in a fight that was almost impossible to win, maybe I shouldn't totally give up on a relationship with my mother. I knew, below all of her narcissistic self-absorption, there was a real person. Maybe there was still a hurt little girl or a damaged teenager? She rarely talked about her family and never with affection. Except her grandma.

That was another thing I'd had that Cass hadn't. My father's parents lived only twenty minutes from us, and I was very close to them. It made up for the fact that I'd never met my maternal grandparents.

Would I ever stop feeling guilty for what I had and Cass didn't?

"Penny for your thoughts?" Cass said as she licked the peanut butter off a spoon in front of my face.

"No. You don't want to know what's in here." I tapped my head.

She dug the spoon into the jar again and just as she was about to put it in her mouth, I quickly leaned in and put my mouth over it. I eyed her as I clamped my teeth on the metal and pulled back, dragging the chunky deliciousness with me.

"Hmmm… that was delicious," I mumbled through sticky lips while I still watched her.

"That was very bad manners, Emerson Hazel O'Connell." She stepped in closer to me. "I think you need to be taught a lesson."

"I would love that," I whispered hoarsely.

Cass took the spoon and touched it to the side of my neck, leaving a tiny spot of peanut butter. I closed my eyes as she removed it with her mouth. When she leaned back, I opened one eye and asked, "Is that it?"

"Oh no. Not by a long shot," she said as the spoon dropped to the floor.

KEELY

14

I should try again with Emerson, I thought as my hand hovered over my phone. I wanted to send her a text apologizing for the night a few weeks ago. I hadn't heard from her, and the silence was surprisingly weighing on me.

My daughter had shocked me with her insight into my life. Was she right? Things Em said kept running through my mind. *You don't know what suffering is* and *Then do what's best for him.* But the most unsettling was *People like you wouldn't be able to make your glorious presence in the world known to everyone who has eyes to see it.* People like whom, exactly? Ones that worked hard to make their lives what they wanted it to be? Instead of wallowing in stale old excuses and lame habits? Was I supposed to do work that sucked the life out of me instead of energizing me? Forever blind to my unique and valuable gifts? And flat broke on top of it all?

Was I supposed to play the victim?

People seemed so good at that now. Experts in refusing responsibility for their lives because of the terrible, and probably not-so-terrible, things that had happened to them. I, too, could have let myself be a victim of my past, but I decided not to. I chose to forget it and move on.

Instead of texting Em, I scrolled through my Facebook page. I knew I should get out my office and do a core workout, but the gym was busy this morning, and I didn't feel like socializing. I smiled as I saw the results of my latest photoshoot at the top of my feed. There were so many good pictures, but I had forced myself to narrow it down to the top ten. I didn't want to overwhelm people. And the best one, a stunning headshot of me looking like I had a sexy secret burning behind my red-lipped smile, was my profile picture. I sighed. These kinds of photos would have to go if the gym didn't pick up. Only fifteen hundred, but still. "Every cent counts," I mimicked Matt's voice.

I had happily watched the comments pour in over the four days since I posted the images. I almost couldn't keep up with the thank-you's I had to write in response.

I decided to creep on Andrew's page. Maybe I could figure out who his *girlfriend* was. My mind crunched on the word. He rarely posted pictures, so I found nothing. I went to his friends list, looking for a Michelle, but of course found none. I knew he wouldn't be that stupid, but it was worth a try. I suddenly decided I needed to know who this chick was. Maybe if I saw her, I could see what I was up against. She must be some kind of goddess to pull Andrew's attention away from me. Visions of young, fresh faces floated through my mind. On the brink of a wonderful new life, his girlfriend must be easy and fun. I started to feel my age as I let my mind wander. I was tired. Tired of working so damn hard. Andrew had always bugged me to do stuff with him. Go for walks. Stop for ice cream. Watch *CSI* together. These were the kind of lame habits that made people stall in their lives. My time was much better spent running and listening to motivational podcasts instead of stopping for ice cream. That's how you got somewhere. But the twinge in my stomach reminded me how exhausting it could be.

Unable to get any information from Andrew's Facebook account, I hit *home* and snooped around, looking for a distraction. I scanned Vicki's feed because she usually had good, motivational posts on her wall and saw that she had posted a sale flyer at one of my favourite home decor stores. "That's what I need!" I whispered to myself, clapping my hands at the idea. I hadn't gone on a shopping spree for months. And most of the items I had at the rental house were from my last home decor binge years ago. "Time to refresh, I think," I said as I got up from my desk, already feeling the start of the adrenaline rush that came with a good shop. I knew, financially, it was a bad idea, but trying to stop a shopping addict once they got the urge was like trying to stop a bulimic once they put that first cookie in their mouth.

"I'm going out for a while, Lacey," I said to the girl at the front desk as I left.

"Will you be back for your four o'clock consult?" she asked.

I stopped and screwed up my face. *No.* I needed time for me, I decided. "No, reschedule it please."

"Um, she was rescheduled last week. Do you want to do it again?"

"If she wants to see me bad enough, she'll get over it." I flipped my hair over the collar of my Gobi bomber as I put it on, pretending to not see the eye roll that went with Lacey's response. "Sure thing."

The saleswoman's eyes lit up when I walked into the store. She saw me as a target, chic and classy looking, but I put up a strong front with them. I *always* kept the upper hand. No one likes to be pushed around.

The temperature had suddenly dropped, forcing me to dig out a warmer coat this morning, but I was barely in the store for two minutes before I had to take it off. *Goddamn menopause.*

"Good afternoon!" she said, walking up to me as I folded my coat over one arm. "What can I help you with today?" I could practically see dollars signs dancing in her eyes.

"Well, I have moved into a new place, and it needs updating. *But…*" I paused, standing as tall as I could, making sure that word sunk in. "I don't plan on staying there too much longer, so I'm looking for move-friendly items." *What did I just say?* Even I was surprised at my statement. I didn't realize how temporary I had decided my situation was. Maybe, deep down, I really wanted to be back with Andrew? Gut reactions are supposed to be the truth.

"Oh, perfect! We have lots of transitional items. What colour are your walls and what is the age of the house you are in now?" She folded her hands together and cocked her head. *That's good.* Her passive puppy dog stance meant I was in control.

"Since it's a rental, it's shades of taupe." I made a noise in the back of my throat. "And about ten years old, with no remodels done."

"Ten years?" She leaned into me like we were old friends, hitting me with her coffee breath. I fought the urge to pop a piece of gum into my own mouth as a suggestion. "Sounds like it's time for a hard update."

"You're telling me. The stainless steel appliances are showing their age."

"Yes, if you can believe it, warm metals are on their way in. Golds and coppers."

"Oh, I love copper." I thought how lovely that would be in the big house against the dark walnut cupboards I'd had installed in a total custom renovation five years ago.

"Me too! And add a new marble countertop and it would be fabulous."

"No granite?"

"Nope. Granite's out too. Besides, these are the big changes, but let's get you started on some small stuff today." She smiled. "How do you feel about ultra violet? It's the Pantone colour of the year." She picked up a throw pillow in a beautiful bluish-purple shade.

"Oh, I love that!" *Shit.* That was a little too excited.

"It's supposed to take our awareness and potential to a higher level. It's a spiritual colour." She caressed the pillow with her left hand.

"*That* is exactly what I need then," I said, touching it, feeling some tension slip from my muscles.

"Now, if we pair that with a grey and a light pink, it would look marvelous!" She walked over to the living room area and picked up a table runner that had the colours she spoke of. "Like this."

I nodded my approval and started picturing them on my coffee table.

"Could you paint a wall?" she asked, lifting a perfect eyebrow.

"Not at my rental, but at the big house, yes."

"Well, this ultra violet colour is just to die for on walls. Then you can add all shades of off-white, handmade vases." She pointed to a set in the middle of a kitchen table across the sales floor. "The trend is to go away from stark, clean white and have a more natural feel."

"I'll have to paint the baseboards, then." I tapped my fingernail on my bottom lip.

She nodded. "And just in case you're the crafty type, DIY is out."

I laughed. "Don't worry about that. I don't have time to craft."

"Artisan rendered pieces are in. Not mason jars turned lamp shades!" She chuckled.

DIY was never *clean* enough for my tastes. "Good. I was never fully on that bandwagon, so I'm happy to see it leave."

She walked over to a bedroom area. "And artwork this year is *moody.* But to be honest, I don't like this look." She nodded towards a neutral painting with a misty, grey landscape. "I think people want their spaces to be inviting and happy places. Not somber and dreary. Too Old English for me. So I would stick to artwork you love, that you are drawn to. In this year's colours if possible, of course. Pops of blue and green, maybe? No one likes to see a painting clash with a couch!" She elbowed me lightly.

I realized the couch at home was black leather and even though only two years old, would not fit with this theme. I could picture it now: A light grey, custom-length microfibre couch set against the ultra violet wall. Off-white baseboards and vases. Dark grey and soft blues and pinks for accents. *Perfection.* Delighted, my blood coursing fully and excitedly through my veins, I felt myself lose control. "I'm going to need a cart," I stated.

"Of course you are," she said solemnly, stalking off to find one.

Almost three hours and several thousand dollars later, I finished loading up the back of my SUV. I slumped into the driver's seat with a smile on my face, fully spent. *That was exactly what I needed.* A little brightening up of my living space was just the thing.

It wasn't until I was almost home that I fully acknowledged to myself that everything I had bought was intended for the big house, not the rental.

I sat in the car for a few minutes before deciding what to do. I had gotten what I wanted from Andrew and it hadn't seemed to work. If anything, I'd felt more disconnected and aimless since the split—as if he had grounded me before. And now with financial problems on the horizon.

Finally I got out, leaving everything where it was, realizing there was no point unpacking all of it only to move it again. I knew my decision was rash, but it had a certain *c'est la vie* feel to it. In a way it was freeing to decide to do something without analyzing it to death. As I unlocked the front door, a genuine smile spread across my face.

MICHELLE

15

I strained my eyes to see the hole in the couch that Ray found last night and demanded I fix before he got home from work the next day.

"You probably did that yourself in an attempt to get some new furniture out of me. You fucking women are always digging for something," he had said.

With my face close to the arm of the couch, I could smell the years of odours it had collected. The dark brown velour had worn well over the years and was easy to clean. Ray always ate in the living room in front of the TV and was constantly spilling food and drinks on it. And it was so soft, I sometimes snuck a nap on it when he was at work. I suddenly realized how much I was like the couch. My hair colour was almost the same. Like me, the couch was soft and worn out but still functioned perfectly fine. I probably didn't smell the best either, but Ray despised perfumes. And I knew that given the chance, I'd clean up well. A little mascara to frame my dark blue eyes would look amazing. But it just was the way it was. The couch and me, used and abused and dirtied, but still functioning. Providing a nice place to rest once in a while.

Like what I give to Andrew.

I had noticed right from the start how he seemed to melt in my presence. As if he went through the rest of his life tight and on edge. If I hadn't known better, I might have suspected he needed me more than I needed him. His face lit up when he told me about his kids. I noticed he was very careful not to say their names, but I knew he had two daughters and a son. The youngest had just finished high school and Andrew assured me his plan was always to leave his wife at this time. He said he had never, in a million years, thought about cheating on her. He wanted to do things the way a good father and husband would. But on the night he met me, all of his well-intentioned plans had been dashed.

I was officially a homewrecker on top of a cheating coward. But this knowledge still didn't stop my heart from fluttering when I saw him. Something had been turned on inside of me that had long been dead, if ever alive. My body wanted him one more time. *Just in case it's the last.* I felt like a person who hoarded food after being rescued from a lifetime of starvation. If I could just bank that feeling for the future, I might survive when Andrew finally realized what a terrible mistake he had made.

I had still been happy when he stopped by the bar quickly the night before to ask me to meet today at noon. I panicked when I got home at one in the morning and Ray had a sore throat and told me he was calling in sick the next day. "Don't wake me up in the morning," he grumbled.

I jolted out of my sleep that morning, my heart racing disturbingly fast, when Ray's cell rang. He fumbled for it, picked it up, and barked, "What!?"

My heart continued to hammer as I lay still next to him. He slammed the phone down. "Stupid fucking idiots!" He marched off to the shower, rubbing his throat. He yelled back at me, "Have my breakfast ready in ten minutes! It seems the world can't function properly without my constant fucking presence!" I heard the water start with a bang in the pipes.

I practically jumped out of bed and got straight to work, humming and smiling while the shower ran.

Thank God for small miracles.

I had a nice, long, hot bath before I met Andrew. I dug out the tiny bottle of Sweet Pea scented lotion I kept hidden from Ray and applied it to my arms and legs. As I dried and arranged my hair loosely around my shoulders, I saw something that made my heart skip a beat. I turned my neck slightly to see three perfect fingertip bruises. I don't know how I didn't see them before, as they were a fading greenish-yellow colour, indicating they were at least several days old. Even more shocking, I didn't remember how I got them. I guess somewhere along the line, I lost track of where all of the marks came from.

These posed a problem though. How was I going to hide them from Andrew? I tried my best to cover them with makeup, which was hard given my odd beige skin tone. I had always wondered about my father's ethnicity, as a rainbow of men had been through our apartment. I rearranged my hair to cover the left side of my neck. The hotel rooms didn't have the best lighting, so I figured I should be okay.

After double-checking the house was in order, I slipped out and caught a cab a couple of blocks away—never in front of the house, as I wouldn't be surprised if Ray had secretly installed cameras to watch my comings and goings.

The cab pulled up to the hotel and I jumped out, proceeding up to the third floor like I belonged there. Which was hard for me, as I was used to ducking my way through life. I set my shoulders back and appeared as though I was simply returning to my room. Ray snarled inside my head, *Slut!* as I knocked on the door, but I pushed him out. I wouldn't let him ruin the hour or two I had coming that would make me love myself a tiny bit more. At least for a couple of days.

The door was ajar, and as soon as I entered the room I could tell that something was wrong. *He didn't get up to greet me.* And even though I knew deep down in my heart what it was, I still needed to hear it from him. Andrew sat on the edge of the bed with his head hung slightly, his hands clasped between his knees.

I sat next to him. "I'm so, so sorry, Michelle," he said sadly. He turned to me and took my hands, swallowing hard. "I really never thought this was going to happen. I was ready to move on with you. Honestly. I even went to the lawyer a couple of days ago. And then she shows up last night at my house with a carload of new things for the house..." His statement made no sense to me. He sighed deeply. "And she was acting the way she used to. When we were young and happy and had fun. She started throwing these hideous pillows into my arms, laughing and saying how well they would match the new couch she had ordered." He shook his head as if not fully understanding either.

He put my hands down and stood up, distancing himself from me. "I didn't even know we needed a new couch!" He lifted his shoulders and hands in unison. "But I saw what I fell in love with in the first place. Her joy was contagious. And I feel like I owe it to that couple to try one more time. And to the kids. Riley doesn't seem to be doing well with the separation. She's been dating this loser and I'm sure it's to spite us. I'm so sorry. I didn't mean to lead you on or hurt your feelings. I hope my honesty with you hasn't hurt you more than I needed to."

What could I say? I had fallen in love with Andrew and he didn't feel the same. Well, maybe he did feel the same, but he had something else to live for. Something that had been a part of his life for so long, it tore him apart to let it go. I felt a rage from within me say, *Well then, you shouldn't have cheated on her!* But I pushed it back down. When had I relied on anyone to keep their word to me? "Third time's a charm" was bullshit. But there was no point making this harder for him than it needed to be. I couldn't manage much in my life, but I could be grateful for what he gave me and release him with some semblance of grace.

Finally, with all the strength I could muster, I said, "I understand." A lie, but what else was I supposed to say? Maybe if I flew into a rage it would help my side. Show him how much *I* needed him?

He looked over at me and I saw his face light up at the prospect of being released without guilt, but it quickly faded. It wasn't who he was. "I wanted to save you. I know it may sound creepy, but it's true. Do you know that?" He reached out and touched the left side of my neck.

I jumped back and barked, "No one can save me."

"But I could have tried. I saw my father take care of my mother when she had cancer and I saw how it changed him. Made him a better, kinder person. He was a workaholic when I was growing up and he realized that's what the world needs more of, people who find joy in caring for others, not just themselves. I saw the way you looked down when you approached our table that night, and my heart broke for you. Here I had this wife who was so strong and so sure of herself, and it just wasn't fair that other people had to live like you do. And then you smiled at me, and I knew there was something beautiful inside of you that never had the chance to be seen. I know this sounds cliché, but it was never about the sex. It was about two people needing something the other had to offer. Does that make sense?"

Then stay.

His words trailed off, and all of my resolve faded. He sat back down and took me into his arms, and I folded into his lap. He cradled me and moved me to the middle of the bed.

I hated and loved him for needing to be with me one last time. It made me feel beautiful and used. He took off my shirt and kissed my breasts and then down to my stomach. I knew he wanted me to let him in. He had tried this several times before, but I had been too self-conscious to let him. But today, everything had changed. I felt torn and lost and reckless and shortsighted. As he pushed my hand away, I stupidly caved. Let him do it, I thought. I'll never see him again anyway; why shouldn't I get something from him that was purely selfish.

My whole body flinched as his tongue flicked over me—a place no one had ever put his mouth since I was twenty-five and first dating Jonathan. I pushed aside my embarrassment at how much hair he would have to wade through.

As he sunk his teeth into me, I greedily took it.

In the cab going to work, conflicting emotions came at me. On one hand, I hated him for using me one more time, but on the other hand, I knew I was ultimately to blame for letting it happen. I hated myself for letting it happen.

I wondered if the contortions on my face prompted the cabbie to suddenly say, "You deserve better."

"What?" I snapped back to reality, which was a sudden Toronto snowstorm raging all around the car. Within two days fall would be back, and everything would be warm again.

"I see it all the time." He tsked and his head wobbled. "You, nice lady. Guy takes advantage just because you think it's normal to be used. Because life never show you anything else. Only pain and suffering."

My mouth dropped open. I couldn't understand how some random guy knew anything about my life. A ringing started in my ears, but I still couldn't formulate a response to his words.

"I see this stuff in my old country. Woman always beat down. They really think they deserve nothing better than what a man gives them. That's why I move here." He laughed. "I know it may look like running away, but I have three daughters and I knew I had to do better for them after my dear Afia died."

My stomach dropped and I whispered, "I'm so sorry."

"Yes. Thank you. It was sad, but necessary, you see."

"Necessary for your wife to die?" I asked incredulously.

"Yes. After Taliban, no more school for women. Well, my Afia not like that. She fight back. And she paid ultimate price. She made me promise long time before to do better by the girls and I did. Even my oldest, Sarah, she went back just last month to do what her mother never finish."

"Doesn't that scare you?" I twisted the corner of my coat, thinking about sending Cass somewhere so dangerous.

"Yes, of course. But how else will all those little girls know they also deserve better?"

He said this with such absolute certainty that I almost, for a second, thought I could do it too. Stand up for myself. Put the broken, hurt four-year-old aside and do something. But then the light of the idea faded. *Why, after all this time, was the world bringing me chance after chance to change?* It was killing me.

The cab driver looked up into the rearview mirror and said, "You just think on it, okay?"

I looked down at my hands and saw the symbol of my prison. The plain gold band on my ring finger reminded me that I wasn't worth more than the cheapest, plainest ring Ray could find. It still shocked me that I actually got him to agree to use all of my bar wages to help Cassie through school. The ring was the symbol that he owned me because he paid my way through this miserable life so I could pay for Cassie's.

Over. Done. Move on.

In a split second, before rational thought could catch up with the impulse, I ripped the ring off and rolled the window down, flinging it out onto the busy, snowy street. *Fuck men.*

"You never find it again," the cabbie said, eyeing me with a smirk from the rearview mirror.

The feeling of freedom that lasted all of ten minutes before we pulled up to the bar was better than any sex with Andrew. The feeling that I had done something to save myself. I would worry about the repercussions later.

CASSIE

16

I feel like a stalker. I lay there silently in the early morning light as Emmy's face was soft and relaxed. Unbothered by the world. I was still struck by how physically beautiful she was. Perfect white skin and long, sleek black hair. And her eyes. *Irish green*, she called them. Like her mother's, she had added sadly.

And a person might think the most astonishing thing about Em was that she had chosen me. Plain. Regular. Average. But the most astonishing thing was that her face didn't matter to her. Or her Victoria's Secret-worthy body. She acted as if all that didn't exist. She joked she just wanted to piss her mom off, but I think it was because she knew the truth.

It's just a shell.

Maybe it was easy for someone so attractive to sluff off what they were given and realize it was fleeting. I should have been able to do the same with my plain looks. I was far from revolting, but what did it really matter, anyway? I thanked God every day that my mom didn't let me have any social media accounts as a teenager. I was sure it saved me from a world of hurt that came from constantly comparing yourself to other people's "perfect" pictures.

Em told me once that the last thing she wanted was to be like her mom, who apparently suffered with *the beautiful curse.* I tried to hide the snort that rose inside me when Em said that.

That was when I told her about curses that were much worse than beauty.

I loved her even more for the way she cried when I elaborated on that. Not in a sadistic way, but in a way that came from a deep understanding of who she really was.

I smiled as I thought about that February when our philosophy class began. Every class, I watched with humour as the boys clamoured to sit next to her. I could tell it was a competition to see who could engage her in the longest conversation. She was polite, but kept her responses to a minimum and her questions back at them to zero. Her body language screamed, *I don't want your attention!* But since when did that ever stop a man with his eye on a prize? The day she saw me watching her fend them off she smiled at me and rolled her eyes. I laughed silently and thanked my lucky stars she even noticed me at all.

The next class, I took a huge chance and sat next to her, to the dismay of several boys honing in on the empty seat to the left of her. I didn't hit on her. I didn't try to engage her in meaningless conversation. I didn't "accidentally" drop my pen on the floor by her feet and brush the side of her leg as I retrieved it. I just sat next to her. At the end of class, she simply leaned over and whispered in my ear, "Thank you."

I had to stop myself from doing a tiny fist pump. Or turning to one of those boys and mouthing, *That's how it's done.* I'd been a bit of a player in high school. My mom didn't know because I never brought any of them home. The first girl I dated, Jenna, was a hard-assed little thing, openly gay. I'd had a suspicion about myself for a long time, but always chalked my disinterest in boys to my lack of good male role models. That or late puberty. I was probably the last girl in junior high school to grow boobs. Not that they ever got very big. I didn't mind though. It meant I could get away with wearing cheap, flimsy Walmart bras.

It was grade eleven, and Jenna had invited me over for a movie. Later I found out her intention was to seduce me. I let her. I became addicted to satisfying her sexually. Maybe it was an effort to gain some control over my life, or someone else's.

Over the next two years, I had sex with no less than seven women. I also confirmed that I was truly gay, that it was not a result of circumstance or fate, the way Em felt it was for her.

It was nice the way Em thought *souls* were more capable of choosing a partner than brains and hormones were.

She stirred next to me and opened her eyes. Smiling, she asked, "What are you looking at?"

"Your soul," I stated, my eyes large.

She giggled and said, "You always know the right thing to say to melt my heart."

I propped my head on my hand. "What can I say, I have a knack for being romantic in a weird and possibly creepy sort of way."

She rolled onto her back and stretched. "So what are we up to today?"

I took a deep breath and said quickly, "I thought you could meet my mom tonight."

Her eyes widened, and she quickly turned back to me. "For real? Are we ready for that? I mean, please don't take that the wrong way. You know I love you, but our parents?"

"I was thinking maybe there's no point hiding it anymore. I mean if shit is going to hit the fan, we might as well get it over with, no?"

"True," she said. "Do you think it's safer to start with your mom? I don't know if my parents are ready yet. I mean, things seem to be going well since Mom moved back into the house a couple of months ago, so maybe it's a good time?"

"Well, let's start with my mom. She's working at the bar tonight, so it will be casual. I don't *think* she will be surprised, but you never know."

"Well, let's give it a shot. Because I'm not going anywhere soon, so we might as well make it official."

"Okay. I'll text her and let her know." I leaned over and kissed her. "I love you, *Emmy-Lou*."

She rolled her eyes at me and threw a pillow at my head. "Just for that, I'm not getting out of bed until you make me some coffee."

I leaned in to kiss her neck and murmured, "That's fine by me."

We chose a table near the back of the bar. I watched my mom slowly go around the tables taking orders with a vacant look on her face. Something had not been right with her the past couple of months. Since I took her to the woman's shelter. What little life she'd had in her was gone. As if she'd seen something that couldn't be unseen.

She finally made it to our table and slid into the seat next to me. "Hi, turkey. Sorry that took so long." She barely cracked a smile.

I smiled. "That's okay, Mom. We're not in a hurry."

She stretched out her hand towards Em. "Hi, there. I'm Michelle, Cassie's mom."

Em smiled. "Hi, Michelle. I'm Emerson."

"That's a lovely name," she said.

"Yours too. Actually, Michelle was one of the runners up on my baby name list."

"Well, I think Emerson suits you just fine. It has a little more pizazz." She finally smiled the way I was used to seeing. "So what can I get you ladies to drink? Pepsi, Cass?"

I looked at Em. "I'll have a pint of whatever's on tap, please," she said. I had drunk alcohol a bit in high school, but quickly lost a taste for it after seeing friends blackout. That, combined with Ray and my grandmother, made me decide I didn't want to risk being like them. I had too much to do in my life to spend it wasted.

Mom's grin grew wider. "Sure." I was certain she had figured us out already.

She stood up and said, "Coming right up." She turned back to look at Em and then me as she walked away. She never had a very good poker face.

When Mom brought another round a half an hour later, I patted the seat beside me and asked her if she had a minute. The look on her face was passive as she sat.

I noticed that her wedding ring was missing, so I asked where it was.

Mom's face flushed and she tried to wave me away. "Oh, I lost it."

"After ten years, you just lost it?" I frowned.

"Well, I don't know where for sure. When I left the house I had it, and then when I left work that same night, I realized it was missing."

I figured she was lying, but I didn't interrupt. She added, "I think it may have been when I was shovelling snow. I couldn't find my mitts, and Ray was freaking out, and by the time I was done, my hands were freezing. I looked everywhere, but I couldn't find it." She shrugged.

I so badly wanted to ask her how Ray had reacted, but I didn't want to make her more uncomfortable, especially in from of Em, so I just said, "Huh."

She leaned over and whispered into my ear, "Before you say anything, just remember how much I love you."

I looked back at her. "So you already know?"

She smiled. "I've been watching you two from the bar. It's pretty obvious you are enamoured with each other."

And just like that, so easily, we happily launched into the story of how we met. Em and I taking turns inserting our favourite parts of the story. Mom sat listening the whole time with a huge smile on her face. It was a relief to see her happy again.

Finally, Em excused herself to go to the washroom. I turned to Mom, excited. "Do you really like her?"

She laughed. "Of course I do. What's not to like? She's lovely."

"And you're not upset that I'm dating a girl?"

She looked intently at me before asking, "Are you happy?"

"Yes."

She searched my face. "Does she treat you well?"

"Yes."

"Then that's enough for me."

I threw my arms around her neck. "Oh, thank you, Mom!"

She leaned into my hair and whispered, "I love you."

"I love you too."

She pulled back from me and smirked. "Didn't you think I would suspect this after you not dating boys your whole life? And then there were all those calls from random girls in high school."

I shrugged my shoulders. "Maybe I'm just that picky."

Her face fell. "I wish I had been that picky."

"It's not too late. We can still work something out," I said quickly.

She shook her head slowly. "You don't understand. It is too late."

I saw a sense of despair no child ever wants to see in their parent's eyes. But I said firmly, "No. It's not."

She smiled weakly. "I did such a good job with you." She touched the side of my face. "You're the only thing that's right in my life."

I renewed my vow to do something about that. Sooner rather than later.

It was late, and we were just about to leave when the front door banged open.

I looked up. "Shit," I muttered.

"What? What's wrong Cass?" Emerson asked worriedly.

I immediately saw the look of fear on my mom's face as she spotted her husband enter the bar, arm slung around the shoulders of a friend.

They sat down heavily at the bar and Ray bellowed to Michelle, "Bring me a whiskey!"

The bartender came over and said something to them that I couldn't hear.

"I don't fucking care what your policy is! I want a whiskey!" he hollered back.

I saw my mom nod to the bartender, who poured Ray a drink beneath the countertop. "This tastes like crap!" Ray said, but quickly got carried away in a conversation with his friend.

Mom made a motion for us to sneak out the door while he wasn't looking, but something rooted me to the spot. Emerson tapped my arm. "Don't you want to go?" Her voice was shaky.

I continued to stare at him, not answering her. Suddenly he turned to my mom and barked, "I'm ready for sex now!" with a wicked grin on his face.

The whole bar drained of noise as my mom's face turned red. The bartender turned angrily toward Mom, but she wouldn't return her gaze. "I said, I'm ready for sex now! Let's go." Ray got up and waited for her to follow.

Michelle said, "I can't just leave. I have to clean up and cash out."

Suddenly, Ray lunged across the bar and grabbed Mom's arm, and before I knew what I was doing, I was across the room and pounding on his back. "Leave her alone!" I screeched, my arms freewheeling.

Ray elbowed me away angrily and turned around. "Well, hello! If it isn't the long-lost Minnie Mouse! Have you come to take your mother's place?" He eyed me in a way that turned my stomach.

Suddenly Em was by my side, pulling at my arm. "Cassie!" she hissed. "Let's go."

"Oh, what do we have here?" Ray slurred, taking Emerson in.

"Don't look at her like that!" I yelled at him, not caring that the noise in the bar still hadn't returned, meaning we were still the centre of attention. I would have thought this sort of thing was a regular occurrence around here.

"Are you two *lovers?*" he said in a high-pitched voice, joking. His face turned mean when we didn't respond.

"You're a dyke?" he practically shrieked. If there had been any air left in the stillness of the bar, it had now completely drained. "I guess I shouldn't be surprised. What man would want your plain ass. But you." He stepped toward Em, shaking his head. "That's unfortunate."

I put myself between the two of them, protectiveness overriding my fear. Mom came around the bar and pulled him away. "Let's go home."

"No, Mom," I whispered, searching her face for a shred of defiance. Maybe that same emotion that had resulted in a lost ring?

Her look commanded me not to stop her as she dragged him out of the bar.

I apologized over and over to Em on the way home. I could have happily lived out my days without her seeing what Mom and I had to deal with. She continually assured me her year at the clinic downtown had shown her an even darker human nature.

"But it's still not the same as seeing it firsthand. Actually caring about someone and seeing how it affects them. It's like straight white people with a gay or black friend. They think they know what it's like to be discriminated against or marginalized, but until you know someone gay or black and see them as just another human, it's not the same."

She nodded and then quickly added, "Not seeing is what keeps people in my socioeconomic class in their privileged lives. I hate to use that term, but it's true. If they can't see it in front of their face, it's easier to pretend it doesn't exist."

We drove home in silence. I didn't need to add anything to that. Em saw. It was other people that needed help seeing.

EMERSON

17

I tried to smooth it over to ease Cassie's mind, but the scene at the bar haunted me all through the night, into my dreams, and for the whole day after. It created a fog around me as I went about my life. I had a hard time focusing on anything that came out of my professors' mouths. I had lied about seeing those things at the clinic, but I didn't want her to feel worse than she already did. Cassie had told me what went on at her house, and I'd *heard* things at the clinic, but seeing Ray's abuse in person was so much more disturbing. Took it from a *conversation* to a *reality*.

I berated myself for accusing my mother of not knowing suffering, because in fact I didn't truly know either. I was ashamed of the "terrible life" I thought I had endured growing up. Poor me. It was still nothing compared to Cassie's. Or her mom's. Or so many other girls and women.

I knew the saying "suffering is relative," but was it only people who had suffered very little in their own lives who repeated that phrase?

What was the worst thing that had happened to *me?* Having to endure five years of Mom forcing me to dance, hating it the whole time? That she made me have my little moustache lasered off when I was only twelve, which was extremely painful even though they said it wouldn't be? That I was scared shitless when Aaron stalked me in grade eleven, sending me nasty letters and calling the house ten times a night? That my mommy didn't make me the centre of her world? I had a pretty great father, siblings, and Janae to make up for it.

All silliness compared to this.

I felt so guilty at the life I had been given. My mother would be furious if she ever knew I thought that. I could hear her now: *It's all about choices, Emerson.* But I couldn't help but wonder if she was wrong. Yes, when you wanted to decide whether you would like Vietnamese or Mexican for supper, there was a choice to be made. Even in my little bubble, I had all the choices in the world at my disposal when it came to deciding on a career path. *I had options.* What would it be like to not have one single option?

Hell.

I jumped off the bus and wandered down the street toward my apartment, trying to fathom the unfairness of life. I mostly rode transit to school so I could read on the way instead of fighting with traffic. See? Even that was a choice. Cassie *had* to take transit. I saw a woman struggling to get her stroller up over the curb without dumping the baby. She had a huge diaper bag slung over her shoulder and a bag of groceries in the basket below the seat. She looked weighed down. And possibly on the verge of a meltdown, based on the way she rammed the wheel of the stroller into the curb, as if hoping it would magically jump up and over on its own. I quickened my step and reached for the front of the stroller. "Here, let me help you with that." I pulled it up the four inches or so it needed to get onto the sidewalk.

I smiled and looked at her face and was surprised to see a truly exhausted person in front of me. I could see it in the lines around her eyes and lips. Her whole face sagged, even though she was probably not much older than me. She smiled gratefully and breathed, "Thank you. These things are such a cumbersome pain in the ass." We both laughed, and then she was gone.

I stood there for what must have been several minutes. I'd done something so simple that alleviated what was causing someone else so much grief.

So easily, I had done something that cost me nothing and gave her everything.

"Well, maybe that's an exaggeration, but you know what I'm getting at," I said to Cass later that night as I tried to explain what had occurred. *How do I sum up such a blinding revelation?* "I know I didn't give her *everything*. But at least it was a tiny bit of relief. She looked so freaking *tired.*"

"That's why you are going into nursing; you are the kind of soul who's meant to see what people need and give it to them. You're a helper." Cassie smiled, as if the answer was that obvious.

"I must have gotten it from Janae." I missed seeing her almost every day. She had been hired when I was about ten. Janae was from the Philippines and had left her own children behind with her brother's family to come to Canada and make some money. She sent every extra cent she earned back to them. How happy she had been to finally bring all three of her boys over last year. I couldn't imagine how hard it must have been to leave them behind when they were still little. She always reassured me that family units were different in the Philippines, that her boys were in good hands, but I saw the sadness in her eyes. Really, what else could you say when you had no other option? She had just gotten on with it.

I flipped the five-egg, ham and cheese omelette I was making for us to split for supper. I knew Cass had avoided talking about the scene in the bar, except to repeatedly apologize, which she did again. I snapped, "I had to see it. Especially given the career path I've chosen." I forced my anger to be replaced by understanding. If our roles were reversed, I wouldn't want her to see it either.

From behind me, I heard Cass shift on her seat at the table. I poked the omelette near the middle to test if all of the jiggle was gone. Finally, she sighed and said, "I know. I would have kept you from seeing that forever, but that's not how the world works."

"No, it's not. The world works when people who can do something do it." I turned back to her. "We're going to figure this out together." I pointed the flipper at her.

She looked down from my intense gaze, chewing her fingernails. "Do you ever think a soul has a purpose in life?"

I frowned, confused by her random comment. "What do you mean?"

Cass looked up and gazed out the tiny kitchen window. "So, take my mom for example. She was completely neglected her whole life. No one has ever taken care of her. First she married my father and then she marries Ray. She has me and she vows to be the mother she never had. Or do you think people make a conscious decision to do the opposite of the way they were raised? Like you?"

"What do you mean, *like me?*" I asked, a bit defensive.

"Do you ever think you are opposite of your mom because you hate that part of her? Or do you think life gave you that mom to make it obvious what you were supposed to do with your life? That you needed to know what it was like to have no one care so that you would know exactly how to care?"

"Oh my God, you are making my head spin." I smiled, shaking my head. "Thanks, philosophy!" I lightly slapped my hand to my head. "Is that why you are going into social work? So you can save abused women?"

She finally looked up at me and I blanched at the pained look in her eyes, immediately regretting my flippant attitude. "Well, yes. But the *why* is what I want to know," she said.

"I guess in the grand scheme of things, it doesn't really matter."

"No." She paused. "But it's a nice thought, isn't it?"

"What?"

"That it was always out of our control. That it all works a certain way for a reason. Do we, as simple human beings, really have that kind of power over our lives?"

"Oh, you and my mother are not going to get along *at all*." I shook my head.

"Maybe you and I were meant to be together for a reason and we just can't see it yet. Or will ever see it," Cassie said, serious again.

I turned back to the stove and turned it off. *Maybe.* I could tell how real all of this was to Cass and that possibly she'd never had the chance to discuss it with anyone. I reached into the cupboard and took out two plates, putting half of the omelette on each one.

I sat across from her. "You're right. Maybe in the grand scheme of things, beyond our day-to-day problems, life is bigger than us. And that regardless what life a person has been given, something specific must happen for us to finally realize this. Maybe our moms' lives are the opposite sides of the same coin."

Cass took a bite. "Like, there's some kind of past trauma for both of them, but they both reacted differently? Do you really think your mom's hiding something?"

"Why else would she be so controlled?"

"Denial versus victim," Cass whispered.

"I know you don't want to see your mother as a victim, in the sense that she blames others for her life." I knew I had to tread carefully here. "But I meant, more in the sense that she feels she has no control over what happens to her."

"Well, in a way you don't have control over what happens."

"No, but you can control how you react. Or in my mother's case, overcontrol."

"Hmmm." Cass smiled. "Do you think this is what normal twenty-one-year-olds sit around doing on a Friday night? Having worldly conversations?"

"Kinda doubt it." I laughed, finishing my supper. I guess I had been more starving than I thought. "Maybe we've just been propelled to figure life out sooner rather than later."

"I think we should lighten things up tonight then. Let's go dancing." Her dark blue eyes lit up.

I laughed at her turn of direction. "Have you ever gone clubbing in your life?"

"Nope."

I pushed my plate away and jumped up, holding my hand out to her. "Then tonight is the perfect night to start."

KEELY

18

I lifted my coffee to my nose and inhaled deeply. Starbucks Gold Coast Blend whole beans, ground fresh and preset every night before bed by Andrew himself. I was enjoying his good old pampering. It helped me look past his underwear I found crumpled up at the foot of the bed the night before. The memory of the day two months earlier, when I showed up here, made me laugh.

I hadn't been able to bring myself to unpack the car once I had realized that everything I bought was intended for the big house. I took that as my subconscious desire to try again. The next day, I drove over to the house and just started unloading the purchases onto the front lawn. Maybe it was presumptive of me, but I decided since I was the one that left, it should be within my power to be the one that came back. I didn't give *Michelle* another thought. *I* was the woman he married. I just had to start trying a little harder. And keep my annoyance under wraps. *It really shouldn't be that hard, he's a good guy,* I told myself repeatedly.

Andrew came out onto the front step with a frown on his face, so I threw a pillow at him. I knew from the responding grin that he couldn't hold back that he would give us one more shot.

He had taken me back so easily. *Like he truly loved me.* And my random crying had mostly stopped, a sign that I made the right decision. I looked around at the gorgeous new living room, filled with my recent purchases. And I had taken the sale lady's advice and painted the focal wall ultra violet. Stunning. Andrew wasn't impressed with the new couch or pink accents, but I simply said, "I'm back, aren't I?" Which I knew was wrong as soon as it came out of my mouth as I noticed that old look that flitted across his face. This was exactly the kind of thing I was going to have to work harder on, I reprimanded myself.

Now I looked up to see him come down the stairs yawning and stretching. He leaned over me and planted a kiss on my forehead. "Good morning."

"Morning." *A little more enthusiasm, Keely. This is your husband, not a grocery store clerk.* I took a sip of my coffee.

"What are you up to today?" He sat down on the couch to put his socks on.

I had tried so hard to keep my food and workout routines to myself. I hated the wince that crossed his face when I detailed my food intake for him. And I made him think I was mostly working when I was at the gym, not training. I was up to four hours a day in preparation for my competition. But I couldn't sugarcoat it this time. "I have to train today, since the comp is in two days. But we could do something after?" I tried to sound genuine.

He looked a little put out, but then quickly brightened. "I'll call Jacob and see if he wants to come work on the bike today then."

"Yes, that's a great idea." *Anything to get him off my case.* My internal snark had slowly crept back here and there since I'd moved back. Maybe just hormones. Even though between menopause and only having twelve percent body fat, I didn't have periods anymore, I didn't think the monthly moodiness had entirely stopped.

Or maybe this was just me.

"I was thinking maybe we could get a last-minute flight to Saint Lucia after the competition," I said. *When I can eat normal for a few days and still have a ripped body.* I never had to worry about a bikini line as I had all of the hair on my body south of my neck lasered off a couple of years ago. It was excruciating but oh so worth it.

His face lit up. "Really? That would be awesome!" His enthusiasm at spending time with me was sweet. "I'll book something this afternoon."

I smiled. "That would be wonderful." *I saved that one by a thread.*

I was in the homestretch of "peak week." The gruelling days that lead up to a competition. Strict didn't even begin to explain the two months prior, but this week was rigid beyond belief. I started dreaming about cheeseburgers and ice cream, and made Andrew eat in a separate room from me. Not that I ever really cooked for him in the first place. Our house was a more of a "fend for yourself" kind of place, especially since Janae was gone. She had been a wonderful cook for Andrew and the kids—comfort food was her forte. I'd had to prepare my own meals since she didn't understand the lean protein, complex carb thing. "Gluten what?" she had asked once when I tried to explain to her what white bread was comprised of. As she flipped grilled cheese sandwiches for the kids' lunch, I went on a spiel about how it was the binding component of bread. Essentially glue. In your guts. She smiled as she listened, but I could tell she didn't really believe me. Finally she shook her head and laughed. "You make food so *dangerous*, Keely!" So I started listing a bunch of technical terms in an effort to boggle her mind. "Inflammation, leaky gut, decreased immune function, damage to gut biome, bloating, gas, poop problems, brain fog, bad skin. Isn't *that* enough to convince you?" I asked, breathless and proud that I'd inventoried all of this information. But she simply shrugged, flipped another sandwich, and replied, "But I like bread. It reminds me of home."

I said, "I thought you ate rice there." Not that rice was much better. I opened my mouth to start on the bad things I knew about rice, which admittedly wasn't much since I never loved the stuff. She stopped and turned to me, giving me the best dirty look she could manage—which for Janae was about as ominous as a Care Bear. "Keely, you really need to get out more."

For a second I had wanted to launch into a verbal reprimand, but then I realized I needed her and didn't have the time or energy to look for a new nanny. Plus, the kids would be devastated. Instead, I shot her a real evil eye and stalked out of the kitchen.

This time around, I was trying a new competition strategy and it had me stressed out. I was pretty ill after my last comp due to the old-fashioned regime. Carbohydrate, water, and sodium intake basically down to nil by show day. This was how I got all of the subcellular water out of my system to show off the beautifully toned muscles I had worked so hard for. The last thing I needed was them hiding beneath fat or a fluid pocket. By the competition, though, I was running on steam, supplements, and vodka. I became dehydrated and had such a bad headache and nausea I almost couldn't compete. And I only placed fifth due to the reverse water retention. I decided I was too old for this and hired a new trainer who agreed that the old ways of prepping were too dangerous.

So this time, I felt much better. It was just as rigorous, but not as dangerous. I ate certain things at certain times, controlled down to the gram and ounce.

The next day, after I was done getting my spray tan, Andrew sent a text: *Flying out at 7:45 Monday morning. That ok?*

I responded: *Yes.*

Great. And I hope you don't mind, I booked for 2 weeks.

I hesitated. Two weeks was a long time to be stranded with him. But if I took lots of books and he brought his golf clubs, maybe it would be fine. I really needed to reread *The Happiness Project* and take some serious notes.

Finally I responded: *Sounds great*

So why was a tiny part of me not looking forward to this? I felt the old tingle in my nose and forced it to stop. Stray tears would ruin the tan. Why couldn't I decide what the hell I wanted? Within a year, I had gone from miserably married to joyfully separated to sadly separated to happily reconnected to increasingly miserable. It was enough to make my head explode. The month after I'd moved back in had held so much promise. I realized it was likely an exaggerated honeymoon phase, but I hadn't expected it to start fading so fast. I'd even let Andrew go down on me a couple of times, which he did expertly. It was nice, but I couldn't fully relax and let myself go like I did in the old days.

I forced the same memory that I always did when these mixed feelings started to rise up in me. Years ago, on a talk show, an old couple who'd been married for like sixty years were asked how they had survived so long together. They both said that they never wanted to get divorced at the same time. So maybe this was just the natural cycle of a marriage?

I figured it was impossible to love someone completely, one hundred percent of the time. "Isn't it?" I asked myself.

Competition day came in a flurry of incremental meals at prescribed times. Three ounces of steak, eight ounces of sweet potato, and six ounces of water six hours prior to comp. Five minutes before walking on stage I was allowed a small candy bar. That part I could get used to. I pumped up my muscles three times before hitting the stage, after meals one, four, and six, to deliver glucose to my muscles. I still did the vodka shot, more out of superstition than anything.

I was in the forty-five-plus category. *Grandmasters* to be flattering. I was surprised to see the calibre of older ladies as we prepped backstage together. I was going to have some stiff competition this time, and for a second I cursed my decision to switch peak week practices. *If only I had trained harder.* I knew I could have squeezed in a couple extra minutes each day.

In the figure class, the judges wanted to see "the total package." That meant along with superior athletic definition, they were looking for tight, smooth skin with a beautiful tone. No cellulite. I excelled in the "total package," as I was naturally beautiful. I had my hair and makeup done to reflect this. And confidence was my best friend. I could walk out on that stage like I owned it. But today seemed different. I was actually looking around at how good the other competitors looked, something I never used to worry about.

I walked out and struck all the right poses in my brand-new, emerald-green, rhinestone-trimmed bikini. I had chosen my second favourite one that was only five hundred, with Matt nagging me in the back of my mind. The one I'd really wanted was nine hundred, gold, and amazing. Alarmingly, the usual high I felt on stage never came. I forced myself to smile and sell my best assets—calves and arms.

But even my third-place finish couldn't lift my spirits as I left the auditorium. *What the hell is wrong with me?* Normally this placing would have left me ecstatic, especially after my last epic fail. I texted Andrew about my results, but never heard back from him. *Strange.*

After driving around town for an hour, I headed home, suddenly more exhausted than I had ever felt. Even when the kids were babies and I was still trying to work. I fell into bed and slept soundly for ten hours straight.

I rolled over the next morning to find Andrew sleeping beside me. *I wonder when he got in?* He stirred, and I asked, "Where were you last night? I texted you after my comp and you never answered." Irritation lined my voice. He knew how important these shows were for me.

He hesitated before saying, "I am so sorry, Keely. I got sucked into a meeting. We had an emergency with some infrastructure in the south, and since we're leaving Monday, it couldn't wait."

It sounded plausible. "Right," I said. *But on a Saturday?*

He yawned loudly. "What did your text say? I didn't see it. How did the show go?"

"Great, I got third."

"That's awesome, Keely!" He leaned over to kiss me on the cheek. I turned to kiss him back, but he jumped out of bed. For some reason I was feeling it this morning, but he was gone before I could make a move. *He just missed out,* I thought sourly to myself. "I'm going to shower and get packing, okay?" he said, walking toward the washroom.

"Sure." I rolled onto my back and stared at the ceiling. Once I heard the shower start, I quickly rolled over and grabbed his cell phone from the night stand. I don't know what prompted me to do it, since we had always valued each other's privacy. *Until Michelle*, my mind snapped. There was a notice for a text message from *Nelson* at 12:42 a.m. It simply read *Thank you*. Nelson was a common last name, I was sure it was a co-worker or someone at the city. But something made me want to dig a little further, so I entered his passcode. It didn't work.

There's only one reason he would change his passcode. But a surprising thought crossed my mind. Did I really care if he was still cheating on me? I was sure lots of women knew deep down their husbands were cheating but chose not to see it. Why? Because they liked the rest of the life the marriage afforded them. It could be worse. I could be beaten to within an inch of my life on a regular basis.

I tried to push the thought away as I got up and forced myself to think about what to pack for the trip instead. But one thought kept coming to me. *How much am I willing to suffer to maintain the life I want?* What do I let go of personally to hold onto the bigger picture?

It followed me all the way to Saint Lucia the next day, too. Why couldn't anything be easy? Even as I saw the clear, turquoise waters I loved so much come into view below me, the internal conflict plagued me.

MICHELLE

19

I didn't want to text Cassie, but I needed someone immediately. And not because I was in extreme pain, but because I had never felt so damaged.

The whole previous night came back in horrific detail. Andrew had showed up at the bar and asked if I could go for a drive after work. He needed to talk to me. I knew it was a bad idea. Not because of Ray, but because of my emotions. In the months since he'd broken it off, I had done relatively well in pretending the whole affair hadn't happened. But I knew it was a crystal image and could easily be shattered if I saw him again.

The crushing heaviness after Andrew broke up with me had been more than I could bear. I started to wish he never came around, that I never had a glimpse of something different. I had let a tiny seed of hope be sown somewhere deep inside of myself. And that was really, really stupid.

Of course my heart leapt compulsively when he came in. My first, immediate thought was, *He changed his mind!* But it turned out he really did just want to talk. No kissing, no touching. Just talking. As he went on about Keely and her continued coldness, I began to see how emotionally needy Andrew was. He needed someone to care for, and I needed someone to care for me, so didn't that make us the perfect pair?

Once he had spilled everything he had been saving, he quickly and profusely apologized.

"That wasn't fair. I'm so sorry, Michelle. You have enough to deal with without listening to some whining asshole." His hands gripped the steering wheel hard.

I looked out the windshield to see the traffic whipping past the parking lot where we sat, even though it was well past midnight. *Does this city ever shut the fuck up?* I repressed the smile that crept up at my cussing. Normally, I would have chastised myself for thinking like this, but I felt anger mix with growing recklessness inside of me. Anger because Andrew had the gall to use me as an emotional leaning post. And after a lifetime of constriction, the recklessness could come from any number of places. I had *purposefully* overcooked Ray's eggs the other day with a wicked grin to myself. This new me scared me.

"I don't mind listening," I finally said, cutting him some slack. I really didn't. I just knew how slippery the slope really was.

"It's just that she says she decided to stay with me, that she wants to try, but her actions and body language don't agree with her statements." He sighed deeply, leaning his head against the seat. "And here I am, telling you, of all people. I must be the most insensitive dickhead in the whole world."

Maybe… but I still love you. I only barely managed to keep that statement to myself. I moved to put my hand on his, but pulled it back upon contact.

He sighed deeply. "We're leaving for our condo for two weeks. I don't know how much of her frowning looks I can take."

I stifled a *ha!* A beach condo. Such a foreign idea to me. I had never been out of the province. Hell, I'd hardly been out of the city. What a pathetic life. I barely knew people with such excess until I met Andrew. I knew he wasn't trying to make me feel small.

"I'm sorry, Andrew, but I really should get home," I forced myself to say. Ray would be wondering where I was. He was playing cards with his buddies tonight and told me to walk home. He didn't like me to spend money on cabs, even though they made me feel safer. But really? What could happen to me out in the cool Toronto night that hadn't already been done? In fact, my own house was probably more dangerous than some dark, deserted alley.

"Yes, of course." He put the car into drive and turned out onto the street. He parked a couple of blocks away from the house and I opened the door. He leaned across me and kissed me lightly on the cheek. "I'm sorry. I'll try to stay away, okay?"

A tiny part of me cried *please don't* as I quietly got out of the car. Before I turned onto my street, I texted Andrew: *Thank you*. It would be best for me if he really did stay away.

Ray was sitting on the front step smoking when I walked up the sidewalk. A beer bottle sat beside him on the step. "Where have you been?" he said smoothly and quietly. His eyes were dark and accusing.

Internal alarms went off in me. "I… I worked a bit late and then… walked home." My lying skills were poor, but it was the best thing I could come up with.

He stood up and crushed the cigarette, grabbing the bottle. "Bullshit. I stopped by the bar and some waitress I've never seen before said you left with a guy. A guy who didn't look like me." He stepped down the stairs toward me.

I quickly looked both ways and started backing up. It must have been that new girl Felicia. She didn't know what was going on. *You knew you were going to get caught sooner or later, didn't you?* my mind pointed out. "No. I don't know what she's talking about. A couple of customers left at the same time as me, so maybe she thought I was with them?" My heart hammered.

"She said she *thought* it was her husband. So that means you were *with* him and *talking* to him." He took two more big steps and stopped, towering over me. "I should have known that the second you didn't need me anymore to help you raise that little brat, you'd start whoring around.

The last thing I heard as he raised the bottle over my head was "this is for the eggs."

Now here I lay, in the hospital, confused and broken. My head hurt more than it ever had, apparently from the concussion. The nurse had kindly told me that a neighbour found me on the front lawn, bleeding from my head and unconscious. Ray said he was inside sleeping when the paramedics questioned him. Wide eyed, he stated he had no idea where the beer bottle that had split my head open came from.

Then the nurse got very serious. "The police can't charge him until you make a statement. There were no witnesses. Of course there were fingerprints on the bottle, but he said that he and his friends had been drinking and one of them probably took his empty bottle and used it as an ashtray outside. We need you to talk, Michelle." Her eyes pleaded with me. I wondered how many women those eyes had searched out for the truth.

Again, my body betrayed me with a flinch. The truth was on the tip of my tongue. I even opened my mouth to speak. What did I have to lose anyway? The nurse leaned in, alive with the expectation of what I would tell her.

But the clamp came down just in time. Before it slipped out.

The nurse finally straightened up, irritated and heartbroken. I was sorry I couldn't do what she wanted me to. I was too weak. I turned my head and pretended to focus on the vertical blinds that hung against the window.

She bumped into Cassie on the way out of the room and they exchanged a few words. By the look that clouded my daughter's face, I knew what the nurse was telling her. Cassie sat down heavily in the chair next to me and stared silently at me.

Finally, I whispered, "Please don't look at me like that, Cassie."

She suddenly started crying, which shocked me. She was such a stoic person. I felt even more terrible that I was the source of her tears.

"Mom," she breathed. "We could build a case. This is your fourth hospital visit. They're not going to let this go." She nodded out the door towards the nurse's desk, where three of them huddled around a computer.

Add in all the times I didn't come to the hospital.

She leaned over me and gently touched my head. "How many stitches?"

I frowned, not exactly remembering. "Thirty. I think?" I finally said, forcing my eyebrows to smooth back out. The frown had pulled uncomfortably on the staples.

"How many is it going to take?" she mumbled, looking away.

"What?"

"How many stitches is it going to take? How many fractures?" She turned back to me, her voice rising. "How many bruises? How many close calls?" She then looked directly into my eyes and growled, "How many *rapes*?"

The ferocity in her tone made my stomach turn. I looked down from the gaze she had me pinned under.

"Don't think I don't know. I know you guys have sex, and I know you aren't an active participant. That makes it rape. You know that, right?" Cass leaned toward me.

I found myself nodding and crying and falling and breaking. I had called Cassie to the hospital to make me feel better, not worse. She seemed as though she couldn't control herself once she had started. "I know you feel as though there's nothing you can do about your life because you don't deserve better than what you get," she breathed heavily. "But what you are really doing is not taking responsibility for your own life. It hurts me to say this to you, Mom, but people all over the world have terrible things happen to them. Worse than you." I wanted to argue that wasn't possible, but she wouldn't let me interrupt her speech. "I *want* to save you. I really do. But I can't." Her voice broke. "No one can. You have to do it for yourself, or you'll never truly be free." She finished with a pant.

I quickly wondered if she knew about Andrew. Why else would she say no one could save me? "But... I—"

Cass cut me off. "I know this is the brutal truth. But that's how much I love you and want to help you." She jumped up and started pacing the small room. "But you have to take the first step. It's a sign to me—to yourself—that you want better and that you realize it's in your power to provide that for yourself."

She stopped at the door to the room and looked out at the nurses, her hands clasped behind her back. "You are not to blame for what happened to you, but it's still your choice what you will live with after the fact."

I knew with that, she had no more to say to me.

Cassie checked me out with the promise of bringing me back in ten days to have the staples removed. I noticed in the mirror the huge shaved spot on my head. I was going to be wearing a hat for a while.

"Can we start making a plan? I know springing the women's shelter on you was a shock, but maybe if we went about it in a more methodical way? Between the two of us, we could start a private bank account? Start putting money into it?" I could tell she wanted to add: *Something? Anything?* "I'll pick up a couple of shifts at the store every week, okay?"

I knew she wasn't going to let it go this time, so I found myself saying okay. Was it just to see the look of relief on her beautiful face? Or was there a tiny spark of hope in it?

As we pulled up to the house, she turned to me. "I can't believe I'm taking you back here. It makes me want to puke. Are you sure you won't come to my place? Even for a few days?"

"No, Cassie."

"I'm taking you inside at least." She turned off the ignition.

"I can go in myself," I said, quickly opening the car door.

But she was younger and faster and was around the little blue "friend's" car, which I realized was Emerson's now, before I was even out. She said in a steely tone, "I'm taking you in. I'm not afraid of him."

You should be.

"Well, well, well. If it's not the klutz and the dyke," Ray boomed as we walked in the house.

"What did you do to her?" Cassie hissed, coming to stand right in front of him.

Ray grew a comical, surprised look on his face. "I." He pressed his fingers to his chest. "Did nothing to her."

"Bullshit," Cassie spat. I walked up and put my hand on her arm.

"I can't help it if your mother got drunk at work and fell on the sidewalk and landed her head on a bottle." He smirked. "Anyway, I'm hungry." He turned to me. "I haven't ate all day. Is your head too broken to make supper?" His glare broke whatever resolve Cassie's fervent speech had given me. Again.

And for the hundred-thousandth time in my life, I dropped my head and did what I was told.

I didn't hear Cassie leave the house as I pulled a loaf of bread out of the fridge, but when I turned to glance back to the living room, she was gone.

That night I woke from a dream, my head throbbing. I was fighting with Andrew, who was strangely my father. We were in my old childhood apartment and I saw my mother sitting in the ratty green recliner. She looked incredibly small, tinier than I remembered. Because I was an adult now? She smoked and muttered to herself, a stained off-white nightie hanging loosely on her frame. When she saw Andrew, she jumped up, screaming, "Why did you leave? We could have made it with you. We could have had a decent life!" She pounded him on the chest, and he looked to me, terrified, as if I could save him.

Anger overcame me, and I stepped toward him. "Why did you leave?" I hissed and spat and finally cried. "It could have been okay, we would have loved you and she wouldn't have turned into this." I looked at my mom, who had now crumpled on the floor at his feet. I looked back to Andrew, who wasn't Andrew anymore, but some dark stranger. "Dad?" I whispered, totally confused.

He reached out and touched my face. "I love you, Elly. You deserve better."

I lay in bed, tears coursing down my face into a tiny pool in my ears. *Elly?* Was this man my father? Did I actually have a memory of him stored somewhere deep inside of me?

Too bad I didn't have the money to hire a therapist, I thought before I drifted back to sleep.

CASSIE

20

My anger had been barely contained when I walked into that hospital room. But it extinguished as soon as I saw her.

How many times can you get over seeing the person you loved most in the whole world broken? *Is she going to make me realize just how many?*

My mother had been lying limply in the hospital bed with a bandage wrapped around her head. She had a black eye on the right side, where he had hit her, cutting open her scalp from the temple towards the back of her head.

"She could have bled to death if the neighbour hadn't found her." The nurse's words hung over me like a cloud, and I realized after seeing her face harden and soften in the same sentence that I wasn't the only one whose heart bled for these kinds of women.

Dead.

That's what she could have been. But hadn't I always known that was a possibility? My mother was only ever one precisely placed blow, one arterial cut, one squarely landed punch, one shove in the wrong direction, away from death. Ray had always been connivingly controlled in his abuse, but this time seemed reckless, even for him.

"What are you thinking about? Or is that a stupid question?" Emerson's voice interrupted my thoughts.

I turned from the window. She tilted her head the way a puppy does when trying really hard to listen, waiting for a command or signal from the person their whole world revolves around. I knew it wasn't her fault, but I blurted out in an effort to release some anger, "Your mom gets to lie on a beach and my mom gets to lie in a hospital bed." The hurt on her face instantly made me regret what I'd said. "I'm sorry, it's not you. It's just that life is so unfair."

She looked at me for a long time. So long I started to worry that I really should never open my mouth again. That I had finally broken the one thing that kept me going and gave me hope. Finally, she said, "You're right. It's not fair. Thank you for saying what you felt."

A huge sigh of relief escaped me. "What am I supposed to do, Em?" I cried, shoving my hands in my pockets and pacing the room. "I almost feel like his accomplice. Taking her back there, I mean. I should have just kept driving."

"Where would you have gone, though? To the shelter?"

I shrugged. "I guess so. Shit, I have about nine hundred dollars in my savings account and a credit card. I could take her west."

"But what about school? Would you throw all of that away?"

I didn't hesitate. "For her, yes." I sat and then immediately got back up and grabbed a cup, filling it with water from the tap. "I'm smart and hardworking. I could find a job at a restaurant or clothing store."

"Do you think you would always feel like you were on the run? Always on guard?" she pressed.

"Probably. But isn't that still better than now?" I took a drink and set the cup down, unconsciously wiping my lip balm off the edge with my thumb.

Em looked at me softly. "Maybe. But I can't help but think there's still a better way. Something we can't see yet."

Her positivity always amazed me. Bottomless. "How long do I wait, though? This is the worst she's ever been hurt. She doesn't have much further to fall until he kills her." I winced at the words, but it was the truth.

"How about you finish your degree? That's only four-ish months. You know your mom would be extremely upset if you didn't finish school because of her. Next spring. Then we can do something about this." Em nodded deeply, believing it a solid plan.

We. She said it like we were going to be together forever.

The next day on the bus to school I saw a mom gripping a little girl's arm tight and hissing angrily into her ear. The child looked terrified, with her huge blue eyes darting back and forth across the aisle. She finally shrank away from her mother in an effort to become smaller and unnoticeable. I'd seen this before. In my second year at school, I interned with family services, and I was allowed to accompany the social worker on less serious cases. I'd seen this little girl's expression then on the children we investigated for possible removal from the home. The same expression I suspected my own mother's face wore all those years ago. If only someone else had seen it. If only someone had cared. If only the authorities had intervened, maybe she could have had a different life.

I inhaled swiftly as the idea struck me, making everything clear. *Why didn't I think of this before?*

"But I thought you were going to focus on women's shelters?" Professor MacDougall asked me as I sat in front of her. I had just asked if it was too late to switch my focus.

"I was. I mean, I may still do that one day. But something occurred to me. I want to work in family services. If I can get the kids out of the abusive home, maybe they can still have a chance at a normal life." *Because once they're adult women, it's almost impossible for them to leave.*

She nodded. "That's the idea, Cassie. And the younger we can get them out, the better their chances are." She leaned forward and gazed levelly at me. "It's not an easy job. You see the lowest of the low. The worst-case scenarios. Things that will make you question what humans are really capable of doing to each other. Even to people they are supposed to love and protect."

I *never* asked for the easy path. "Can't be much worse than what I already know," I said, looking past her shoulder at a family picture. They looked normal and happy, with two parents and two smiling kids. Sure, I had seen terrible things happen. One time I came home from school to catch Ray shoving my mom's head in the oven. He held her by the hair—her face right inside the oven—saying, "This is what you call clean? Do it again." Seeing my mom's limp body, as if she had given up and let Ray shove her in there, had made me want to scream, "Fight back!" but I stood there silently. Ray didn't even see me as he strode out the back door. Mom turned to look at me, tears running down her face, but said nothing as she turned back to the oven, picking up a scrubber from the floor. I must have watched her methodically scrub the bottom, then the sides, then the top for half an hour, my emotions fluctuating from anger to sadness to empathy to disbelief. I knew she needed financial help raising me. I was in grade eleven, and she frequently promised, or rather commanded, I'd go to college. Finally, I turned and went to my room, knowing I was the reason she stayed here. She sold herself out to guarantee my future. I vowed to get her out—one way or another.

Now Professor MacDougall frowned deeply. "Cassie, I hope you have no idea how bad it really can be."

There's only one way to find out. "Someone has to do it."

She closed her eyes briefly, then said, "Yes. And things are really changing, making it harder for people to hide the terrible things they do. And knowing where your motivations lie, I have no doubt you will fully capitalize on this fact."

I smiled. "I'll take that as a compliment."

"As it was meant."

"I know this is your special thing, but can I help you decorate?" Em asked as I pulled the cake out of the oven. She quickly added, "I know you are perfectly capable of doing it yourself. I just feel like... I want to do something special for your mom too."

I smiled as I closed the oven door. I had made my mom a birthday cake every year since I was nine years old. I remember how devastated I had been when she sadly told me that she'd never had a birthday cake. I felt huge guilt for all the years she had done it for me. I vowed that day to never, ever forget her birthday. I would even put up with all the moaning and groaning I had to hear from Ray about the big, useless deal I was making about the whole thing. I think that was the first time the words *fuck you* ran through my mind towards him.

"You are the sweetest thing. Of course you can help. Plus, you're way more artistic than me."

She whipped out her phone. "Oh, I was hoping you'd say that! I was thinking this." She showed me an image. A far cry from the plain, iced-in-the-pan cakes I had made for Mom over the years.

"Em! You can't pull that off, can you?" I laughed. "I mean, it's not that I think you can't do it, but that's pretty fancy."

She ran to the front door, where she had left a shopping bag. "I already have all the stuff." She came back to me, smiling from ear to ear.

My heart melted. *How is this possible? And how many times can I ask myself how a person can be so lucky?*

EMERSON

21

I was so excited to decorate the cake! I was pretty crafty and loved doing this kind of stuff. I didn't want to tell Cass that really, this was revenge on my mother. When I was fourteen and Riley was eleven, we decided to start a cupcake decorating business. Our first "event" was Mother's forty-second birthday. We thought it would be such a wonderful surprise for her. We went to great lengths to think of a theme she would like. We settled on white cupcakes with hot pink icing piled up as high as we could get it and black nonpareils scattered around each of them. We used black-and-white brocade cupcake liners with the special aluminum lining so they would retain their colours during the baking process. We stood back and admired our creations piled on the tiered tower Dad had bought us specifically to display cupcakes. It was a mountain of professional-quality deliciousness, or so we thought. "They really are stunning," Dad said, standing back to admire them.

That night, we presented them to Mom while singing "Happy Birthday." The look on her face as we entered the room destroyed us. She went on and on about how beautiful they were. And her favourite colour, too! She exclaimed they were so stunning that she didn't know if she could bring herself to eat them, and that if she could, she would preserve them forever as a symbol of how much thought we had put into her birthday. The joking faded to tension as Dad hissed at her, "Just eat the cupcake, Keely."

You'd have thought we were feeding her arsenic by the look on her face as she took minuscule bites. With her mouth pulled back and her nose wrinkled, she finally—probably ten minutes later, with half of the icing scraped onto the edge of her plate—finished it. "That was delicious, girls. I just couldn't eat all the icing; it was too sweet."

Dad, Riley, Jacob, and I all exchanged bewildered looks over our second cupcakes.

The next year, Dad helped us make a sugar- and fat- and gluten-free cake for Mom's birthday. She enjoyed it much more. I didn't realize at the time how heartbreaking the cupcake memory would be. My mom couldn't even fake appreciation for the moment. It was the kind of tiny moment that breaks something between a parent and child, possibly forever. It was a drop in the bucket of a lifetime of relationship "misses" between us.

I set to work, and two hours later, a full hour after Cass walked out of my "decorating class," the masterpiece was complete. "It's done! Come look!" I called to her, unable to contain my excitement.

Her jaw dropped when she saw it. Tears actually came to her eyes. "It's the most beautiful thing I have ever seen, Em," she whispered. It was a lemon cake with two tiers. White buttercream icing sculpted into small peaks, sprinkled with coarse sugar, lemon zest, and pale green silk flowers. And for the finishing touch, I had added a semi-transparent, light green ribbon around the bottom of the tiers. It was actually to hide the imperfect seal between the layers, but no one besides me needed to know that little detail.

Exactly the response I was gunning for. "She deserves it," I said, nodding quickly.

"Yes, she does."

"I wanted to do something classic and soft, yet beautiful. Like her." I stood back and looked over the cake for any flaws.

"We are *not* taking this to the house," Cassie said firmly.

"What do you mean? Isn't that what you normally do?"

"Yes, but he's not getting any of this masterpiece. I'll text her and see if we can bring it to the bar. Then more people can enjoy it too."

"Oh, that's a good idea! Maybe we should decorate the place?"

She laughed. "Slow down there, lady. That might be too much for her. You know, she doesn't like to be the centre of attention."

I just rolled my eyes. *Could our mothers be any more different?*

I snuck out of the apartment for a few minutes to finish fully executing my plan. I knew Cassie was probably right about Michelle not wanting a big to-do made over her. But there was one little gift I just had to get her.

I drove to the little gem store that I had fallen in love with when I was sixteen. I could spend hours wandering up and down the two aisles, touching every stone I passed. The feeling was indescribable. As if each and every stone brought with it an energy intended to lift people higher.

I wandered around for half an hour before realizing that I was running out of time. I homed in on the stone I had come for, hoping it came in a carving I was also looking for.

There it was! Perfection.

I had Tristan wrap it up in a tiny box and I practically skipped out of the store, my mission fully completed.

That night as we sang to Michelle, surrounded by her co-workers and even some regular customers, I saw the modest person she was. The tears in her eyes danced with candlelight, and her smile was lovely and sweet. She exclaimed over and over that the cake was the most exquisite thing she had ever seen. When she said that it was too beautiful to eat, I knew that she meant it for reasons entirely different than my mother had. And then, when she actually did bring herself to cut it, I watched with open-mouthed anticipation as she put the first forkful into her mouth. Her reaction was everything I had ever wanted. I saw her transported, if only for a brief second, to a place she deserved to stay forever.

And then I saw the way Cass looked at her. It broke my heart. Love and despair and the intense desire to do something for her mother were obvious.

If only I could figure something out. I tapped my foot, my mind spinning. There must be something I could do with everything I had been given. How was it possible in this day and age for one person to have so much and another to have nothing?

We stayed for several hours, drinking and chatting. I hadn't forgotten about the present, I was just waiting for the right time. Finally, when Cass went to the washroom and customers weren't demanding Michelle's attention, I snuck up on her side.

"Here. Just a little something." I pressed the small black box into her hand.

"Oh! Emerson! You shouldn't have," she said.

"I had to. It was a divine intervention, out of my control." I grinned and put my hands up in a helpless gesture.

She opened the box and pulled out the light-pink crystal angel. It was less than two inches tall. I wanted it to be small enough that it could be easily carried around, or hidden if necessary.

Michelle hadn't spoken yet, so I said, "It's made of rose quartz. It's the crystal of unconditional love. I just wanted you to know that you have more people in your corner than you think. *Unconditionally.*" I emphasized the last word as much as I could. "It also represents healing." I noticed her hand drift unconsciously to the scar on her head. I turned to leave, not wanting to make her more uncomfortable than she probably already felt, but she suddenly turned and pulled me into a hug. Surprised at first, I quickly relaxed into her, feeling that this was how a mother should embrace a child. I wrapped my arms around her.

I looked over her shoulder to see Cassie watching us from across the bar. The look on her face wasn't complicated like when she watched her mom eating the cake. This time it was very simple.

KEELY

22

I couldn't begin to explain how much I loved the Caribbean. The contrast with my regular life was stark. No wonder people were addicted to vacationing. I could get on a plane and relax, even though I didn't love flying. It was the anticipation of the uncomplicated, stress-free days coming.

But this time, over the course of two weeks in paradise, I started to realize something. *Andrew isn't trying as hard.* Now, was this because he knew I didn't always appreciate his efforts or because he had other things on his mind? Like when he went out to jog on the beach every morning. He always asked if I wanted a smoothie on his way back. But one day in the middle of the trip, he showed up with one. Just one. For himself.

"Why didn't you ask me if I wanted a smoothie?" I asked, trying to sound casual as I put down my book, *How to Win Friends and Influence People.* This was my go-to read when I needed to feel good about myself and remember that I was doing the right thing in my life for myself. The fact that I had to pick it up again after probably five years was unsettling, but I pushed the feeling aside. Maybe it was time I updated my self-help library. I glanced over to the bright yellow *You Are a Badass* laying on the balcony chair next to me.

Andrew raised his eyebrows and said, "I've asked you every day this week and you've said no. So why would I bother to keep asking if you obviously don't want one?"

Because I like to know that I'm still a priority to you. God, I was glad that thought didn't come out of my mouth. Instead I just shrugged my shoulders and said, "Whatever." I looked out over the ocean to see a pelican drifting on the updraft over the beach.

"I'm just taking a page out of your book. When was the last time you made sure I was fed?" I swear his bottom lip stuck out a bit.

Could he be any needier?

I had also caught Andrew staring off into space several times. I almost asked him what he was thinking about the last time, but had stopped cold when I saw a slow smile spread over his face. I had never seen him like that. The smile lifted his eyes and smoothed the skin between his eyebrows. It made him look ten years younger and more handsome than ever. It was extremely suspicious.

Nelson. My mind kept wandering back to that name. I tried to tell myself that it was just a co-worker, but my hesitancy to ask him about it directly raised my sense that it wasn't. I'd actually had the exact conversation that floated through my mind with a group of ladies from the condo last night at the bar downstairs.

Gloria had flipped her hand when Rena asked her if her husband's affair bothered her.

"And lose all of this?" Gloria motioned out to the ocean. "No way. He can keep her, I don't care, as long as I get to keep my life. In fact, he's been bugging me less for sex, so I'd call that a win-win!" She threw her head back in laughter, her fake blonde hair flying exaggeratedly. "She can do the dirty work for me." She wrinkled her nose.

"Sounds like the ideal situation," I said, drumming my fingers on the arm of the blue wicker chair.

"Yes, it is. The only thing he had a hard time with was that I started making him wear condoms. I'm not catching some disease from whatever that filthy little slut is packing around.

Maybe that's the real reason he's not coming to me for sex anymore." She winked at me.

Why didn't I think of that? I barked at myself. Michelle could have AIDS for all I knew! And then he came home to me? Not that we had sex that often, but still.

That thought sealed the idea for me. I needed to hire a private investigator. I needed to know for sure. Either that or make Andrew wrap it up and forget about it.

But it was not in my nature to let go so easily. To let *her* have any semblance of control over *my* life. I needed to know what I was dealing with. Was it so bad to want it both ways? Freedom *and* devotion from Andrew? My idea of the perfect marriage, actually.

As soon as we were home in Toronto, I set to searching. I needed to give the PI something to go on, so I searched Andrew's Facebook friends list again, this time looking for a Nelson.

And there it was. *M. Nelson.* Maybe it was a work person. I clicked on his profile, saw nothing posted on his wall, and started going through the pictures. All I found were nature shots. Close-ups of bugs and flowers. Sweeping landscapes and storm clouds. No selfies. Not one single person. I almost gave up when I finally came across an actual photo of people.

A grainy, dimly lit shot. Possibly in a bar or something. A woman about my age and a girl. Probably her daughter, I decided, seeing how closely they pressed together. They looked very similar. *Plain.* Straight, medium-brown hair down past the older woman's shoulders and more of a curly bob for the girl. No makeup that I could see, which I decided would do them both a world of good. I looked more closely and saw something withdrawn in the woman's eyes, like she was trying to hide. Poor thing. She had probably never taken a selfie in her whole life, and this was painful for her. I could tell from the angle that the girl was holding the phone.

This couldn't possibly be her? I imagined Andrew attracted to some young, blonde, goddess-warrior type of woman. Maybe a CEO of a big company. Someone who could kick some balls. *Someone more like me.* Except for the young and blonde, of course.

Maybe she was easy? Like Gloria said, guys were all about getting laid, weren't they? But this woman didn't look easy. She looked like a nice mom who loved her daughter and possibly had some issues of her own.

I passed what I had found to the PI I had hired, recommended by one of the other women in Saint Lucia. His name was Ralph, and he came to my office one afternoon to meet. He seemed a bit sleazy, but what did I care? I did not appreciate the way he looked at me though, and told him so by crossing my arms and looking sternly at him.

"So your husband's name is Andrew O'Connell and his mistress is named Michelle?" he asked, writing notes in a disgusting brown notebook with a mustard stain on the cover. All I could picture was him shoving a greasy, cheese-laden burger into his mouth, the book catching the drips.

I forced the appalled look I must have had off my face and nodded. "I should add that's my last name. Andrew took it when we married. I wanted to keep my last name to honour my grandmother and he was very modern about it." I narrowed my eyes at him. "It doesn't always have to be the woman who gives everything up for the man."

Ralph raised his eyebrows but said nothing, just took more notes.

"And he had a text from someone named *Nelson* that said *thank you.* I couldn't get into his phone because he changed the passcode, which is suspicious. I looked on his Facebook and only found an *M. Nelson.* The M might be for Michelle." I still had a hard time believing the woman in the shot was who Andrew was dating, probably just Andrew's co-worker's wife and daughter. "There was a picture of a woman and her daughter, but that was it." I pushed the grainy picture I had taken a screenshot of and printed across the desk to him. Jeez, I sounded like a stalker. *You are!* my brain yelled at me. "It's my right to know," I muttered.

"What?" he asked.

"Nothing. Just talking to myself." I tried to laugh it away. I placed one of Andrew's business cards on the table. "This is his company; he's a civil engineer."

"Okay. Do you think that's it?"

"I think so. I know it's not much to go on."

He smiled and stood up. "I've worked with less. I can set up invoicing and payments privately, so he doesn't figure it out."

"I'll run it through the gym. I handle my own finances." *Thank you very much.*

The look he gave me on the way out the door showed his appreciation of a woman who ran her own show.

I had chewed my pencil eraser clean off before I realized I had been fantasizing about eating the biggest burger ever. *With double bacon.* The meeting, combined with the extremely pushy man who had shown up at the gym asking for donations for a woman's shelter across town that was struggling, had stressed me out. He had insisted on talking to the owner, not Amber at the front desk. I had to finally get short with him, saying that if people used their brains more effectively in life, there would be no need for shelters. That had sent him packing.

On my way home from the gym, I forced myself to drive past the Five Guys burger joint and stop by the grocery store instead to grab proper, healthy groceries. I'd had my two weeks of eating crap, now it was time to get back to business. I sucked in the tiny gut that had grown while I lounged around in paradise, not running every day and drinking too much wine.

"Keely?" I heard from behind me.

I froze. I knew instantly who it was. Why, in a city of nine million people, could I not avoid this woman? I slowly turned around. I forced myself to smile. *Not too big!* "Hi, Cadence. How are you?" I felt my right eye twitch. I immediately noticed that some little age spots were showing on her cheekbones. Strangely though, they didn't age her.

"Oh, I'm great!" she said happily, pushing up her dark-rimmed glasses. "I was hoping to run into you again since you didn't have time to talk at grad. Jesse just started engineering at U of T. What's Riley up to?"

Fuck all. "Oh, she's taking a year off to figure out what she wants to do. You know, she has so many options! Maybe too many, in fact. You know, she's smart, artistic." You'd never know it by the grades she pulled in this last year. My smile grew a little bigger and I could feel my face flushing.

"Yes. Jesse was always talking about how good Riley was at computer stuff. You know, nowadays, all kinds of jobs exist that weren't available for us. I'm sure she'll find something she loves soon enough." She stepped a micro-inch toward me, leaning into the conversation. I caught a whiff of pineapple and mandarin. *Must be Burberry.*

I refocused on what she had just said. *Computers?* Maybe I should hire Riley to do the gym's website if that was true. Save myself a couple of bucks. Cadence opened her mouth and then closed it, her eyes imploring me to say something.

The silence grew uncomfortable, so I quickly said, "Well, it was nice seeing you. But I should get home and make supper. You know how the family gets when you don't feed them properly." I needed to get away from her as quickly as possible before I said something stupid.

Her shoulders dropped a fraction. "Oh, yes! Okay, well, I'll see you around sometime?" She looked up at me, obviously hesitating over her next words.

But I wasn't going to let her speak them. "Yes. See you." I quickly turned and walked away, not looking back.

I couldn't relax until I was safely back in my car. I forced myself not to think about that night. But it came to me anyway.

Five years earlier, in an effort to expand my horizons, I'd joined a book club. Cadence was another member of the club, and it happened that our kids went to the same school. I was desperate for people to talk to outside of the house and work, and we started getting together in the evenings in addition to book club meetings, mostly for wings and a few drinks, but it slowly evolved to clubbing. Eventually the partying started getting a little out of control. Guys became very aggressive when a group of drunk moms were causing a riot on the dance floor. We started pretending we were "together" in an effort to keep the men at bay. Of course we should have known it would only pique their interest. One or five drinks too many and I tumbled into Cadence while we danced. She held me up and then quickly leaned in to kiss me. I didn't pull away. Her lips were as soft as I'd thought they'd be.

After that night, I purposely removed myself from the group. To me, it was a drunken kiss. That was it. But to her it was more. She tried to call and text, but I told her repeatedly that I was married and not interested.

She was recently divorced and had decided she was done with men, so it was easy for her.

I did miss the book club, but leaving was for the best. Plus, drinking and binging on late-night pizza and ending up too hungover to exercise the next day seemed like a waste of a life to me. Shortly after that, I settled into project ME.

It seemed like so long ago. So much had happened since then. Where had the time gone? And how did Cadence still look so gorgeous without a lick of makeup?

MICHELLE

23

Again, I awoke with a start. These dreams really were starting to disrupt what little quality sleep I had. This time it was about Jonathan, and not so much a dream as a memory.

For all these years I had lied to Cassie about her father. I felt so guilty, but convinced myself it was for the best. Jonathan didn't die in a car accident. I ran away from him. He was never the sweet father figure I'd told Cassie about. He had been, well, really not much.

I'd fallen for Jonathan so young, twenty, right after my mother died. I was working in a restaurant and a bar, and still struggling to get by. Honestly, Jonathan wasn't that bad. I could say that in hindsight. He hadn't been abusive, but more neglectful of our relationship than anything. He didn't care what I did or where I went, as long as he could have sex with me when he wanted and I fed him when he was hungry.

Really, a saint compared to Ray. I should have stayed, but I naively wanted more, and look where being greedy got me.

What Jonathan and I had wasn't so different from many couples, surely. What many women endured to make it in the world. And then Cassie was born, and I wanted better for her. Jonathan hardly noticed a child had been brought into our life.

For a year, I scrimped and saved. Jonathan and I could provide a better life for Cass than I'd had, but I still wanted more. I wanted love. For me and her.

I left him one day when Cass was two, and I never looked back. I know he never looked for us, because I stayed in touch with a neighbour. I knew it was dangerous, but I needed to know if he noticed we were gone. Deep down I wanted him to get mad, to come looking for us, saying he couldn't survive without me. But he never did.

And four months later, another woman moved in with him.

That's when I started telling Cassie he was dead. It was better that way. I kind of screwed myself though, because to perpetuate the lie, I didn't ask for child support.

Thanks to a retired teacher in the building who watched Cassie for free, I made it almost six years on my own before my bank account drained, my credit card racked up as high as it could go, and my heart needed more.

Things seemed a bit better after the wonderful birthday party the girls had thrown for me. I hadn't put the crystal angel down since that night two weeks ago. She even came in the shower with me. A nice reprieve from the reality of my life.

I sat in the rocking chair until the sun came up, trying to process the realization. Trying to understand my past decision. I sifted through all of the terrible encounters I'd had as a child, wondering if anyone gets over seeing their mother have sex with strangers for drugs, or waking to a guy pulling the sheet up, or scrounging for food to stop her stomach from screaming during the silence of social studies class, or learning so young how to care for a parent.

First I'd lied to Cass and then I placed her in a horrific new life. I was possibly a worse mother than my own. My mother had drunk herself to death, maybe to escape her own pain or maybe to save me from her.

Strangely, I felt a bit less heavy after I acknowledged this fact. I had finally owned up to what I did to Cassie, to myself at least. I knew I wouldn't be free of the truth until I told her. What if she could have had a better life with Jonathan? I'd obviously made the wrong decision.

But this new state of mind was more dangerous than I realized. It gave me just enough energy to do something I'd wanted to do for so, so long.

I was going to do what Cassie had said so plainly. I was finally going to take responsibility for how I lived my life. A new page one.

I realized how tired I was. So tired of thinking and wondering and waiting. I just wanted out. *I'm done.* "Uncle," I whispered.

When you're flat on the floor, continually trampled over, you haven't enough energy to get up. But suddenly, I felt the trampling stop, if only for a second. It was still long enough for me to at least stand up.

"What are you leaving me for supper tonight?" Ray asked as I collected my things and got ready to leave for work. I stopped at his question and straightened my back. Finally, I said, a little quieter than I had intended, "Nothing."

"What?"

A little louder. "Nothing."

He was out of his chair in my face faster than I would have thought possible. "What?" he growled. I could clearly see the black pores on his red and slightly swollen nose.

I took a step backward and put my hand on the doorknob, stealing myself. "I'm sure you can figure something out." I pulled the door open and quickly stepped outside before he was able to grab me by the arm. He pulled me roughly into him so that our foreheads were almost touching. His breath smelled terrible as he said, "Did you already forget your little accident a few weeks ago?"

Stand your ground, there's not much more he can do to you. Death would be welcome anyway. "No."

Surprisingly, he backed up and laughed. "Little mouse has grown a set of balls, it would appear! I think I like it. More of a challenge," he said to an imaginary audience. His eyes flipped to black again. "I'll deal with you when you get home."

With that, I ran down the step with a wry smile on my face. *No, you won't.* I felt the lightness of knowing where I was going.

I dropped a letter in the mail and headed to the Leaside Bridge. The same bridge that Blair at the women's shelter had talked about. It was high enough to do the job.

I walked quickly to the centre of the bridge, the highest part. Even a foot could mean the difference between success and a horrific survival.

Could I really do this? And more importantly, did I need to? There were options for women like me, and Cassie wanted to use them.

Cassie.

I had dropped the letter in the mail for her and tried to push her out of my mind. I'd written out the whole truth. The terrible neglect I'd suffered at the hands of my mother, the lie that was Jonathan—that I'd left him, and he was probably still alive. But not Andrew. She would never know about him. There was no reason to tease her with that information. I apologized a hundred times in the letter. I had written it over and over, until I'd gotten a hand cramp, and then I forced myself to write it at least fifty more times. I wanted to push myself to emotional exhaustion. The letter ended up more like a six-page journal entry than a suicide note, but the very least I could do was give her the truth.

She was the only thing that could stop me. But hadn't I done my job? I got her out of the house safely. In one piece.

Now, for the first time in my life, couldn't I be selfish? And if selfish meant ending it, wasn't I allowed that? I was done letting Cassie feel responsible for me. It was time I took that upon myself. And if Emerson was serious about her unconditional love, she would direct it to the one person who needed it.

My greatest fear was that Ray would go after Cass if I simply disappeared, but I was certain if he had my broken body to stand over, he would leave her alone.

Pulling my old wool coat around myself, I stood staring down at the ravine that ran under the bridge for a long time, frozen in indecision.

Now that I was here, I started to wonder if I wasn't just being melodramatic. One time when I was about seven, I remembered my mother standing over me, red and panting from the exertion of giving me the strap. My little naked bum was on fire as I faced the wall. I don't even remember what I had done to deserve it, but I had learned to take it, as it seemed to relieve some of my mother's demons. The transfer of pain helped her function for a couple of days afterward.

But now, I was done hurting.

I set my purse on the ground and the handles crumpled into a pile, like I soon would. A couple of cars honked as they passed, but no one stopped. Another sign that I was on the right track. With both hands free to climb the rail, I reached up. As I prepared to pull myself up, I heard my phone ring. *Don't answer it.* But it kept ringing. It stopped for about ten seconds, then started again. Whoever it was, they were really persistent. *What if something is wrong with Cassie?*

"Damn it!" Sighing, I climbed down and bent to retrieve the phone out of my purse when I noticed a man approaching me. He had a camera slung around his neck and a sketchy look to him. I busied myself answering the phone, not looking at who was calling. As I said "Hello?" The man walked by me, nodded, and then kept going.

"Michelle!" I heard Andrew bark. "What's wrong?"

"Andrew?" I asked, surprised and dazed, a car whizzing past.

"Michelle, where are you?"

"Why are you calling me?"

He sighed. "I just had this feeling. It was weird. That something was wrong and I should call you. Like you know when people have a feeling they shouldn't get on a plane and don't and then it crashes? It used to happen all of the time to me when the kids were little, but I had to learn to ignore it because I was usually wrong," he babbled.

I crumpled to the ground and put my head between my knees to stop the feeling of passing out that was trying to overtake me. I couldn't decide if this was the best or worst thing to happen to me right now.

"Michelle? Please tell me you're fine, that I'm overreacting," he pleaded.

I didn't answer, and he added, "Where are you? Why is it so noisy? I'll come get you wherever you are." His voice bordered on hysterical.

Honest. That was what we had promised to be with each other from the beginning. But I knew if I told him the truth, there would be no going back. It wasn't fair to him to deal with my silliness. I opened my hand to see that the little angel had left dents. *Unconditional.* But Andrew's love hadn't been. It had all been conditional on Keely. She had what I needed and wouldn't let go, regardless of love or need.

"Michelle?" He tried one more time. "I love you."

Anger boiled up inside of me. How dare he say that after leaving? But what if all this worked out? If he was my escape? I didn't deserve it. I was a mess. No one would ever want to spend the rest of their life with me, would they?

"Are you still there?"

But you do deserve it, something deep down inside of me said. I could only get my breathing under control long enough to whisper, "Leaside Bridge." *Page one.*

"Michelle," he choked. "What the hell are you doing there?" The fear in his voice was raw, but I couldn't answer. "I'll be there in fifteen minutes. *Please.* Don't go anywhere."

I laughed to myself. *That will be easy. I don't have anywhere to go. Literally.*

I couldn't actually believe that after all these years, I had finally given myself the permission to start a new story. One that I was responsible for. Even if Andrew and I never worked out in the end, would it be so bad if I used him to help me up off the floor?

I stood up and waited, my hammering heart slowing. I wanted to look like I was simply waiting for someone, not like someone who was on the brink of the end. I hoped that if I acted like I deserved a place in this world, I would believe it too.

Andrew's black SUV squealed to a stop in the middle of the road. It had barely come to a full stop before he was out of it, collecting me in his arms. *My rescuer.*

"Michelle?" he said, tears rolling down his face into my hair. "Why?"

"Why not," I said, using a casual tone to test his honest response.

He made a choking sound, and I immediately regretted my words. "Let's get you out of here, okay?" More cars honked as they swerved around his car.

I nodded as he held onto me fiercely. From the outside, I may have appeared to have disappeared into his embrace, but to me it felt more like accepting his help and everything else he had to give me, freely. Wasn't that what a good relationship contained—give *and* take? I felt safe in his arms. I felt that maybe things would be okay. He finally let go and helped me into the car, ran around, and drove me away from the place where my future had been unknown.

I could feel him looking at my head. The hair had started to regrow over the wound, but it was still red and angry. His hands clenched on the steering wheel and he started driving a little faster down the road.

"Andrew, please slow down," I said.

"I'm driving straight to your place, and I'm going to fucking kill him."

"Andrew! Please don't."

"Why the hell not, Michelle? We could make it look like self-defense. You can't tell me the police don't already have him on their radar."

I shook my head. "No. It could go badly. You don't know him. And he has a gun."

He didn't answer, but slowed the car down slightly.

"I can't risk losing you," I said, knowing I meant that on more levels than he could understand.

"You're not going back," he said firmly.

"No, I'm not." *Cassie would be so proud of me.* "Shit!" I said suddenly, making him flinch.

"What?" he asked, new alarm growing in his voice.

"I did something really dumb."

The letter.

KEELY

24

"Jesus Christ, Andrew!" I screamed into the empty house as I tripped over his shoes. He always came in the house, turned around, closed the door, and took his shoes off. Leaving them right in the path of the next person going out the door. *Who fucking does that?* Suddenly in a rage, I picked up both of his shoes, opened the front door, and flung them out into the yard. Slamming the door closed, I slumped against it, my breath coming hard. I couldn't stop the old voice from sneaking in. *If I was single, I wouldn't have to deal with crap like this.* Shoes would only be where *I* left them.

"Shut up!" I yelled at myself, pressing the heels of my hands into my eyes. "If I was single, I would be living back in that shitty little house again." I forced myself to take deep breaths until the rage passed.

What I was actually angry at was the way Andrew had just left the house. We were both sitting in the living room, me reading and him watching some kind of sports, when he stood up suddenly.

"I have to go to work," he said in a robotic voice. There was a vacant look in his eyes, but I could see his chest rising and falling rapidly. I looked quickly for his cell phone, but it was far away on the kitchen counter, so I knew he hadn't received a work call.

"But it's Saturday, Andrew. What is so important that it can't wait?"

"I forgot to finish something yesterday," he said vaguely, mechanically walking to the kitchen to grab his phone and car keys.

"Will you be back in time to help me build those racks at the gym like you promised?" I called toward him, but he didn't answer as the door closed.

Asshole. But what I was really wondering was if Michelle had anything to do with this. I didn't know how it was possible, since there was no call or text, but something didn't sit well.

I tried to get back into my book, but after half an hour, I gave up. I wandered into the kitchen and started pulling all of the glassware out of the cupboard, which looked as if a three-year-old had last put them away. After the cupboard was empty, I started putting every piece back in an orderly fashion. Arranging the glasses by type and height and use. I hadn't realized I had twenty-seven crystal wine glasses.

"Anal, much?" Riley's voice made me jump, almost breaking one of the glasses.

"Jesus," I said. "You shouldn't sneak up on people like that."

"I didn't sneak. I actually made lots of noise coming in, but you were too focused on your... what are you doing, anyway? Taking inventory of your most precious belongings?"

I clenched my teeth and forced myself to reply nicely. "No. I'm just bored. Is that okay?"

"Yeah, sure. I just thought it had something to do with the fact that Dad's shoes are lying on the sidewalk."

I didn't have to look to know the smirk on her face. "Where were you last night, anyway?"

"Now you want to know about my comings and goings? I'm eighteen. You should have asked me that, like, five years ago."

I put the last glass carefully in place and then turned around. "Look, Riley. I'm not in the best mood, so cut the attitude, all right?" I crossed my arms over my chest, trying not to comment on the ripped joggers and baggy T-shirt she wore.

She squinted an eye at me, then walked past. "I'm just here to grab a couple of things."

I called after her as she went up the stairs. "You could at least check in once in a while! The only way I know you've been home anymore is when all of Dad's ice cream is gone." *Crap. That's not the right thing to say, Keely.* I heard Riley stomp around upstairs for a few minutes and then come lumbering back down the stairs. She was almost out the door when she stopped. I noticed she forced herself to stand up straighter as she turned back to me.

"When you want to talk to me like a person you respect, call me." She slammed the door. *She's the one who wants respect? How about me?*

My phone started ringing, and I rushed to find it, hoping it was Andrew. It was Ralph. "Hi. You're not supposed to call, only email, I thought," I said, my irritation surging again.

"Well, I thought you would be very interested to see what I discovered today."

So it was Michelle he left for! Ralph continued without waiting for me to speak, his manner brisk. "I just have to get the pictures uploaded. How about I meet you at the gym in two hours."

"Yes. That would be fine." Maybe we were going to get to the bottom of this bullshit once and for all. I turned back to the cupboards and started on the china.

I flipped through the pictures for a second time, slowly scrutinizing them. I couldn't put a finger on which emotion I felt the strongest. Pity, revulsion, anger, fear. I poured over the photos as Ralph went on and on about how great his timing was and that he was so awesome for figuring out who Michelle was only two days before. He would have missed the whole scene.

The first half a dozen or so shots showed a rundown little house and then a woman coming out of it. The same woman I found on Facebook. She had the same limp hair and meek presence. Then a man was in the next shot, grabbing her tightly by the arm. Her face was trying to hold back a look of pain, like she'd done it a million times before. At first, a primal urge rose in me. *How dare he grab her like that!* If anyone ever touched me like that, they would regret it. But in the next shot, his face was pressed to hers and I could see by the tendons standing out on Michelle's neck that she was trying to back away from him. He looked like he wanted to kill her. I suddenly felt tears prick at my eyes for all the women who went through this. Even though I had never, I could imagine. In the next shot, a close-up, I could see a long, angry red scar running across her head, the hair just starting to grow back. Then she left as he glared at her from the doorway, hands on his hips. It reminded me of my power posing. *He's trying to take up as much space in her life as he can.* I was surprised at how much I wanted to punch this asshole.

The next image shocked me as badly as it did the first time I flipped through. *She's going to jump.* I could see it all over her body. She was on a bridge, and her purse lay on the ground as both of her arms prepared to heave her up the rail. *Have I ever in my life felt this kind of pain?* So much pain, that the only way out was to end it. No, my mind rallied itself back together. I would never live my life on someone else's terms, that much was true.

"That's when I couldn't just stand there taking pictures anymore," Ralph interrupted my thoughts. "I started walking towards her, but luckily right as I passed, her phone rang. I'm guessing it was your husband, because he was there about fifteen minutes later." I had a fleeting thought that Ralph wasn't as slimy as he looked.

Again, sympathy was quickly replaced by anger. He ran away to *rescue her?* What kind of weak woman needed a man to rescue her? Then the pictures showed Andrew leaning toward her and her looking up at him with pure anguish on her face. She looked completely wrecked, and my heart heaved for her. *I'm having sympathy for my husband's lover?* I almost couldn't believe it myself. The oscillation of emotions in me was enough to make me nauseous. The last picture was the one that conflicted me the most. Andrew embraced Michelle more fiercely than he had ever held me. His arms were wrapped so far around her that he was almost touching his opposite shoulders. She disappeared into him. Just a fluff of hair poked out of the top of the embrace and her feet out the bottom of her worn-out brown coat. Andrew looked like he was trying to press her into his very soul. The look on his face was tortured but peaceful at the same time. In the last shot, a tear hung on the tip of his nose as he lay his head on top of hers.

I felt that this picture could win the Pulitzer prize for all of the emotion it captured.

"That's it?" I looked up at Ralph, reining in my emotions.

"What do you mean *that's it?* The poor woman almost fucking killed herself! She's obviously abused and looking for a way out. I'm fairly certain your husband wants to provide that for her."

"Yeah. *So* obvious," I said coolly, rolling my eyes.

Suddenly, almost knocking his chair over, Ralph stood up, his heavy brown eyebrows knit together. "You know, I don't consider myself a warm and fuzzy kind of guy. You can't be, doing what I do. Seeing the things I see. But sometimes, it's not what I capture on film that disgusts me the most, it's the people footing the bill. Good day, Ms. O'Connell," he said as he left my office.

I'm the monster here? That's real fucking rich. Who was the one who got paid to spy on people? *Jerk.* I grabbed the pictures and then pushed them into a desk drawer, slamming it shut.

MICHELLE

25

First, Andrew asked me if I knew Cassie's phone number by heart. "Yes, why?" I said. He quickly pulled over and asked for my phone. I watched him put it under the tire of the car. He got back in and drove over it probably twenty times with grim satisfaction. He then threw the remains into the ditch beside the road and got back into the car. Smirking, he said, "That felt really good for some reason."

I was officially cut off from my old life. I suddenly felt light-headed and had to put my head between my legs again. *Is this really happening?*

Finally, I lifted my head to see him watching me closely. "Can we stop and fish the letter out of the mailbox?"

"Absolutely not. That mailbox is only one block from your house. You're not going anywhere near that place." I begged him again, but he refused. Really, it was the truth. One way or another, Cass should know. I didn't know what she'd be madder about, Jonathan or the fact that I'd wanted to kill myself.

The memory box! I had really failed Cassie now. Not only was she going to be livid with me, but I wasn't going to be able to rescue her childhood memories either. An image came to mind, and as terrible as it was, it brought a little smile to my face. I saw myself throwing a match on the house and standing back to watch it go up in flames. With Ray inside.

"Now that's better." Andrew smiled at me.

"What?"

"That smile I love. What are you thinking about?" He laughed when I told him.

My amusement spilled into the truth. I didn't stop talking for ten minutes straight. "How can you possibly love someone who doesn't have the first clue about who they are? Someone who has been through so much…" I said, struggling to say the word abuse. Because, as a child it had simply happened to me, but as an adult I *let* it happen to me.

"What does it all matter in the end?" he said. "I love *you*. Not what's happened to you or what you've done to yourself. Maybe one day you can learn to realize that for yourself. Do you know how kind and smart and strong you are?" I couldn't find an answer as he drove me to a hotel way across town and rented a room for two weeks. He proceeded to sneak me in the back entrance so no one would be able to identify me if Ray came looking.

As we sat down on the bed, he put his arm around my shoulder and took a deep breath, finally able to relax. "I know it's only temporary, but we will figure the rest out later. Okay?" He turned to me and lifted my chin with his finger.

"Okay." I leaned into his embrace. I had never felt so safe in my whole life.

For the next hour, we talked. I continued to spill more childhood memories that had resurfaced, which brought fresh tears to my eyes. When I tortured myself over the what-ifs of Jonathan, Andrew reassured me that I did what I thought best. He said if all of that hadn't happened, I wouldn't be here. The truth of his statement hit me like a ton of bricks.

He actually laughed when I told him about throwing my wedding ring away and cried when I told me about the beer bottle to the head.

"We need to call Cassie tomorrow. You need to tell her everything. About me. What's in the letter. All of it."

I nodded. "I know."

"It will be hard, but you have to know that after it's all said and done, she will be happy for you."

Again, I nodded.

Finally, he whispered into my hair, "I'll never forgive myself."

I looked up at him. "For what?"

"Him hitting you with the beer bottle. It was my fault, wasn't it? You never said it was the night I stopped by and spilled my guts, but I know it was." His left hand clenched tightly, turning his knuckles white.

"Andrew, it wouldn't have mattered one way or the other. Something potentially fatal would have happened to me eventually. Maybe it was a blessing, because it sped things up. Maybe I can try and start over. Forty-seven isn't too late, is it?"

"No. No, it absolutely isn't," he said finally.

I paced the room while Andrew went out shopping. He returned an hour later with enough supplies to last me a few days. He dumped a shopping bag full of food and drinks on the bed. And then he handed me a couple of books. A pay-as-you-go phone. And finally, a hunting knife.

I looked at him, shocked. "Well, I didn't think you wanted a gun. Not that I could get one. This isn't the States." He smiled. "I just thought this would make you feel safer." He picked up *East of Eden* by John Steinbeck. "Not the most uplifting read, but one of my favourites from my youth."

I touched the cover of the book softly. *Me, read?* I had never read much more than textbooks and cookbooks and storybooks in my life. I picked up *Eat, Pray, Love* by Elizabeth Gilbert. "I thought that one was a bit lighter. I know Keely loved it," he trailed off, putting *East of Eden* down.

"You don't have to avoid talking about her. She still exists, okay?" I touched his sleeve.

He nodded. "We'll work it out. Please trust me. I know what she wants, so I'll just give it to her," he said with look of deep concentration on his face.

The next morning, while Andrew left to talk to Keely and apparently give her what she wanted, a tiny seed of fear told me that she wanted only him and that she would do everything to keep him away from me. What if he caved to her now? I'd only have two weeks security to figure myself out. But I knew I would, regardless. A tiny warrior had been born in me and the slippery slope had begun. It was either move forward or die. Strange how I could swing from wanting to die to wanting to fight in a matter of hours.

I steeled myself and called Cassie. She picked up on the first ring. "Mom? Mom, where are you? Are you okay?" Her words tumbled out in fear.

"Cassie. I'm fine," I said firmly. I knew Ray and the bar were probably looking for me. "Is Ray there?"

"No, why?"

"Has he called you?"

"Yes. Where are you, Mom?"

"I'm safe," I said again. *How many times am I going to have to repeat that before I believe it myself?* "I'm at a hotel."

"Thank God." She sighed. "Based on Ray's anger, I'm assuming you finally left him?"

"Yes. But there's more to it than that. I need to talk to you. Do you think if I gave you the address you would come here? Can you borrow Emerson's car?"

"Yes, of course!"

"But only if you don't think he's following you. Or anyone. And don't bring Emerson yet. She doesn't need to get tied up in this."

"She already is, Mom. She wants to help you too."

I smiled, glancing over to the little angel on the nightstand. "That's very sweet of her, but not for this visit. This number I called you from is a new phone. But don't add me to your contacts in case Ray gets a hold of it. Here's the address of the hotel."

"Got it."

"Please be careful. Take every twist and turn in the road so no one can follow you, okay?"

"Why now?" Cassie suddenly asked. "Why did you leave all of a sudden."

"My knight in shining armour arrived."

"You have a boyfriend!?" she squealed.

I laughed. "I guess I do."

"I'll be there as soon as I can."

"I love you. I can't wait to see you."

"I love you too, Mom. I'm so proud of you."

That makes two of us.

When I finally heard the light tap on the door, I barely looked through the peephole before I flung it open and grabbed her. "What took you so long? It's been an hour!"

"You told me to be careful. I must have taken fifty-four turns, drove through about seventy-six lights. I even backtracked twice to really throw off any would-be stalkers." She grinned.

"Good girl." I pulled her inside and locked us tightly in.

She sat down on the bed and picked up the book. "Hmm, *East of Eden*. One of my favs."

"Oh good, then you and Andrew have something in common then." I beamed.

Cassie frowned and stared at me for a long time. Finally, I asked nervously, "What?" My hand instinctively going to the scar on my head.

"You're different. *Finally.*" She jumped up and grabbed me into another tight hug and started crying. As she sobbed, she said, "I've dreamed about this day for so long."

"Me too, sweetie," I said as I stroked her hair.

She pulled back from me and asked, "Are you sure you're safe?"

I sighed and sat down on the bed, pulling my legs under me. "As safe as I can be, given the circumstances, Cass."

"I understand. Living free and scared is better than just living scared."

I laughed. "Okay, wise one." Actually, how would I ever be fully able to express how much she had helped propel me forward with her speech at the hospital? Even if the end I had intended and the one that had happened were totally different, she was still the spark.

She shrugged and said, "Philosophy was one of my favourite classes. That's where I met Em."

In that instant, I knew that she would never have to suffer as I had. Not because she was dating a girl, although that probably did help, but I knew for certain that I had endured enough pain for both of us. Our karma had finally been fulfilled.

"So, I have to tell you something that will upset you." I took a deep breath.

She didn't answer, so I let it tumble out of me before I chickened out. "I sent you a letter yesterday. A *goodbye* letter."

Her face fell. "Oh, Mom." Her eyebrows wrinkled in an effort to not lose it.

"But please remember when you read it, I'm still alive," I quickly continued. "It won't be easy for you to read, but what's done is done. He saved me." It was so cliché. I would be frowned upon by feminists everywhere. But when it was the only option you could see, what else could you do?

I hesitated. "Are you disappointed that I needed *a man* to save me?"

Her eyes grew angry. "Why would you say that? I don't care what it took to save you. All I care is that it's done. Everyone needs *someone* or *something* to live for. It's what makes it all worth the fight. Everyone has to have at least one thing that matters to them more than anything."

In her eyes I saw with finality that I was her thing to fight for. "Oh, my baby, you don't have to worry about me anymore." Tears of guilt filled my eyes. *God! I need to stop crying.*

"It was my *choice* to worry about you. So don't even think about taking that one on yourself," she said hotly.

"I don't deserve you." I looked down.

"Look at me." She leaned into my face, demanding. I worried for a second the fire in her had rubbed off from Ray. "*You. Deserve. Everything,*" she said firmly, but softly.

I nodded, trying my hardest to believe her.

CASSIE

26

I left the hotel room with an earnest promise from Mom that I'd meet Andrew the next time I came by. I felt that she was actually excited for me to finally meet him. She told me it had only been six months since they met, with a break for the last three. So really, they hardly knew each other, it seemed to me.

"But even if they break up after a while, he still got her out, no?" Em reasoned with me later that night as we sat watching *Stranger Things*. Even though we had already watched both seasons, we loved it and had started over.

How could I argue with that kind of logic? "As long as she doesn't go back to Ray," I said. Or someone like Jonathan. Within three minutes of her briefing me on that part of her letter, I went from anger to understanding. Even though she had said he hadn't been a saint, I would be lying to myself if I didn't admit I was a little excited at the prospect of having a real father out there.

"Well, from what you've told me, Andrew sounds like a pretty decent guy. Most Andrews I know are pretty awesome." She laughed.

"Yeah, well, we'll see when we meet him." I knew I had to keep my optimism under control about what this guy could do for Mom in the long run. "I know my mom doesn't want me to bring you, but I think it would be better for me if you came."

She raised an eyebrow. "Does my tough-as-nails little girlfriend need me to hold her hand?"

Em barely ducked in time to dodge the pillow I threw at her, while saying, "Consider it a compliment."

"Oh, I'm flattered for sure." She winked at me.

"She seemed to think I would be mad at her for letting a man save her. Am I that much of a man-hating bitch?" I asked.

"Seriously, Cass. Don't ever say that. There are tons of great men in the world, my dad and brother included. And if someone isn't able to save themselves, what does it matter if someone else has to do it for them? Remember—no man is an island." She used air quotes to emphasize the cliché.

"That's exactly what I told her. It's such a fairy tale in a way. I just hope that it comes with the quintessential happy ending." I frowned.

Em scooched over on the couch and put her arm around my shoulder, pulling me close to her. "Me too."

A loud knock on the door. I looked at Em with worry. I knew who it was. "Go hide in the bedroom, okay?" I pushed her shoulder.

"I am not hiding, Cassie." Em crossed her arms across her chest, not moving.

"This is not a fucking game, Emerson!" I hissed at her. "I've told you what he's capable of."

"Just don't answer it then."

"He'll never go away," I said.

As if on cue, he banged again, yelling, "Let me in, *daughter*. I know you're in there. I can hear you whispering to your hot little girlfriend. Or it that your cheating whore of a mother?" This had to be the first time in my life he'd called me his daughter.

Ray started laughing uncontrollably, the sounds surely echoing up and down the hallway, alerting the neighbours that a lunatic was here. Finally his laughter stopped with a couple of snorts and sighs. I could almost see him wiping the tears from his eyes. "Cassie. Dear. Why don't you come out here and have a little drink with me?"

I didn't answer him, but managed to get Emerson up quietly. "Go to the bedroom and call the cops. Please." I wanted her as far away from the door as possible.

"Okay. But be careful!" She eyed me. "And do not open the door."

"Don't worry. I'm just going to try and talk to him." Again, *now* was the first time since I'd come to live with Ray that I was going to have a real conversation with him? I walked over to the door and sat on the ground next to it. I wasn't stupid enough to be directly on the other side of it—I knew he had a gun at home hidden in the nightstand.

I took a deep breath, using all of my willpower to not unleash on him. I wanted to scream and list all of the things I knew he'd done to my mom over the years. The sexual, emotional, and physical abuse he'd tormented her with.

"She only got with me to provide for you. You know that, right?" I heard Ray whisper through the door, slurring a bit on the last word.

I also swore I heard some sadness in his voice. I decided honest was best right now. "I know."

"I was good to her, in the beginning. I probably loved her. But how was I supposed to know what that really looked like? I grew up in a family of drunken losers." His tone was rising again. "I was beat almost every day of my life, alongside my mother. And that's what I got dealt in life, why did anyone else deserve better?" I heard something metal clink against a bottle.

"And I put up with you! I didn't want kids around, but Michelle was so goddamn *obedient*." I cringed at the word. "And now, after putting you through college, she fucking cheats on me? Even I never did that!"

I heard some shuffling and a bottle hit the floor. "No way, man. No way she gets to do that to me." He started pounding on the door. "So you open this door, you little bitch, or I'm going to shoot it down."

I quickly crawled toward the bedroom, hoping the two walls in between it and the front door provided enough safety. I saw Emerson was still on the phone. She smiled in relief at seeing me.

"She's mine, Cassie! And no one is ever going to have her. She'll be dead before that happens."

Em asked the operator, "You didn't happen to hear that, did you?" She nodded and smiled.

What the hell have I gotten her into? She did not deserve this. But then again, what doesn't kill us makes us stronger. I almost burst out laughing at the timing of my epiphany. *This must be what extreme stress does to a person.*

I heard sirens outside pulling up. I would have thought the cops would have descended silently for a domestic.

"You called the cops?" Ray yelled. "Good. Maybe I can file charges against your mother for back payment for raising you. She'll pay, Cassie! One way or another."

"Put the gun down!" I heard an officer shout.

"Yeah, yeah," Ray said, and within a few minutes, he was handcuffed and we were giving our statement to the police.

"You have to get your mom to come forward and testify," one police officer said, closing his notebook as the other took Ray down the hall in handcuffs. He tried to throw a glare back at me over his shoulder, but the officer pushed his head roughly forward. *Too bad she didn't punch him.*

I shook my head. "I can't see it happening."

"Look, right now, all we can charge him with is reckless use of a firearm, public intoxication, and harassment against you. I looked up your mom's records, and with her testimony we could add assault, rape, attempted murder. All kinds of things that would secure him a nice long stay in jail. Not just a couple of years."

"I know all of that," I said shortly. I took a deep breath as Em took my hand. "I'm sorry. But she just left yesterday. She hasn't even had a day to enjoy her freedom."

"If she doesn't testify, she will never truly be able to enjoy her freedom. She will always be looking behind her. And not to mention endangering anyone else Ray might go after who's connected to your mother," he said, trying everything in his power to convince me.

I chewed on my top lip. "I'll go see her tomorrow and talk to her. Alone." I looked at him pointedly.

"Okay. We'll hold Ray without bail until we hear from you. His hearing will probably be near the end of the week."

I wanted so badly to tell the officer what he wanted to hear, what I needed to hear. But I knew a lifetime of not believing in yourself could not possibly change overnight. Being brave enough to stand up for what you deserve was a gradual process full of starts and stops, lurching forward and falling backward, wasn't it? *Or maybe it does happen in one huge jolt?*

I hoped, one way or another, something else would happen to seal the deal for her. True change comes only out of wanting it badly enough for yourself. Not from anyone else. I felt a small amount of guilt over the contradictory theory I had previously told her about everyone needing something to live for.

At the time, I could only tell her what she needed to hear.

KEELY

27

On Sunday, Andrew showed up back at the house unannounced midmorning. He didn't even knock, just walked in like he owned the place. *He does!* my mind hissed. Of course, I knew technically that was true. But I had rationalized that the way he walked out the previous day, knowing that he was going to her, he had forfeited any rights he had to our stuff. I was not going to make this easy for him.

He sat down at the kitchen table after helping himself to a cup of coffee. He tried to hide the face he made as he took a sip. *Well, you should have been here to make it yourself.* Somehow, Andrew's magical coffee grounds-to-water ratio always seemed a bit more right than the watery brew I came up with.

He took a deep breath and spilled everything. I was shocked that he effortlessly told me about her and how they met. As his speech went on, his shoulders relaxed inch by inch. He ended his words on a small omission. He told me he saved her from her abusive husband, a ploy on my feelings, I was certain, but skipped the bridge scene. He put his hands on his thighs and sat back. "So, you see, she needs me. I know how much that may turn your stomach," he said as I tried to smooth out the frown that must have crept onto my face.

Slowly, the realization sunk in. *He loves her.* It was the only logical explanation. Andrew was always the emotional one in our relationship. I remembered how he had cried each time I gave birth. I had cried with Emerson, more out of the pride I had in myself for enduring the whole thing. But when the other two were born, the product of the wonderful advent of scheduled c-sections, all I saw was more work and less time for myself. It almost seemed strange in hindsight that Andrew and I connected in the first place. I guess he'd had what I needed on a physical level, but maybe not emotional.

Andrew truly did things that mattered to others. A concept that, at this point in my life, was foreign to me. But he was totally showing his cards, and if I was going to win this one, I had to pull out all the stops.

I knew it was a dirty move. "I need you to take care of me, Andrew," I said in a surprisingly convincing and needy tone.

I could see from the shocked look on his face that I had hit the nail on the head. *Bingo.* It was the exact opposite of what he needed to hear from me. *Like I would release him so easily.* I called the shots around here.

"Keely," he started, fidgeting with his wedding band. I could practically see the sweat start to form on his hairline as it did when he was stressed.

I forced a tear to come to my eye. "I'm so sorry, Andrew. I know I can be mean." I poured it on. "And sometimes I act like I don't need you, but I do. There will never be anyone else who loves me like you do." I smiled internally at the convincingly pathetic tone in my voice.

"Keely," he started again. "I hope you understand that with this coming out of nowhere, I can't help but be suspicious of your motives."

My eyes widened, an honest response to the sudden courage he seemed to gather. "Motives? I have no motives. I have just been thinking really hard since we got home from our trip. I've been trying to imagine what my life would be like with you truly gone. And I don't like it." I felt myself scrambling between my lies and the actual truth as real tears escaped my eyes.

His shoulders slumped, but he didn't move to comfort me. He stayed rooted to the kitchen chair he was occupying. I knew I'd have to cinch this before *she* did. I pulled out the final straw. "I was actually thinking of quitting competitions and hiring a manager for the gym."

He raised an eyebrow. *Perfect.*

"Really?" he said.

I sighed and got up, walked to the window, and looked outside, dragging the suspense with me. *Could I really quit competing for him?* It was getting to be a grind. I mean, I wouldn't give up the lifestyle, just the insanity of comp. My last success had sat emptily in my stomach. And maybe stepping away from the gym wasn't such a bad idea. I had no hobbies to speak of. I was sure I could find something to occupy my time.

"I don't know, Keely. I really thought your move back in wasn't working. Honestly, I feel like you hate me sometimes," he said, his voice dropping off.

"Hate is a strong word, Andrew." *But maybe not too far off.* I sighed, figuring being genuine couldn't hurt at this point. "It's really not you. It never was. You are a great guy. I just feel like sometimes I want to be alone. Even if we did break up, I probably wouldn't even try dating. Too much bother."

"Wouldn't you get lonely?" I was pretty sure Andrew hadn't been without a girlfriend since he was sixteen.

I shrugged. "Right now, I'd say I doubt it. Maybe after being alone for a couple of years, that would change." I turned back to look at him.

Andrew opened his mouth and then closed it. Something he wanted to say obviously hung on the tip of the tongue.

"What?" I asked.

"Have you ever done something for someone else that was completely selfless? Like volunteered at a shelter or food bank?" he asked randomly.

Why was he attacking me all of a sudden? "You sound like Emerson," I spat. "Why would I do that, anyways?" I took a deep breath through my nose. "Look, Andrew, I grew up figuring how to get shit done on my own. No one helped me. So why would I ever help anyone else?" *Especially for free?*

He looked at me for a long time, as if he was deciding something. "Never mind," he said finally. He stood up and said, "I'm going out for the night."

"Where?" I barked. "Are you going back to *Michelle*?" I couldn't help but snarl her name.

He looked at me sadly and said, "You have a lot to learn about compassion, Keely. I hope it's not too late when you do finally figure it out." He turned to leave.

"I'll never let you go, Andrew!" I hissed at him, my fury at having apparently lost coming fully to life. I quickly lost all rationality. "I'll sink my claws into everything that we have between us and won't let go. I'll bury you in legalities and paperwork. You'll be left with nothing." I clenched my fists tightly at my sides, nails biting hard into my palms.

He shrugged his shoulders and said, "Take your best shot. I'm too old for your bullshit games anymore."

Something inside of me snapped and I uttered, "*Maybe* a story or two will arise about how you treated me. *Maybe* I'm scared of you. *Maybe* I'll show up at the police station with a bruise or two. Given what's come up in the news lately, I'm pretty sure they'd listen to me."

I was shocked at the speed and rage with which he turned on me. In a heartbeat, he was up and in my face, growling. He leaned into me, blue eyes flashing and hands pressing on the arms of the chair. "You have no fucking idea what it means to be abused. What it truly means to suffer at the hands of a man. I *tried* to take care of you. I *tried* to love you the best I could. And it was never good enough for you. But that effort, given to someone who truly needs it, could make a world of difference.

For years now, you have put yourself before every member of this family. You couldn't tell me what selfless meant if your life depended on it." He then turned and walked out the door.

I called after him, "I'll win this Andrew! You just wait and see!"

"Fuck you, Keely!" he said over his shoulder.

My jaw dropped open as I saw something I had never seen in Andrew. *Defiance.*

I was surprised how much it turned me on.

All of my life, I had told myself I didn't need a man to take care of me. But as I thought about the photo of Andrew wrapping Michelle in a safe embrace, I again wondered if this marriage was not the right match from the start. *For him.*

I had been attracted to Andrew because he was handsome and successful. And he doted on me. Bought me everything I wanted, payed for my on-and-off trendy and excessive self-care regimes. He didn't complain when I spent a thousand bucks on the latest miracle skin care line or five hundred on a state-of-the-art juicer. He just wanted me to be happy. I tried not to think about the amount of money I had spent on trying to slow my aging down. That money alone could have bought a less demanding person a comfortable life. Someone like Michelle.

But was there ever love? I didn't doubt he felt it for me, but what about me for him? Had I ever truly loved anyone? Yes, I loved the kids, but it felt like more of a responsible, necessary love.

But that photo. Had I ever felt *that* for anyone else? I knew the true answer, that one person, but I stuffed the memories back down where they had hidden for thirty years.

In the other pictures, I had noticed Michelle's clothes were old, dull, and about ten seasons ago. Nothing about her screamed "I take care of myself!" All it said was "I barely exist."

So was I really supposed to feel bad for her? Should I have sympathy for her obviously terrible choice of a husband? Was I to take pity on her that she never bothered to get a post-secondary education and had to work in a bar? My mind briefly slipped to Riley. I reminded myself to harass her about choosing a college.

Could I help it if I knew that I deserved everything I had worked for? Maybe Michelle never tried hard enough at anything. Maybe she was lazy or completely unmotivated. So what attracted Andrew to her? *I suppose she's a good person with a heart of gold!* Hearts of gold were for obese, unattractive women or 1950s housewives who baked pies for the neighbours and happily watched each other's kids. Women today were independent and fierce. *We were killing it!* Just like men had been for—well, forever.

Somehow, our roles had reversed over the years. Andrew was the nurturer. He was the one who made it to each and every awards ceremony, sporting event, and band performance that the kids had ever been a part of. He was who they went to when they were hurt or scared or needed advice. The only thing I ever did was made sure the kids' lunches contained complex proteins and vegetables instead of store-bought cookies and goldfish crackers.

My gut wrestled with the knowledge that I did everything right in my life. That I did it my way. It was the quietly growing whisper from my heart that suggested maybe I had completely missed the boat.

EMERSON

28

The next day, as we pulled up to the hotel, I was still shaken from the ordeal with Ray. Cass turned to me, seemingly to say something. But she just stared at me silently for a minute and then got out of the car.

We walked quietly down the hallway of the hotel, Cass squeezing my hand. Her mom had insisted I not come, but since when do kids listen to their parents? Even if they love them unconditionally.

The door to room 438 opened, and things became very unfocused. I blinked my eyes several times and shook my head violently, my messy bun falling from the top of my head.

"Em, are you okay?" I heard Cassie's voice come at me from across a huge void.

Finally, Dad said, bewildered, "Emerson, what are you doing here?" He looked quickly down the hallway.

His voice snapped me out of it, and I said, "I'd like to know the same thing. *Dad.*"

Cassie gaped, looking from me to him.

"Get in here." He pulled me by the arm with Cass following, and quickly closed the door behind us.

Andrew. I had a hunch Dad cheated on Mom. Why, I wasn't sure. Maybe it was because deep down I felt like he deserved better than her. When I was little, I'd catch myself in a daydream about Dad marrying my best friend Jesse's mom, who was divorced. She was so nice to me. Cassie had told me her mom's boyfriend's name last night, but how could I have put two and two together?

Suddenly I started laughing. I felt a delirium rising in me.

"Emerson, this isn't funny," Dad said sternly, crossing his arms. But I could see a slow smile spread across Michelle's face.

"What are the chances?" Her eyes grew wide, and she blinked several times. "It's like it's fate or something." Her mouth moved silently, as if she was trying to put everything together.

Cassie suddenly turned to me and blurted out, "Yes. I told you there was a reason we were together."

"I said that," I argued back at her.

"No, I did. I'm perceptive like that." She tapped the side of her head, to which I rolled my eyes.

Dad sat down heavily on the bed, trying to take in the scene. "So… you two are *dating?*"

I looked sideways at Cass and grabbed her hand. "Yes, Dad."

"But…" He shook his head. "Why didn't you ever tell me you were gay?"

"We were going to tell you, really. But things were such a mess with you and Mom." I shot Michelle an apologetic look. She nodded reassuringly at me.

He turned to her. "And you knew?"

Michelle said defensively, "Well, I didn't know she was your daughter. But yes, they told me a few weeks back. I know it's really unimaginable. But when I saw them together for the first time… " She paused.

"Well, yes, but…"

"Do you have a problem with me?" Cassie asked, stepping forward.

"No. Of course not!" He put both hands up. "It's just… this is a lot to wrap my puny mind around." He jumped up suddenly and touched my elbow. "Can I talk to you outside please, Em?"

"Sure." I followed him out of the room.

He closed the door gently and quickly said to me, "Em. This is a very dangerous situation. Ray is very volatile, and we don't know what he's going to do next."

Cassie must not have told her mom what happened at the apartment. "It's okay, Dad. He's been arrested."

He started. "What? How do you know that?"

I filled him in on the incident, trying to not make it sound like a big deal. He stifled a sob anyway. "*He had a gun?*"

"Yes. But he didn't shoot it. Really, it's okay. I'm tougher than you think," I said.

"I know how tough you are. I just… if something ever happened to you." His voice hitched.

"There's Cassie to worry about too," I added.

"Well, yes, of course. I don't want her to get hurt either, but you're my daughter!"

I felt defensive. "Does it matter? Like, we're all people who deserve to be safe. It doesn't matter who's related to who."

He grabbed me into a fierce hug. "Oh, bug," he gently said my baby nickname. When I was born, I had huge eyes that seemingly never blinked. "My little crusader," he whispered into my ear. "I guess I have three women to protect from this psycho now."

I smiled into his shoulder.

As we came back in the room, Michelle shook her head at me. I shrugged. "I couldn't let her come alone again," I said.

"Cass filled me in on yesterday." Michelle looked up to my dad, worry lining her face. "I'm so sorry your daughter is caught in the middle of this."

He sat down and put his hand on hers. *He loves her.* "It's not your fault."

"If I had just made one crucial decision differently all those years ago, we wouldn't be here."

"You're telling me." Cassie laughed. "That's right, Mom. *I* wouldn't be here. Nothing can be changed, we can only move forward. So once and for all, stop beating yourself up, okay?"

"Here, here." Dad clapped loudly.

Cassie knelt down in front of her mom. "This is why you need to testify. To protect everyone in this room. I hate to put that kind of pressure on you, but he will get way more jail time if you do. You'll be free of him for real. Not running and hiding."

I looked at Michelle and quietly added, "You may have felt alone and unprotected your whole life, but right here, right now, you have an army behind you. And we are a tough bunch of mofo's."

"Emerson!" Dad said.

"It's true. She's Taylor Swift." I pointed to Michelle. "And we're her squad." I spread my hands to Cass and Dad.

"You don't know how much I hate that analogy," Cassie groaned.

"I do. That's exactly why I said it."

We smiled at each other as our parents watched intently.

Finally, Dad said, "We need to talk about your guys' safety."

I nodded. "Yes. We already have a plan. Cass packed a bag and is going to stay with me. At least until everything settles down."

Dad stood up and started pacing the room, his fingers laced behind his back. "Yes, that's a good idea." He stopped to look at Michelle. "I think we should get Cassie a new apartment."

"What?" Cass jumped in. "I can't afford that. With moving costs and a new damage deposit. No way." She looked at Michelle. "And we all know that if he wants to find me again, he will." She eyed Andrew. "Same with you two. Is your long-term plan to live in a hotel?'

"Cass," Michelle warned.

"Well, I have a right to know, don't I?"

"Yes, you absolutely do, Cassie," Andrew jumped in. "Maybe let's wait until everything settles down for a few days and until we find out about what the police are going to do with Ray." He turned to me and Cass. "Are you certain he doesn't know where you live?"

"Yes," we both answered at the same time.

Dad looked like he wanted to believe us. I suddenly realized how much stress he must be under. There were deep lines around his mouth, and I knew that the continual grimacing over the past while hadn't helped them.

"Right." He took a deep breath. "Right," he repeated, forcing himself to relax a little.

I felt that someone had to take control to make everyone feel like it was going to be okay. As I was the most unaffected by this whole thing, it should naturally fall on me. I felt a bit of my mom in me as I stepped forward. "So, let's just stick to the plan."

"That sounds good." Michelle stood up. "He's locked up and we're safe," she said, I think, to mostly convince herself. "Maybe one of you should text or call every couple of hours? I know it's overkill, but if I can't be there myself to check on you… and I have Andrew. I'm okay," she said, repeating what I would assume had been her internal mantra since the bridge incident Cass had told me about.

"I'll do regular drive-bys," Dad said.

That was another thing that had never occurred to me in my privileged, perfect life. Killing myself. I had probably had fleeting thoughts of it when Brody dumped me without reason in grade eleven. Or when I realized that I had never really had a mom. Sure, I had a mother, but I felt that I and my siblings had missed out on that quintessential nurturing, biologically related female. But that opening had left room for others like Dad or Janae to take over, so I wouldn't have changed it.

So, no, things had never been so bad that I wanted to end it all. Tears came to my eyes at the thought of how hopeless a person must have to feel to get that far. "I just... I don't know what to say." My tears finally spilled over. "How did I get through twenty-one years of my life not *seeing* any of this? It must have gone on all around me and I just skipped through life blissfully unaware."

"And you could have kept going." Cass leaned into my face, making eye contact. "But you didn't. That's the best anyone can do."

"Does that make people like my mom a terrible person?" I looked at Dad.

"No, Emerson, it doesn't. It just means she's not there yet. And I bet most people don't realize until it's too late." Dad sighed. "It still doesn't make them *good* or *bad*. It's just survival of the fittest. Animal nature."

"We'll leave you two alone," Cass said, interrupting him, seeing that I needed a break.

"I'll walk you out," Dad said.

Michelle embraced Cass and me tightly. "*Please* take care of each other," she whispered and released us.

Down at my car, Dad opened the driver's side door and he said, "You're going to have to tell your mother you have a girlfriend." I was sure I detected a hint of humour in his voice.

Cassie got in the passenger side and closed the door. "I know. I'm just not looking forward to it," I said quietly.

"Maybe wait a couple of days. She wasn't in the best mood when I left yesterday."

"Why her?" I asked suddenly. *I mean, I can see why, knowing how my mom is.* There was something about Michelle that was so soft. And nurturing. Like him.

"Michelle?" he asked.

I nodded.

He leaned on the open door. "It's so hard to explain, Em. I know you're young, but sometimes you just see someone, and it clicks. Or one little thing they do makes you think something you didn't expect. Honestly, it was the way she smiled at me. Like she could see the good in anyone. Lame, I know, but yet so beautifully simple. I had to go back just so I could see it again, and then I was screwed. Look, I wasn't out to cheat on your mom, it just happened."

I grinned. "I didn't mean to fall in love with a girl, it just happened."

He kissed me on the forehead as I got in the car. "Then we know exactly what the other person is talking about."

I looked up at him, shielding my eyes from the sun and said, "It's the best kind of love, no?"

"I think it is, Em."

MICHELLE

29

As Andrew walked the girls down to the car, I tried not to let my guilt get control of me. Not only was Cassie dragged into this mess, and then Andrew, but now his daughter? Who happened to be Cassie's girlfriend? My mind swam as the information rolled around, desperately trying to be processed. How could I have not figured this out earlier?

I turned onto my side and curled up, trying to fight the tears. *Why didn't I just jump?* I should have let my phone ring. Sure, Andrew and Cass would have been sad, but they would have gotten over it. Ray wouldn't have harassed the girls. And Andrew would have probably never found out his daughter was wrapped up in everything.

Now, because I was too scared to jump, I had put all of them at risk. Fat tears finally rolled down my face.

I should just go back to Ray, I thought. I could probably provoke him into killing me, having his revenge, and leave everyone else alone.

I didn't hear Andrew come back in the room. He quietly curled up behind me. "Don't even think about it."

I stiffened. "Think about what?"

"Running away. Going back to him. Killing yourself. Whatever half-baked idea you have to try and save the rest of us any more pain."

My pretty tears instantly turned ugly.

"You deserve happiness just as much as the rest of us. If everyone spent their lives running from what terrified them, we would be a bunch of selfish assholes who only looked out for ourselves and gave nothing to anyone else." He sat up suddenly.

"What?" I asked rolling over, wiping my nose on my sleeve.

"Oh, nothing. Something just occurred to me. About Keely."

"Tell me. I want to know."

"I just had a thought as to why she's so obsessed with herself and always tries to control every aspect of her life. She's hiding something." He nodded, apparently liking his idea. "Anyways, what does it matter? My life isn't about trying to figure her out anymore." He smiled at me and lay back down.

He kissed my neck and murmured, "I'm here. I'm whole. And I'm not running from anything. Especially you. I was meant to protect you. You *think* that you needed me to save you, but did it ever occur to you that it was *me* who needed *you*?"

How could I answer him? There was nothing I could say to top this. No words could elevate the feeling between us. I kissed him softly on the lips and gave him the only thing I had left to give. Myself.

KEELY

30

E merson: *Mom, I need to talk to you. Can I come over later?*
Me: *Sure. I'll be home from the gym after 8*

Emerson: *K*

Me: *Are you going to tell me what this is about?*

After two hours, I still hadn't received a text back. "Why is she being so secretive?" I muttered to myself.

I arrived home from the gym to see Emerson and a friend sitting on the front step.

Weird that she would bring someone over. "I hit construction," I said, not mentioning that I hadn't left the gym until seven-fifty. A huge company had approached me about buying gym memberships for all two hundred and fifty of their employees for Christmas. I wasn't going to let that one get away, and I figured if it was important, Emerson would wait.

They stood up in unison. Strange. I frowned as I approached them.

"Hi, Mom," Em stated. She didn't make a move toward me, so I brushed past her into the house.

"Hey. Want a drink?" I asked. "I could use a glass of wine to celebrate."

"Celebrate what?"

"I just landed a big deal at the gym. It's just what we needed to pump up our revenues."

"Oh," she said.

I turned and said, "A *congratulations, Mom* would be appreciated. The gym hasn't been doing well lately."

She asked, "Were you risking closure?"

"No, Em. I would have to lose most of my clients for that to happen. I am a great businesswoman, you know. I run a tight ship. It's just that I would have to start cutting back on *unnecessaries* if things didn't pick up."

She snorted. "Oh, so you were risking gel-nail and designer-shoe losses."

I turned to her and put my hands on my hips, noticing the other girl stepped closer to Em's erect frame. *Great posture.* "Have you come here to fight with me? Because frankly, I'm not in the mood for it."

"You were never in the mood for it."

I sighed and let it go. Maybe a glass of pinot would relax her. I walked into the kitchen and automatically poured three glasses.

"Oh, thank you, but I don't drink," the girl said quietly, but firmly.

I laughed. "Why on God's green earth not?"

Em stepped in. "Because her dad is an alcoholic and her mom has spent half her life serving other alcoholics. Let's just say, she's not going there."

I waved my hand and muttered over the rim of the glass, "Oh, you young people! You're so idealistic." I inhaled the bouquet and drank half of the glass in one swallow. "Just wait. In ten, fifteen years, you'll be married with kids. Tired and beat into acceptance just like the rest of us. Then you'll want a glass of wine."

"No, she won't." Em levelled her gaze at me.

She is full of piss and vinegar tonight! "We'll see." I smirked and turned to close the kitchen blinds.

"I'm gay."

I froze, hand on the twister-stick thing. The wine rolled in my stomach. The air around me became void of oxygen. Before I could stop my mind, it flashed back to when I was eighteen. We were screaming at each other, Mother and me, over breakfast. I straightened my shoulders and turned around, forcing myself back to the present.

I saw that the girl had pressed herself even closer to Emerson, as if she was trying to protect her. As I looked at both of them, I realized Em wasn't lying. Finally, I said in the flattest tone I could muster, "I can't accept that."

She laughed roughly. "You've never, in my whole life, accepted me for what I was, so why would this be any different? You only ever wanted a mini-Keely. You wanted someone just like you, so we could be friends, because you don't have any. You never let me be me."

I had no friends because I didn't have time for people that had no plans for their life besides sitting around complaining about their husbands and kids. I narrowed an eye at her, my heart hammering in my chest. "It's not natural," I said, eerily echoing my mother's voice. My mind was back in the summer after grade twelve.

"It's as natural as anything else."

"If God thought it was natural, he wouldn't have made men and women with specific reproductive organs," I said down the tunnel of time.

"*God?* Since when do you give a shit about God?"

My own mother's face, red and angry, loomed before me. My hands clenched, and I now repeated the exact same words she said to me years ago. "If we weren't put on this earth to procreate, then why make us different?" Adding my own twist to her lecture. "Should we all be androgynous blobs then?" I looked pointedly at the girl beside Emerson.

"We are not gorillas anymore, Mom!" Em said, her tone fierce. "We are past that. The world is overpopulated with humans anyhow. Our sole purpose in life isn't to make more babies. Has it ever crossed your mind that *spirits* can fall in love?"

Spirits. I looked past Emerson. In my mind, I saw Deanna, standing beneath the lone maple tree between our farms. I snuck up from behind her and quietly wrapped my arms around her waist. As the wind rustled the wheat around us and I inhaled her scent, I knew there was no other place I would be. I snapped myself out of the memory before Em noticed the tears that had started to accumulate in my eyes.

"Are you crying?" she asked incredulously. "Are you that upset that I have a *girlfriend*? I guess you can add that to your list of fails on my part." She turned to leave.

I lowered my head and whispered again, "It's just not natural."

"How would you know? There's not a single natural thing about you, Mom," Em hissed. "One day, maybe you will strip all of that crap off yourself and show me a real person." She softened suddenly. "*I know she's in there*. Beneath all of the false layers you have built upon yourself, there's a soul I could love, if you would only give me the chance." Turning, she took the girl's hand and pulled her out of the kitchen.

As the door closed, I crumpled to the floor, sobbing, trying to decide if I should push the memory down where it had been hiding all those years or if I should let it have its way with me. The way Deanna did so many years ago.

It was 1985 in rural Saskatchewan, and these things were looked upon with disgust and anger. The acceptable expressions of fear. I had been a real person once, I told myself, despite what Em said. I was happy and soft and in love. *With a girl.*

Deanna and I had been neighbours and friends all our lives. One day we were talking beneath the maple tree about what we were going to do with our lives when we left high school the next year. I had decided that I was going to pursue a modelling career, despite my mother's disgust at the idea. Deanna wanted to be a vet. Her dream was to return to that dusty place to start her own practice. I realized we were on totally different trajectories. What surprised me was that it made me very sad. Suddenly, we both stopped talking and stared at each other. I knew we both knew. Maybe it was the lingering sadness that I'd felt since my grandma had passed away two years prior. I desperately wanted to be connected to someone again. As we leaned into each other, my heart leapt with a joy I had never felt before.

For a year, we managed to keep our relationship a secret. We were both preparing to move to Toronto, and I thought I had nothing to lose by telling my mother right before I left. Being a steadfast Irish Catholic, she lost her mind. She hurled words at me that broke me in so many places and in so many ways, I never returned to the farm after I graduated, not even for the fall ceremony. She told me this wasn't my home anymore, while my father stalked silently out to the barn.

Deanna and I lived together for a year in Toronto. I tried to get into the modelling world, but they said that although I was certainly handsome, I was too *solid*. All they were looking for in those days were wispy, ethereal things, and I was a farm girl. I tried to groom myself accordingly, but I could never rid myself of my edges. I could not tame my black hair, I couldn't make my sharp green eyes fade. And I couldn't soften the muscles I had from years of hard work, even after starving myself for months. So I decided to take drafting at the local college after Deanna brought home some brochures. I was surprised by how much I loved it. The precision of the work. That it had to be precise and exact. Controlled. There was no room for error or bridges would collapse and buildings would crumble.

But it was mostly a man's world. And Deanna and I started to drift apart. She stayed true to herself, and I created a new self. I didn't realize I was constructing a bulletproof persona. One that would survive in this new world.

"You're different," Deanna said to me one afternoon as we sat on our deck, sipping iced tea.

I hated hearing that from her and my gut reaction was to say I'm sorry, but I couldn't bring the words to my lips. I wouldn't apologize for who I was. I simply shrugged and said, "Maybe this is the real me."

"But I feel like I can't see inside of you anymore. Remember when we used to lie beneath the tree and talk for hours about our dreams?" Deanna said.

"That was teenage idealism. That was a time in our lives that was still make-believe."

"That was us as we naturally were. The city has changed you into something hard."

I turned to her and glared. "The city has changed me into something that will thrive." I had been watching the women in the city. They were strong and confident as they marched past me. This was the future for our gender, and I knew I could be one of them. One thing was holding me back. The fact that I had a girlfriend instead of a boyfriend. I didn't need a man to complete me, but I knew I would need a husband to stand by my side. How many lesbians did you see making strides in the world? *Zero.* The world wasn't ready for so much change at once.

"Maybe, in the future, things will be different for gay people," I finally said. "But for now, it doesn't fit with the plan. It's not natural." My mother's words left my mouth before I could stop them.

It broke my heart to do that to Deanna, but if I was going to be the most successful version of myself, it wasn't going to be with her by my side. I forced back the tears that automatically responded to the ones falling down her face.

I later heard through a mutual school friend that Deanna had finished her veterinary training and moved back home. She had started a practice and was doing well, they said. The friend leaned in and whispered with malice, "But did you hear? She's a dyke. Disgusting, isn't it? Apparently, Deanna and one of her techs are dating, but it will ruin her business, I can guarantee."

This information should have saddened me, but instead it fuelled my belief that I had made the right choice. That I was on the right path.

I buried those two years of my life, from Andrew and the kids—from everyone. And now here I was. I looked around the kitchen. I had arrived, hadn't I? A trophy husband, three kids, big, beautiful house. Luxury cars. Vacation property. Respected businesswoman.

And then that night with Cadence happened. I tried to tell myself it was just a drunken mistake, but I knew I had been attracted to her for a while. I forced myself to forget how natural it felt. How beautiful it was to be with a woman again. I tried to convince myself that it was just a glitch in my system. I tried to forget about it and move on. But Cadence continued to make regular appearances in my dreams. I was certain this was what had sparked the retreat from Andrew—realizing my heart was not in the relationship anymore.

I concluded subconsciously, if I couldn't be with a woman and I didn't want to be with him, I would just be alone.

For so many years, I had tried to be what the world would accept. I thought of Em and her girlfriend and realized women had been allowed to evolve out of the barefoot and pregnant trope, but men just would not let themselves be cut entirely from the picture. I knew Em was right, women could live without men. It was men who couldn't survive without us— but they still wanted it on their terms. We were allowed to be A, B, or C, but never, ever D. And women played into it, happy for a least a little wiggle room. We thought we had made it so far making money and running our own show, but that was just men with boobs. I had wasted half of my life trying to ignore what I once knew in my deepest heart was the true me.

No wonder I was so fucking tired.

Finally, I picked myself up off the floor and found my way to the bedroom. I curled up in the middle of the bed and cried myself to sleep.

Maybe this is what a midlife crisis looks like.

I didn't like it one bit.

CASSIE

31

"She's gay," I said to Em as she drove us away from her mother's house.

"What! Are you crazy? My mom is as tight and controlled and straight as I've ever seen someone."

"Exactly." I stared out the window, adding, "You know those kind of people who you can't tell if what they're saying is actually their own opinion or they are simply regurgitating what someone else said?"

Em nodded.

"When your mom said 'it's not natural,' that was a repetition. I could see it in her eyes. It came from a distant memory, far away and detached from herself."

Em quickly glanced at me and said, "You're going to make a wonderful social worker. You see things no one else can. Maybe you should go on to be a therapist."

I shook my head. "No. They just sit in their offices and mostly help people that can afford them. Social workers are on the ground, in the real situations, getting bloody with them."

"You don't make it sound very appealing." She looked back to the road.

I shrugged. "It's not. That's why it's a calling, not a desire. Same as nursing."

"So, we are going to be broke and covered in blood, plowing through case after case together?" Em laughed.

"Yup. And we're going to be the happiest, most fulfilled couple I know." I dug in my coat pocket for my phone, checking to see if Mom had called or texted. Nothing.

Em took her hand off the shifter and took mine. "I couldn't imagine anywhere else I would rather be, even if it has turned into a real shit show." I smiled, thinking she was starting to sound like me.

Several days later, I stood near the edge of my mom's bed in the hotel room. Andrew had to go into work for a couple of hours, so I promised him I would stop by and check on her. Too bad I had to bring bad news with me. "Officer Kent called to inform me yesterday that they're going to release him soon."

She sighed deeply, "I know."

"You can't go back to him. That would be suicide." I quickly winced. "Sorry." The letter had arrived yesterday. I had snuck out for a walk to read it privately. I didn't want Em to feel like she had to comfort me as the sobs wracked my body. Really, I had been upset over nothing—Mom was still here. But the despair in her words was overpowering. I couldn't even begin to know what that would feel like. And the lie about my father? Well, I couldn't change the way it had gone. Maybe he had been a real loser and she left because that's what she thought best. I put any ideas of tracking him down out of my mind for now.

Mom smiled. "It's okay. You're right, I can't go back. So it's either stay in hiding or testify."

"Mom. I'll come with you. And Andrew. And Em."

She focused on smoothing out the wrinkles in my index finger knuckle. She finally said, "I'm so glad you found someone who loves you and treats you well. You don't know how happy that makes me." I saw a tear run down her cheek.

"I do, actually. But you deserve it too. And if you hide from Ray, you'll never have the peace you truly deserve. He thinks you owe him." I tried not to remind myself that *I* was the debt she had to repay.

She swallowed hard and opened her mouth. I leaned in slightly, anticipating her response. She then closed it and slumped forward, head in her hands. Finally she whispered, "I can't."

I closed my eyes and fell to my knees in front of her.

I held her shaking body. Suddenly I was filled with a rage I couldn't explain. I hated Ray. I hated my grandmother. I hated Jonathan. I hated the men that came and went from my mom's childhood home. My hate spread to every person that had ever ground down another human's soul in an effort to make themselves whole. Even Em's mom wasn't spared in my internal rampage.

How fucking *hard* was it to own your own crap instead of beating another person down? I suddenly envisioned the door of Ray's cell unlocked and my mother escorted inside in his place. He stood outside the bars smiling maliciously as he locked her up.

She will never be free.

KEELY

32

I woke up the next morning and felt that my resolve has returned. *Thank God.* Where had all that man-hating come from, anyway? I didn't have the energy to face that demon. I pushed yesterday out of my mind and got up and picked out my best outfit and spent an hour perfecting my hair and makeup. I was going to do what every person did in times of self-doubt nowadays.

I put on my best workout clothes and I took about a hundred selfies. I tried every angle, setting, and light source direction I could think of. As I scrolled through the pictures, a couple stood out as perfect. I narrowed it down to three and then started messing around with beauty filters and contrast, cropping out the annoying door handle from one and the edge of the microwave in another. I finally settled on one. I was holding the phone slightly up and over my head so that my chin looked sharp and my cleavage immaculate. You could see great muscle definition in my bicep as it framed the one side of the photo. The top of my abs looked chiseled and hard. The light from the kitchen window turned out to be the best for making my eyes look like emeralds. The filter I chose made the little wrinkles around my eyes disappear and there I had it! The perfect selfie.

I posted it on Facebook and Instagram and typed, "You are strong. You are capable of facing anything life throws at you.

Remember your goals and make a conscious effort today to only think and speak of yourself positively. Only look forward." I knew my wisdom may be a thinly veiled attempt to garner what I was really searching for, but enough people fed into it, and I watched as the love I so desperately needed rolled in. I needed justification for the path I'd chosen. I sat back and took in responses like "Beauty goals" and "Your abs are what dreams are made of." My favourite was one that said "Perf! If I looked like this about 95 percent of my problems would be gone!" *Exactly.* To these people, I existed as a beautiful, sculpted goddess. As I deserved. I finally looked at the clock and was surprised to see it was one. "I better get to the gym," I told myself.

I was expecting to have explicit dreams involving Deanna and Cadence, but instead my dreams were sad. I kept walking around the farm looking for dead birds. I would then take them home and bury them in the huge garden my grandmother kept. I couldn't see her, but I knew she was there somehow, watching me go about my work. I did it over and over. There seemed to be an endless supply of broken birds that needed me to see them to their final resting place.

"Cancel my consults today, Mindy," I said as I walked past the gym's reception desk. "I'm training all day." I had decided I was going to make my muscles work until they forgot about everything Emerson had told me. And everything her speech had dredged up.

"But you have Zoe coming in at four, remember?" Mindy reminded me.

Right. We were just supposed to revise her training schedule, but I needed to kill two birds with one stone. "Okay. Can you text her and tell her to wear workout gear? We are having a working meeting today." I smiled at Mindy.

"She'll love that! I'll let her know."

And she did love it. Zoe practically bounded into the gym, clad in the skimpiest thing, next to a bikini, she could find in her closet. She had on the burgundy Varley mesh racerback crop top that I'd had my eye on for weeks and simple black Lulu speed shorts. I was temporarily jealous of Zoe's wide thigh gap. Being naturally slim gave her an advantage over me in this department. My adductor muscles were just too defined to leave more than a couple of centimeters. Zoe was built to be a bikini competitor.

Heads turned wherever Zoe went, and the gym was no exception. Long, straight blonde hair, sapphire blue eyes, lightly tanned and blemish-free skin. Everything about her caused desire in men and women. The women maybe leaned more towards a desire to strangle Zoe in her sleep. She was one of those perfect creatures born looking radiant. She was perfectly proportioned and worked hard to keep it that way.

Luckily, Zoe idolized me. Unlike my own daughters. So when I found myself unexpectedly spilling my guts to her, she was thrilled to listen. Everything that had happened over the past couple of months fell out of my mouth—with a minor omission. Zoe's face went from shocked surprise to tears of empathy to anger-fuelled comradery.

"But you have done everything right in your life, Keely!" she gushed. "You don't deserve to be treated like this by your family."

"Thank you, Zoe, but sometimes life is complicated." I shook my head solemnly, watching myself do bicep curls in the mirror.

"Do you really think your daughter is gay? I mean, it seems more people are *trying it out*, especially girls. She may get over it. Especially when she meets the right guy." Zoe winked at some young, buff guy who had been watching her since she walked in the gym. He smirked and nodded back before doing another pull-up.

"I don't know. Sometimes I think the kids, especially her, do things to antagonize me. She could have been you. Modelling, living a jet set life at twenty-one. Having the best of everything before most people even know what they want to do with their lives. But she tossed it all aside to become a nurse."

"A nurse?" Zoe's face didn't hide her repulsion at the idea. "Why would anyone actually want to do that? Especially when you had better options?"

"Who knows, Zoe." I shrugged.

"Choosing those *caring* professions is like being a nice person because your face sucks!" Zoe practically fell over, laughing at her own joke.

I felt myself get slightly defensive at that. Em's face didn't suck. But I knew what she meant. Nursing and policing and teaching were jobs you chose because you didn't think yourself worthy of being amazing and self-sufficient and successful. There had to be an element of selfishness in entrepreneurship. You couldn't let anyone get in your way. Unlike the other jobs, where everyone got in your way. Just like if you didn't have physical beauty to ride on, you better work on your personality. Michelle floated into my mind at this thought, but I quickly booted her out.

I watched as Zoe assessed herself in the mirror while doing squats. The whole place was surrounded with mirrors for this exact purpose. To see how you looked. I turned back to the mirror and noticed how tired I looked. I could see the bags beneath my eyes without looking closely. I had managed to hide them in the selfie, which last time I checked, was on fire. But not one response from my family, just people I knew from the gym or strangers that followed me. *I don't need their approval anyway,* I tried to tell myself.

But didn't I?

The twenty-pound free weights hung at my sides as I quietly watched as Zoe's quadriceps flexed over and over again. Up, down, up, down. They were perfect. I looked down at my own legs, which I had neglected since the holiday, and saw only flab.

The realization of how much *work* I made my life started washing over me again. It was never fucking ending. The calorie counting and food weighing and protein-to-fat ratio analysis and the lifting weights and the putting down the bite of cake hovering on my fork in front of my face. Even when every cell in my body *wanted* to taste it, but deep down I knew it was no use anyway, because I wouldn't actually let myself enjoy it even if I did eat it.

Blinking hard and digging my nails into my palms, I looked around the gym and saw beautiful people. I saw the most toned bodies in the city. All because of me. Posters of advertising campaigns with me plastered across them stared back at me from the walls. A new one for every year of business. *You must keep things fresh, you know!* My mind felt as if it were spiralling into a delusional abyss. You had to continually reinvent yourself, stay one step ahead of the competition, create something people begged and paid for. *Coin the new phrase, be the latest inspiration, invent the best marketing strategy.* If your brand didn't have the most innovative and cutting-edge content, you quickly fell behind the trend.

As my head whipped back and forth, I saw hundreds and thousands of dollars spent on top-of-the-line athletic apparel. And possibly even more money spent on products and services to fight the aging process. Unlike the clothes, most of these purchases were kept a secret. It was best if you could make your impossibly slow decline into old age look natural and effortless. Not painful and unending. The way it really was.

I was sure some people were actually in the gym to ensure their good health, but right now, all I saw were people pretending to be perfect. *Like me.* More of Emerson's words came screaming back to me from another argument we'd had last year. She had claimed the competitions I worked so hard for were about putting value on how my body looked, not how it functioned. I knew, deep down, that she was right. How many times had I hurt myself training? Pushed myself to exhaustion or even puking? I suddenly remembered one line I had purposely forgotten: "What are you trying to heal?"

No, no, no, no…

I had felt myself cracking last night, but I thought coming here, getting back to what I did best, would make the crack fuse back together. But it only seemed to have made it worse.

I stumbled towards the exit, grabbing my purse on the way past my office. As I opened the door to leave, I heard Zoe call, "Where are you going, Keely?!"

I don't know.

MICHELLE

33

I just couldn't do it. I was the weakest person I knew. Even with Andrew and Cassie by my side, I was too terrified to come forward and testify against Ray.

Andrew had found me an apartment to move into soon, but was I supposed to stay locked up in there the rest of my life? The voice inside my head said *yes*. I forced myself to accept that it was still better than going home. Maybe in a couple of years, after Ray calmed down and even moved on, I could work again. Or volunteer. Anything to make my pathetic life worth something. In the end, what would I look back and see? Nothing. What would I have brought to the world to make it a better place? Again, nothing.

But what about Cassie?

Would she be safe from Ray while I hid? Probably not. I could try to get her to come live with me, but I knew she wouldn't. She wasn't a coward like me. She had her own life to live.

Maybe if I spent the next year of my life praying, he would leave her alone.

My phone pinged. It was a text from Cassie.

Mom, I love you.

And then she sent a meme. In it was a quote. It had a red background with a strong white font. It read: *"Life shrinks or expands in proportion to one's courage"* — *Anais Nin*

Did she mean this to help me to find my own courage?

Something deep inside of me, maybe a mother's intuition, knew the answer to this.

No. She was giving herself courage.

I immediately picked up the phone and called her, but of course it went directly to voicemail. I called Andrew, and he answered right away. "Hello? Michelle? Anything wrong?"

"Andrew, what is Emerson's phone number?" I breathed.

"What's wrong? Is Em okay?"

"I don't know, Andrew, but I need to call her. I think Cassie is going to do something dumb." I scrambled around the hotel room, holding the phone to my ear with a shoulder.

"I'm on my way right now. DO NOT GO ANYWHERE. Do you hear me?"

"Yes." I put on my shoes.

"As soon as I hang up, I'll send you Em's info."

"Thank you."

"Michelle, I love you. Please wait for me to get there," he begged as I hung up.

I grabbed my coat and purse and was halfway down the hotel stairs when Andrew's text came through.

I immediately called Emerson. "Hello?" she answered, breathlessly.

"Emerson? This is Michelle. Do you know where Cassie is?"

"No. I was just going to call you. She has her phone turned off." Her voice broke. "I'm worried, Michelle. She was in a really bad mood last night. She wouldn't talk to me at all and just pretended she wasn't feeling good. I was scared to leave her today, but I had a class I couldn't miss. When I got home, she wasn't here."

"Listen, Emerson. Stay there. I think I know where she is. I'm going to find her. I'll call you as soon as I know anything."

"But—"

"Just stay there," I cut her off. I hung up the phone, ran out to the street, and hailed a cab.

CASSIE

34

I sat in Ray's stinky old recliner in the semidarkness of the living room, waiting for him to come home. Evening was approaching, helping me to blend into the dusk. I had come for the memory box, I told myself. But a deeper part of me knew I had come for much more.

I could feel a cool draft on my ankles from one of the windows. This old house was far from airtight. The old clock ticked loudly in the kitchen, making me think of a cheesy horror movie scene, impending doom and all.

I flipped through the contents of the box, seeing memories of my childhood before me. Love letters to my mom, report cards, awards, artwork. All the things a good mom keeps. My mom had told me she didn't have one single thing from her childhood. Not one family heirloom, not one keepsake. She smiled sadly when she told me, as she tried to spin the fact that she had no history as positively as she could. She said it was for the best and there was nothing worth remembering anyway.

I gently placed all the items back in the box and put the lid on. I looked around the house, which was a mess. He had only been out of jail for two days, but it looked like a bachelor had lived here for years. Pizza boxes and beer bottles and an overflowing ashtray littered the coffee table. Dirty clothes lay on the floor and over the couch. And it smelled. I had thought the stench had wafted up when I sat on his chair, but now it seemed to permeate the entire house.

This is what oppression smells like.

I clenched my teeth at the anger that rose in me and tried to control it. *I must remain calm.* I didn't really know what I had planned to do when Ray got home. Yell at him? Try to beat him up? Threaten him? He easily had a hundred pounds on me, so I knew physically forcing him into submission was out. I *should* have looked for the gun. But I wasn't a violent person at heart. Yes, maybe an angry and rash one, but I didn't intend to kill him.

I just wanted to reason with him. "That isn't too much to ask, is it?" I asked myself.

KEELY

35

I drove home in a fog. How, in such a short amount of time, could everything go from crystal clear to mud?

I stopped by Starbucks and recklessly ordered the most decadent drink on the menu. A venti, whole milk cafe mocha *with* whipped cream. And a muffin. I sat in the parking lot and ate with an ecstasy I hadn't felt in years. I let the chocolate chips melt individually on my tongue, alongside the coarse sugar crystals. Heavenly. "This gluten-filled, sugar-infested monstrosity is to die for!" I cackled wildly to myself.

I finally started the car and made my way home. I noticed the sign outside the Catholic high school near our house had a new quote on it. They always had sayings up about how to live your life and how to be kind to others. Crap that I had thought never actually got you anywhere in life. Today it read: "You have never really lived until you have done something for someone who can never repay you."

I snorted out loud and rolled my eyes. *Why would I do anything that didn't benefit me in some way?*

But inside, something moved. My stomach rolled, and I cursed myself for eating the entire muffin. But the feeling was deeper, as if a wall had shifted, ever so slightly, away from the thing it was protecting. Unannounced, a moan escaped me followed by a torrent of tears. I barely had enough time to pull over before I totally lost it.

And, possibly for the first time in my adult life, I let go of my need to control myself.

CASSIE

36

A shadow moved outside the front door, and I tensed. As a key clicked and the door opened, my hands clamped down on the arms of the chair. For a second, terror washed over me. What was I getting myself into?

"Ray," I said as the door opened, trying to control the tremble in my voice.

"Huh?" He blinked. "What the fuck are you doing here?" he finally said once his eyes had adjusted. "Did you bring her, or is she still hiding with her *boyfriend*?"

I ignored the last question. "I thought we could talk." I could chalk this up to on-the-job training for my career.

He snorted and closed the door. "Didn't we talk enough the other day?" He went to the fridge and grabbed a beer, not bothering to offer me anything. He fell onto the couch and took a long gulp. "So. What do you want to talk about?"

I opened my mouth, but he cut me off. "Let me guess. You want me to leave your mother alone?"

"Yes. That would be perfect, actually," I said, my heart slowly returning to a normal rate.

"Then who would look after me?" He leaned forward slightly. "You want to take her place?" He raised his eyebrows and tipped the bottle toward me. "Repay your debt yourself?" He smirked as he looked me over. "I'm sure you would put up more of a fight then your mother ever did."

I jumped out of the chair, fists at my side. "That'd be the fucking day." I tried to push images of Ray forcing himself on my mother out of my head.

"It was so easy, you know. I even babysat you a couple of times when you were little, so she could work."

I shivered, knowing that I had been left alone with him at such a young age.

"Don't worry, I didn't touch you. I'm not *that* kind of creep. I like women, not little girls that still look like boys." He took another swig of beer. "But then one time, your mom didn't want it and I gave it to her anyhow. That's how it goes between men and women. She broke so easily, and I got a taste of the control I could have." He looked at me. "Is that why you're a dyke? So you don't have to worry about men taking what they want?"

My lips pinched at his revelation. Mom had never actually told me Ray raped her, even though I knew. Marital rape really was a thing, despite what men like Ray thought they were entitled to. "Maybe." I shrugged. I wasn't about to try to explain myself to him.

"But now, you're all grown up. You sure you don't want to do your mother a favour and give in? How about this?" He stood up, now only a few feet from me. "One time, and I let her go. That's a small price to pay, I'd think, for the person you so obviously love more than anything in the world." A look of sadness passed over his face, and I realized that love was a foreign concept to Ray. I had a flash of sympathy for him.

I unconsciously took a step back as he moved forward and bumped into the chair. Why did it always have to be about control and sex with guys? Even I'd had a run in with a boy in high school who wanted to prove to his friends that he could "turn" me. I had to get pretty vocal as he trapped me in a bathroom at a party and pinned me against a wall. His hand slid between my legs as he whispered into my ear how much I would enjoy it—in the end.

A loud pounding sounded up the steps and my heart dropped as Emerson flew through the doorway. "Cass!" she cried.

Ray lunged and grabbed me by the arm before I could go to her. I was shocked by how strong he was—it felt like he could crush the bone if he squeezed any harder.

"You." He pointed first to Emerson. "Sit." And then at the couch.

But she stood frozen. She'd obviously thought this through as much as I had. I wanted to hug her and strangle her all at the same time. Ray squeezed my arm and I twisted. "Ow!" I couldn't help saying.

Emerson's trance was broken, and she sat on the couch. Ray pushed me roughly down next to her.

"Now what?" Ray asked.

I looked to Em, and then back to him. "We'll just leave." I went to stand up.

He grabbed me by my throat and pushed me back down. "Oh, no. That will not work for me." He leaned over and whispered into my face, his eyes crinkling at the corners from the grin that formed. "Let's finish what you came here to start."

MICHELLE

37

If I'm too late, I'll never forgive myself. I burst through the door to see Ray looming over Cassie and Emerson on the couch, his face inches from Cassie's.

I know that look.

He looked up in surprise. "Well, well, well! If it isn't the mouse, home at last. Come in and join the party, Michelle." Ray reached for the empty beer bottle and held it up. "We don't need a repeat of last time, do we?"

I shook my head, trying to stay calm. Why was I not surprised neither of the girls had listened?

"Sit, Michelle." He pointed the bottle toward the couch next to Cass. When I didn't move, he said, "Well? Do I have to go get my gun?" His voice rose.

"Oppression is as good a weapon as a gun," Cassie said. I closed my eyes and waited for Ray to lose it.

"Ha! Good one, Cassie." Ray actually seemed to relax as he sat in his recliner. "So, I've been thinking." His foot tapped the floor. "What should I do with two dykes? I mean, it's a porn lover's dream come true, don't you think? Especially with one so beautiful," he said to Emerson.

"Leave them alone," I said, suddenly standing. "I'll come back, just let them go."

"You're a true mother, Michelle, I'll give you that." He stood up again, facing me.

I felt myself snap. Maybe courage does come in one huge burst. *This ends here.* The thought of him touching either of the girls was too much, and I lunged at him with all I had. It was enough to unbalance him, and I turned back to Cass. "Go!" I yelled as Ray regained his balance and grabbed me by the throat. Before I could say anything else, he had me pinned against the wall. "You stupid cunt," he hissed into my face, spit hitting my lip.

I had nowhere to go. I looked at Cass and opened my eyes wide, indicating they should leave. Cass moved behind Ray, picking up the beer bottle he'd dropped when he jumped up.

Ray didn't even notice. He eyes were intent on me. Focused on the task of finally killing me. He put his other hand around my neck and started lifting me up the wall, his nose touching mine. "You'll never be free of me. I won't let go until you've stopped breathing."

I gasped and choked. I could feel his hands crushing my windpipe; the grinding of cartilage was unmistakable. I saw Cass move again behind Ray, then things started to get grey and swimmy. I didn't like the noise that was coming out of my throat.

Right before I passed out, I heard the door bang open once more. My eyes rolled sideways, and in my oxygen-deprived delusion, I saw Andrew.

38

"Dad!" I couldn't help but yell when he came in the door with several police officers right behind him.

His eyes grew large when he took in the scene. Then he lunged, head down and with all of his weight, at Ray. Ray went flying halfway across the living room and Michelle crumpled to the floor. A police officer grabbed Dad's arm to stop him from advancing on Ray again.

Dad quickly turned to Michelle and collected her head into his lap.

Cassie and I went over to them, and I started crying, relief sweeping over me. Everything was finally going to be okay. Michelle looked like a broken rag doll. And I couldn't stop thinking of what Ray was going to do to us. I had never been threatened with such violence in all my life.

I could tell by the dead look on Cassie's face that she wasn't as shocked as I was, and this broke my heart further. She reached for me and stroked my head. "It's all right. Everything's going to be okay."

We all sat against the wall as Michelle regained consciousness and the police handcuffed Ray, who went surprisingly quietly. A paramedic asked us to step aside so they could assess Michelle. As she held Michelle's head still, she turned to us and asked, "Is everyone else okay?"

We all nodded, and she turned back to tend to Michelle.

Cassie continued to hold me, whispering, "It's over, it's over, it's over," into my hair. Finally, I pulled away and looked at her. "Yes, it is," I said, touching the side of her face.

Cassie broke before my eyes. And I was so thankful I was there to hold her together.

KEELY

39

It took me a full hour to get myself together. I must have looked like a lunatic, idling on the side of the road having a nervous breakdown. Thoughts, the likes of which I have never had in my life, pounded through my brain.

Had I never really lived because I hadn't done anything truly selfless?

My ego raised all kinds of counterattacks to that thought. Raising kids was a selfless act, wasn't it? I'd never get repaid for all of the things I bought them. And hadn't I stayed home with the kids, at first at least, because Andrew wanted it that way? And I gave away tons of freebies at the gym.

But I knew the truth, deep down. So why couldn't I bring myself to admit it? I was the only one in this car. The revelation didn't have to leave here.

But it does. It's kind of the whole point of an awakening, isn't it? I sniffed. But admitting I was wrong all these years, or worse, acknowledging that I was a horrible person, was terrifying.

I remembered back to a conversation I had with the kids and Andrew a few years ago. I had just gotten back from the funeral of a gym member, where they played a song that struck a chord with me. I announced to my family that I wanted that song played at my funeral.

"What is it?" asked Jacob.

"'I Did It My Way,' by Frank Sinatra."

Riley coughed a laugh and Emerson said, "Of course. You couldn't find a song more fitting if you tried."

"No, you couldn't," I defended myself. But I saw the looks they exchanged. That moment refused to leave me, even though I tried to ignore what it was telling me.

My way.

I had been so hell-bent on doing things my way, I didn't see anything else. But had I punished myself all these years to avoid acknowledging who I really was? Had my rigid self-control actually been an effort to hide the fact that I was gay? If I focused on what I could change or control, I could ignore what I knew was my true nature. The way a man with a small penis might drive a cherry red Porsche—a hot, young blonde in the passenger seat.

I thought it had just been a teenage phase. But then why did Emerson's revelation evoke such a rage in me? And what about Cadence?

I got out my cell phone and texted Amy. I hadn't talked to my life coach for a while, but I needed someone to tell me what to do. You get the privilege of their cell number when you give them as much money as I had. I asked her: *I'm not a bad person, am I?*

I sat for five minutes awaiting her response, wiping my tears and checking how puffy my face was in the rearview mirror. Finally it came: *Of course not! Where is this coming from?*

Me: *I don't know. I just am thinking maybe I haven't done enough good in my life. That I'm selfish.*

Amy: *Keely! Don't you ever think that. You have made a life for yourself you should be proud of and I don't ever want you to think twice about that.*

Me: *But what if I could do something for someone that would change their life? Even if they've wronged me?*

Amy: *Would doing this thing advance your growth? Because if it doesn't, they aren't worth it.*

"That's the exact opposite of what the sign said," I muttered to myself.

Amy texted again: *No one is worth that kind of self-sacrifice Keely. Don't give that power to someone else. You know how to leave people behind and look forward, so do it. Nobody is worth stressing over.* She added in another text: *You know what they say: Take what is valuable to you and release the rest.*

The words of Ralph came crashing back into my head. He said I disgusted him. And if Amy's words rang true, I was certain that now, after fifty years of life, I was finally realizing how much I disgusted myself as well.

Amy: *I'll just add a half an hour to your monthly invoice for this.*

Me: *I don't get a free bonus here and there?* I added a winky-face emoji.

Amy: *I don't do anything for free.*

I hunkered down in my house for almost a week trying to figure out what to do with my life. I ignored all calls from the gym, feigning some horrible, contagious disease. Andrew had totally disappeared and wouldn't answer my texts. Emerson kept putting me off, saying she was busy with school. Riley came and went from her basement bedroom so stealthily that I never saw her. Jacob… well, he had his own life to live.

What I had to do to move forward came to me one sleep-deprived night.

I need to meet her. It was the only resolution.

MICHELLE

40

I opened my eyes and my pulse leapt. *How was I here, again?* I looked around to see the pale-yellow walls and the beeping machines and the tube in front of my face. My eyes bulged as I realized the tube was down my throat, and my hands flew up to tear it out. Suddenly Andrew was beside me telling to not touch it. "It's okay, Michelle," he reassured me. "You're safe. For real and forever." He added, "Your throat is really swollen."

It came back to me in a fog. Had Ray hurt the girls? I felt that I had gotten there before he did anything. And then from somewhere, a courage, or rage, rose in me that I had never felt before. I was not going to let him hurt them. He did what he wanted to me all those years, but I decided right there that it would have to be over my dead body before he did anything to them. Before my mind could talk me out of it, my body had lunged at him.

I looked out into the hallway and saw them. Emerson was holding Cassie the way Andrew had held me when I wanted to jump off the bridge. I looked back to him and wondered how both of us ever got so lucky.

Then I drifted off again.

CASSIE

41

The hospital corridor was fairly quiet around us. Emerson left after making sure I was going to be okay. She said she had something she needed to take care of.

"You promise?" I held Andrew in my gaze until he became uncomfortable.

His lips were set in a firm line. "Yes," he stated simply. As if it took him no effort to answer that way.

I nodded. "I trust you. That's a big one for me, okay?"

Suddenly Andrew leaned in and hugged me. I was surprised at how strong he was and how convincing his arms were. "I promise to protect you *and* her," he said over my head. "Neither of you ever deserved this. It makes me sick to think about what you both have suffered. What so many people have suffered at the hands of demented people."

I pulled back and asked, "What are you going to do? You know, with Keely?"

"I'll talk to her, don't worry. I'll give her every cent I have if it comes to that."

"Well, Emerson may beat you to it. I think she's on her way now to talk to her."

"Oh, that kid." Andrew leaned against the wall and rubbed his temple.

EMERSON

42

I banged on the front door louder than I needed to. I could hear footsteps inside, but it didn't stop me from hammering harder.

Mom flung the door open and yelled, "What!" She looked shocked to see it was me. "Emerson Hazel. Why are you making such a racket?"

I didn't wait for her response and pushed my way past her. "I need to talk to you."

She jumped aside and called after me, "Okay, fine, but you still don't need to make so much noise."

I spun and hissed at her. "Oh, I do think I need to make some noise. Maybe then you will listen to me." I sat down hard on her new grey couch, sneering at the gross purple wall.

I saw her take a deep breath as she sat in the chair across from me. "Emerson, I haven't had a great week, so I'd appreciate it if you toned it down a bit." She rubbed her eyebrow absently.

"You've had a bad week? Did your stupid selfie post not get as many likes as you wanted?"

"You see those?"

"Of course I see them. But why would I actually *like* them? Do you know how many people post crap like that? Staged pictures of themselves with otherworldly and wise comments and quotes? The only people you're fooling is other people with the same narcissistic problems as you." I dug my phone out of my pocket and scrolled through the pictures. Finding the one I wanted, Michelle in the hospital with Cass leaning over her, I shoved it in her face. "This is what *strong* looks like. This is a real person who needs help and not a pat on the back for lifting weights for four hours a day."

The pained look on her face was satisfying, but I wanted more. "Should Michelle post this picture and say something wise about how she's capable of anything life throws at her, if only she stays positive?" I couldn't stop. "You live in such a fucking bubble! Do you know what she's suffered all of her life? *Just because it isn't happening to you doesn't mean it isn't happening somewhere.* Have you ever heard of that one?" I started madly typing in my Instagram account, veering toward hysterical. "Here, let's post *this* picture with *that* caption and see how many likes we get. Do you think your gym friends will like it?" Tears finally ran over my bottom lids.

Mom gently took the phone from my hands. She put it aside and knelt in front of me. "Emerson, what happened?" I actually thought she sounded concerned.

I blubbered. "You don't know how good you, we, have it. I'm just so tired of seeing all of this you-go-girl pseudo-feminist crap. It's strictly intended for the haves. And it does nothing for the have-nots. The people who truly need help. We go to the gym clad in four hundred dollars worth of high-end sports apparel and buy only local, organic food, and some single moms can't even feed and clothe their kids. It's not fair." I sniffed loudly.

"No, it's not fair. But do you think it's all about choice?"

"Don't give me your "life is made up of choices" speech! Did you ever think about people's starting points? Your starting point was pretty good. Mine was excellent. People like Michelle? Their starting point was about as low as it can get. She has so much more to overcome just to get to the place where we began. Where you're born, that's pure luck."

She nodded. "You're right."

I looked at her, surprised. "So you see how this new wave, me-first feminism is a luxury to those who can afford it? That it doesn't help the women who need it most? Like Ivanka Trump fighting for white-collar women's workplace rights but not letting her working-class employees have any maternity leave?"

She sighed. "Yes. But it's hard to let go of it now that I have it."

Seeing that she was trying to understand, I finally softened. "I know, Mom. But it's never too late." I looked directly at her and said, "You could start by releasing him."

"Your father isn't some pawn to be passed off to another person."

"Really?" I said in my most sarcastic tone. Mom didn't respond, so I continued with a more cooperative attitude. "No. But he's torn by guilt. He's a good person, and at this point he's willing to walk away from everything to be with her. He told Cassie that he would give you every cent he has and would start over so that he could take care of Michelle. And I know you probably hate her, but she needs him. And I also know it probably disgusts you, but she's not strong enough to do it on her own."

She frowned and shook her head, as if not understanding.

"It's okay to need people you know, Mom," I said.

Her lips pinched into a line, but she remained silent.

I left my mom a short time later with a question I had thought long and hard about. I had even asked it of myself, as it could be applied in any number of situations. A warm coat from last season's line or one of many boxes of KD my pantry held. Or in Mom's case, the husband you were not certain you were in love with anymore.

Would you give to someone who desperately needed it, that which you could live without?

Mom had opened her mouth to reply automatically. I was happy she closed it to give the idea some true consideration.

MICHELLE

43

I had asked Andrew about a hundred times how he knew to come to the house instead of the hotel room that night he saved us from something so terrible I had to force my mind around the scene. I would sit back and smile as he said that it was another one of his *feelings* or maybe because he heard me banging around the hotel and then I hung up on him. He had sat in his car for a few minutes, trying to decide what to do when he realized I wouldn't be at the hotel. Logic, he said with a grin. I couldn't doubt now that that this was the way it was supposed to go. And neither would Cassie.

I walked around the apartment touching everything, still amazed that I was here.

I'm free to exist. I no longer went through my days feeling like a prey animal. Always on high alert, ready for danger.

I walked through the tiny living room into the kitchen and noticed the dishes from last night's supper were still in the sink, and my heart unconsciously leapt. Before I could stop the words from coming out of my mouth, I whispered, "Oh crap. I better clean those up before Ray gets home."

But then I froze in place and reminded myself. There was no more Ray. There's only Andrew. I looked wildly back to the living room for confirmation of this. I couldn't see any of Ray's clothes or dirty magazines or ashtrays. I only saw Andrew's running shoes and a stack of engineering drawings and a crumpled up bag of his favourite chips, Dill Pickle Lays.

I breathed. Deeply and slowly. Many, many times.

Six months had passed since the attack. Ray was still in prison awaiting trial because no one would put up bail for him. Or he was considered too dangerous. One of those. I never really paid attention to what my lawyer had said. All I needed to hear was *still in prison.* And I had finally agreed to give a statement against him.

The knowledge didn't entirely stop the random thoughts and panic attacks that were ghosts of my past life sneaking up on me daily. But slowly, the space between them was growing. Even if only in minutes, it was increasing steadily.

"At this rate, I'll be a new person in about... oh... five years." I started laughing crazily. A wild, freeing noise that came from somewhere inside of me I never knew existed. *Joy.*

I had managed to finally pull myself up off the frozen concrete floor of my life. I was on my way up. And just in time to enjoy Cassie's graduation. She had been glowing in her navy cape and hat. Emerson still had one year left, but it had been a lovely family affair with her and Andrew present.

As I sat and watched my daughter walk up on stage and accept her degree, I willed myself not to cry, even though I wanted to. I had shed enough tears in my life. Instead, I beamed and clapped. Cassie, at twenty-two, had already gotten further in life that I ever would. And with a lot of sacrifices and finally courage, I had made that happen.

I jumped when the front door buzzed. I fought my immediate thought of *he's back.* The rational part of me knew it wasn't possible.

Still cautious, I pushed the intercom and said, "Yes?"

"Oh! Hi. Um... is this... Michelle?" a woman's voice asked.

Should I answer truthfully? I knew I shouldn't, but I had a sneaking suspicion I knew who was attached to the voice. "Yes."

"Michelle, I'm sorry, but this is Keely. I was wondering if I could talk to you?"

I laughed to myself, quickly making sure my finger wasn't on the button. "What the hell?" I asked. Today was a good day for progress, wasn't it?

Without answering, I buzzed her in.

KEELY

44

I had stood in this exact spot ten times in the last three months. But I was never brave enough to push the buzzer. I had begged Em to give me Michelle's address, and today I had waited until Andrew went to work. This wasn't between him and me anymore. That was done. This was between me and the woman who took him from me.

As Emerson had unloaded on me that day, it all became clear. I didn't know how I hadn't put it together before. Maybe because it was so unreal? Em was dating Cassie, the daughter of the woman my husband had cheated on me with? What were the chances? It reeked of things like *fate* and *destiny*. Things I didn't believe in.

I had actually kept my mouth shut—trying my best to let Em say what she needed to. She would have probably been exasperated that I hadn't figured it out earlier.

Things had been rocky since Andrew officially moved out, happily leaving me the house and its contents. And the Saint Lucia condo. Literally, the only thing he took with him was his car and personal items. And he seemed to do it cheerfully, whistling while he packed his old blue and black hockey bag.

The door buzzed and clicked, signalling that she let me in after my pathetic little speech. I took a deep breath and headed up the stairs with one gift for them tucked beneath my elbow while I balanced the other carefully on my right palm.

242

MICHELLE

45

I braced myself for the vortex of destruction and insults I expected Keely to bring with her. I opened the door and frowned at what I actually saw.

Keely looked different from the pictures I saw of her online and on Andrew's phone. I had realized a while back that the woman I had shuffled past in the park what seemed like ages ago had been her. That was the person I'd expected. That coiffed and contoured and sneering woman. What I saw now was nothing the same.

She looked... *tired.* I couldn't figure out if it was because she wasn't wearing any makeup to hide the bags beneath her eyes or that her body did not hold an upright, confident air. The second thought was that she looked completely normal. *Someone I could be friends with.* What she pushed into my arms made this feeling even stronger.

"A cake?" I asked, smiling, yet slightly incredulous. It looked delicious. Chocolate buttercream icing was piled high above what spongy goodness must have laid beneath.

She replied hurriedly, "I know it's weird. I understand if you don't want it, but I promise I'm not trying to poison you." She forced a tiny smile.

Poison? The thought hadn't crossed my mind, but now I was wary.

"Look, I know this is out of the blue, but can I come in and talk to you?" Her voice wavered, and her eyes darted around the room. Somehow, knowing she was nervous made me feel a bit better.

"Yes, of course." I stepped back and let her in. I braced myself for a decorative critique; Andrew told me how obsessed Keely was with the latest trends. Instead she said, "It's nice in here. Feels cozy."

A voice inside me told me there was something wrong with her. Maybe not wrong so much as not right. Even though I didn't know her personally, I could tell how uncomfortable she was. I motioned for her to sit down at the gold-flecked Formica-and-chrome kitchen table. Since Andrew had walked away from her with nothing and insisted that I go to school for social work, we were keeping the budget pretty tight. We had found this cute little thing at the used furniture store down the street for thirty dollars. Andrew told me this was what it felt like to be a broke college student, and I told him it felt better than anything I had ever experienced in my life.

I went to the kitchen and grabbed plates and forks. As I sat, my head down, I said, "Is this a peace offering?"

She smiled and sat back. "Yes, I guess so. Cake is an offering of neighbourliness. A peace treaty between women."

I had already started cutting into the cake, unable to wait. "Were we warring?" I stopped cutting and looked up at her.

She laughed. "Well, I thought we were, but maybe you didn't. All I hear from Em is how *truly* nice you are." She squinted her eyes at me. "But I can already see she was right." She quickly pointed a finger at me. "But don't think this means we are going to be friends. I just needed to do something so I could move on. So really, it's for me. And I desperately wanted to eat this cake but didn't trust myself alone in the house with it, so I thought I'd bring it to you to share."

I realized how hard this must be for Keely. And based on what I knew of her personality, she was letting go of a lot of her own issues to be here and do this for me. "Thank you," I said simply.

We dove into that cake like it was the best thing we had ever both tasted. Halfway through the second piece, I got up and poured a large glass of milk for each of us. She said, "Yes, perfect!" I let the icing melt on my tongue, bite after bite, until I thought I was going to be sick. I was almost embarrassed to look up and see what Keely was doing. It was like we were each having our own little moment with the cake and didn't want the other disturbing us.

Finally Keely closed her eyes and sat back. "Do you know I've wanted to do that for probably five years?"

I frowned at her and she continued. "I don't ever, and I mean ever, let myself indulge like this. But." She looked at the clock above the stove. "I think it was high time. I've missed out on a lot of stuff, and I'm not getting any younger." She took a quick breath and added, "I'm sorry."

I raised my eyebrows. "Shouldn't I be apologizing to you?"

"No, not that. I'm not here to talk about Andrew or the cheating or the divorce. That will never change between us. We are never going to be friends."

I was surprised at the slight hurt I felt at her words. She must have seen it and quickly added, "It's not that I don't think we *could* be friends. I just think, given the situation, it's not a good idea. If our daughters stay together, we will see each other here and there, and I don't want it to be too awkward. What I'm sorry for is the life you've been given. It wasn't fair." She looked levelly at me.

I felt my nose tingle at her words. I knew she was sincere when I saw her eyes shining. All I could say was, "Thank you."

She opened her mouth and then closed it. Instead, she simply stood up and put an envelope on the table. "This is for

Andrew," she said. "And you." She straightened her shoulders and continued. "I know it doesn't change everything that has happened to you, but at least you can move forward from a higher place. A place, I realize now, I took for granted every day of my life."

Keely simply turned and left, leaving me sitting with a half-eaten cake and a mystery I'd have to wait until Andrew got home from work to solve.

"Oh, Keely!" I called just before she closed the door.

She turned back to me, questioning.

"Can you please do me one small favour?"

For a second, I thought she was going to tell me to go to hell as her face contorted. She finally breathed, as if with great effort. "Yes, of course."

"There's someone I haven't seen since I left Ray and I'm worried about them. Could you check on them for me? And give them a message?"

She nodded as she listened to the details I spoke out loud while writing them on a scrap of paper.

KEELY

46

I walked out of the little apartment building feeling better than I ever had, putting the piece of paper in my purse.

Emerson's words had echoed in my mind for months after she left them with me.

Would you give to someone who desperately needed it, that which you could live without?

I didn't really *let* Andrew go to Michelle so much as he simply just up and left. I had no say. He gave me everything and walked away.

After processing all of the connections, I had raged at him over the phone about the ordeal that Em had been through. I was livid that he put our daughter, that Michelle and Cassie put our daughter, in that situation. He simply replied, "It was *one* occurrence. Think about that happening daily for your whole life," and hung up on me. Eventually, Emerson had given into my asking and told me exactly what Andrew was referring to. The details turned my stomach.

I tried to return to my former glory. I had the time for it now, but nothing seemed to work. In an effort to lift my mood, I gifted myself a trip to the condo. That worked for all of two days. One night, I was sitting with the ladies, aka the housewives of Beverly Hills, when one of them started complaining that the Lexus parking at the airport, which was closest to the departure gates, wasn't going ahead. "I'll still have to schlep through the parking lot like a *Ford* owner!" she cackled.

But one comment really made me lose my appetite for them, and for everything I thought I had above Michelle. Gloria had passed her phone around with a meme on it that said, "Money can't buy happiness, but it can buy diamonds and botox and that's basically the same thing." They had all laughed incessantly over their own appreciation of this sentiment, sighing and gently dabbing at their eyes—not wanting to damage their lash extensions. The thought of Andrew and Michelle living happily, minus the money, sent me over the edge. I stood up and said, "You guys suck." I turned and walked away from their gasping and wrinkle-free faces.

I only got 1.4 million for the condo, but I was in a hurry to get rid of it. Minus taxes and realtor fees and so on, the final cheque came in under a mil. I was sure Andrew needed the money now, and waiting for a better offer may have taken months.

As I slipped the cashier's cheque made out to him in the envelope, I felt something I had never known before. Or at least not for a long, long time.

I had whispered to myself as I licked the envelope closed, "*Now* I have lived."

I stopped by the homeless shelter that Michelle had given me the address to. I was surprised how close it was to the gym. And Michelle's bar. It had been right under my nose, and I hadn't given it, or them, a second thought.

I saw who I was looking for. He was right where Michelle had said he would be. I approached him and noticed one of his shoes was held together with duct tape. As I crouched down in front of him, it broke my heart that he flinched away from me. Like I was poison. I forced myself to talk. "Jim?"

His eyebrows went up as he looked at me.

"Michelle sent me."

"Michelle?" He sat up straighter. "Where's she been? I miss seeing her lovely face every day." He smiled, showing a large chip in one top incisor.

"She wanted me to tell you she's doing great. That she got out."

"She did?" His eyes started to water.

"She wanted me to tell you that today is a good day to start over, that she has faith in you." I added to Michelle's words a few of my own. "There really is hope, Jim." I hoped he knew I meant it.

"That's what she said to me almost every day!"

I stood up and dug in my pocket. It was funny how so quickly my "bucket list" had changed. I handed him the wad of money; twenty-five twenties. "She wanted you to have this, and she said when she's able, she'll stop by again."

He took the money and thanked me profusely, tears cleaning a path down his dirty face. I was certain then that my monetary addition to Michelle's message was the right thing to do. I had turned into a regular Ebenezer Scrooge. I quickly turned and walked away, afraid he would see the tears on my face too.

I drove to the park and walked around it a few times. Spring had fully sprung, and I enjoyed the twittering birds and the wind rustling through the new leaves on the trees. It reminded me of the maple tree Deanna and I had fallen in love beneath. I had stepped back from the day-to-day operations of the gym, and even though I still loved it, it felt good to make space for things like reflection. I was finally able to breathe. As a bonus, the pain I'd had in between my spine and left shoulder blade for as long as I could remember seemed less severe.

One matter still needed my attention, I felt, before I could really move on.

I sat at my favourite bench and took my phone out of my pocket, scrolling through my contacts. I knew it was too late for any kind of reconciliation with Deanna. I had a feeling my reappearance in her life would probably cause her more grief than it would do me good. *Look at me grow!* I smiled to myself.

I found the number I was looking for and took a long, drawn-out deep breath. And then another one. I thought going to see Michelle had been hard! With shaking gel-nail free fingertips, I pushed the little call button. *I could hang up now! It's not too late.* But what good would that do anyone? And before I could think any further, I heard her sweet voice answer the phone.

"Hello?" Cadence said.

My voice trembled. "Hi," I blurted out. "Cadence? It's Keely."

I wasn't sure I deserved it, but what she said next was the greatest gift she could have given me. I knew, however this went, that I would never be able to repay her. "Keely," she exhaled. "I'm so glad you finally called."

I sighed and closed my eyes, tilting my head towards the warm June sun.

DISCUSSION QUESTIONS

1. Many people born into middle class families that work their way up economically feel that they deserve it and that they have worked hard for what they have. Although this is undoubtedly true, have you ever given thought to what that would look like if you started life at Michelle's level?

2. There is a stark contrast in the mother daughter relationships in the story. Do you relate to one or another more strongly? Either as a daughter or a mother?

3. Do you think Keely's rigid and self-inflicted health regime is a direct result of her childhood or simply her personality? If she had felt free to date women from a young age, do you think she would have taken the body-building path?

4. Andrew obviously is the kind of person who is happier taking care of someone. Do you think it is based on the need to identify as a hero or saviour or can it naturally be in someone's character to help those who need it simply because they can?

5. Cassie's motivation for helping Michelle get out of her abusive relationship with Ray stems from genuine love for her mother, but do you think it's the child's responsibly to rescue a parent who cannot do it for themselves? Would you do the same in Cassie's situation?

6. Is Emerson's dislike of Keely's lifestyle warranted? Shouldn't people be able to do what they want without such harsh judgments from the people that are supposed to love them regardless?

7. The news states that the economic gap is growing between the classes, particularly between the lower and middle classes. Have you seen evidence of this in your own life?

8. Do you agree with Emerson in that people can fall in love with spirits regardless of gender? Have you ever experienced feelings beyond friendship regardless of how you had previously sexually identified, i.e. someone the same gender as yourself?

9. Do you think Cassie and Em are overly idealistic in their world views? Do people grow out of this as the "real world" brings all of it realities with it or can we choose to keep young ideals?

10. There are four different viewpoints in this novel. Did you identify with any one more strongly than the others?

11. Keely's obsession with how she looks seems to be a more and more common thread among women today. Do you think that social media has made it worse? In which ways? What do you see as the future for self-worth for the younger generations? Do you ever feel that your real self is not good enough to show in public?

12. Cake is symbolic in several different ways in this novel. What do they mean to you?

ACKNOWLEDGEMENTS

Again, I have to thank my wonderful husband, Jeremy, and my two amazing daughters, Julia and Erica, for just smiling and nodding as I pushed this writing thing further than I ever thought possible.

Thank you to Naomi K. Lewis for her editorial genius and cheerleading skills. And thank you to my friends, family, and first readers for the overwhelming support and encouragement. I had no idea where this journey was going to take me after my first book, but so many people have stood beside me, continually asking when the next one was going to be ready. That means a lot to me. Specifically, Troy, Deepa, Keri, Jamie, Tara, Liz, Sabrina and Jeanette—I appreciate all of you tremendously.

Thank you to Dane at ebooklaunch for bringing the cover of this book to life in a way I only imagined. It was a tall order and you filled it perfectly. And thank you to John and Deborah, also at ebooklaunch, for making the inside beautiful and error-free.

And last, I want to acknowledge the hopeful and idealistic seventeen year old inside of me that has not lost belief in equality. This is not a zero-sum game. There's enough for everyone.

ABOUT THE AUTHOR

Nicole Brooks' first novel, *Just Because We Can* (2018), inspired by her career as an Environmental Scientist, was a Next Generation Indie Book Award Finalist. Her work continues to explore the truths that are hard to see in our day-to-day grind. Now a full-time mother, Nicole tries to fit writing into her life every minute the kids are at school. She is a hobby artist and nature enthusiast who lives with her family just outside Calgary, Alberta.

If you love a book, authors love to hear about it! Please tell your friends and post a review.

CPSIA information can be obtained
at www.ICGtesting.com
Printed in the USA
LVHW091151291119
638855LV00004B/565/P